REMAINS TO BE SEEN

J.M. Gregson

Severn House Large Print
London & New York

This first large print edition published 2008
in Great Britain and the USA by
SEVERN HOUSE PUBLISHERS of
9-15 High Street, Sutton, Surrey, SM1 1DF.
First world regula
Severn House Pub

Copyright © 2007

All rights reserved
The moral right of

British Library Ca

Gregson, J. M.
    Remains to be seen. - Large print ed. - (Detective
  Inspector Peach mysteries) (Severn House mystery)
  1. Peach, Percy (Fictitious character) - Fiction 2. Blake,
  Lucy (Fictitious character) - Fiction 3. Police - England -
  Lancashire - Fiction 4. Detective and mystery stories
  5. Large type books
  I. Title
  823.9'14[F]

  ISBN-13: 978-0-7278-7669-0

Printed and bound in Great Britain by
MPG Books Ltd, Bodmin, Cornwall.

To Bernie and Bernard Gaunt.
For their many kindnesses to my family.

One

No one took much notice of him, in this part of the town. He shuffled along with his head jutting forward and his eyes cast upon the ground in front of him.

It would have suited him to pass unnoticed, but he did not seem to be giving any thought to what was going on around him. He was an unprepossessing figure, huddling his arms against his chest, feeling the cold of the keen March wind. His quick, shambling gait was that of an older man; his narrow-chested body was thin and unkempt. He wore a torn green anorak and his filthy jeans were frayed at the bottoms as well as torn at the knees. When he occasionally glanced up at the street ahead of him, his complexion revealed the sallow look of skin that saw too little of the outdoors. He wore nothing upon his head; his lank black hair looked in urgent need of washing and cutting.

No one watching the emaciated body move along these quiet streets would have thought that he would be a key character in a sensational crime by the end of the week.

The soft country of the Ribble Valley stretched to the very edge of the old cotton town, and here there were signs of spring. A pale sun picked out the first rich green of the new season's growth in the fields running down to the water's edge. The first lambs bleated, tottering on uncertain legs towards their observant mothers. On this fine day after the rains of February fill-dyke, the three rivers ran full but softly where they met at Mitton. In the small front gardens of the stone cottages which huddled together in the villages of the valley, the snowdrops were over and the crocuses were in full and flamboyant bloom.

But the man who shuffled along with downcast eyes was a creature of the town, and in the mean and narrow streets of the older part of Brunton the hazy March sun was too pale to lift the grimness. He clutched his plastic bag and hurried onwards, his paces small but swift, his lips muttering a silent litany which even he probably did not understand. People who deal with the seamier side of twenty-first-century life – social workers and policemen, for instance – would have recognized the preoccupied mien of the drug-user.

But this was a Monday morning, and the town was reluctantly resuming work after the excesses of the weekend. As midday approached, there were few eyes cast upon the rapidly shuffling figure with the single plastic bag clutched in its lean fingers. There were fewer still who had the slightest interest in his progress along these mean streets of blackened brick, which had been built to house the workers in the cotton mills well over a century earlier.

Had there been any observers, it might have surprised them that the man moved beyond the worst streets of the town, the ones earmarked for clearance in the next stage of its redevelopment. He seemed such a furtive creature that one might have expected him to dart like a feral cat into the obscurity of one of these narrow terraces. Instead, he moved on, at the same unvarying pace, into streets which were wider, with houses which sat squarely behind small front gardens. A hundred years earlier, these residences had been in their heyday and highly desirable.

They were late-Victorian houses which were now inexorably on the way down. Whole districts went down fast nowadays. Not as fast as in the cities, where areas lost or gained prestige with a rapidity which was often bewildering to the older residents, but fast enough to keep Brunton's burgeoning regiment of estate agents on their toes. These once substantial houses had been turned first into flats, then into warrens of single rented rooms, where few lingered longer than they were forced to stay.

This was a district which had changed its

ambience; that was the phrase offered by the sociologists in the town's newly titled university. The social workers to whom the academics pontificated did not view the place so dispassionately. They confronted the daily reality, and the reality made them fearful. They feared for the few survivors of a previous and more prosperous era who had chosen to spend their last years here. They feared for the futures of the wild-eyed, resourceful children who were growing up in these streets, mostly with single parents. And finally, they had learned to fear for themselves. There was little sympathy and less security for those whose work took them into these run-down places.

The man, still looking neither to his right nor his left, turned without pause into the last house at the end of a cul de sac. Casual observers would have thought the house was unoccupied and semi-derelict. It was a decaying Victorian semi-detached, with all but two of the panes in its ground-floor bay windows missing. But the spaces once occupied by glass had been boarded up, a sure indication to those experienced in such things that this was a squat, a house illegally occupied by residents who paid neither rent nor rates nor any kind of service charge.

The man in the frayed jeans went down to the extensive cellar, pausing for a moment at the bottom of the stone stairs, allowing his eyes to refocus and make what use they could of the dim light available in this eerie place.

It was the smell which he remembered most of all about the house. He felt the revulsion twitching his stomach now, controlled the urge to retch, as he had to do so often in the last few months. It was a stink, not a smell: a stink which had many elements in it, none of them pleasant. Damp plaster, dusty bricks and decaying mortar. Stale sweat and staler urine, rotting clothes, damp mattresses and filthy blankets. The sweet, heavy smell of cannabis, and the other, more elusive scents of the harder and more dangerous drugs. These were scents which came and went during the day, as people moved in and out of the place. And overlaying it all and comprehending these other scents, the complex of smells which accumulated in a crowded place where water had been cut off with the other services, and people could wash neither themselves nor their clothes.

In twenty minutes, the stink wouldn't matter. In twenty minutes, you would have become accustomed and inured to it, unable to distinguish either that awful odour or your own contribution to it. The man wasn't sure whether that was a consolation or not. He was no longer sure about a lot of things, since he had moved in here.

There was a brick wall in the centre of the cellar, which divided it into two spacious areas, each equally damp and cold. The front one had originally held the tons of coal needed to heat this high house to the temperature acceptable for the comfort of its Victorian middle-class owners and their servants; the rear section had been designed to store wines and the furniture which overflowed from the crowded rooms upstairs.

The man went and peered into this rear section, which appeared at first glance to be unoccupied. 'You awake, Lucy?' he said. 'It's Jack.'

You always identified yourself in these places, with their constantly changing flotsam of humanity. And you used your own name, if you knew what was good for you. Jack Clark: anything else was dangerous. If you gave yourself another name to wipe out your past, you were likely to forget it when people shook you roughly awake, or roused you from a haze induced by drugs. There were a lot of knives about, and it didn't do for people to think you had been trying to deceive them. Most people here were desperate, in their different ways. But some of those who came and went in the squat worked for powerful people. It didn't pay to be caught deceiving them, so Jack Clark used his own name.

There was no sound from the shape on the thin mattress in the corner at the back of the cellar, but he caught the glint of white from an eye, and knew that she was looking at him. He went slowly forward – sudden movements could seem threatening to addicts – and perched on the tea chest beside the mattress. 'I bought some bread and marge. You can share it, if you like. You should eat, you know.'

At first he thought there would be no response. Long seconds passed. It was not until he pulled out a slice of the stale white bread and began to munch it himself that the girl levered herself up and pressed her back against the wall behind her. She shivered violently with the cold of it against her spine, then pulled the blanket up against her neck. He held out a slice of the white bread, with its thin coating of margarine. She looked at it for a moment, then thrust a gaunt wrist from beneath the blanket, seized the bread from him, and tore at it like a hungry animal.

He was revolted by this action, he told himself, rather than by the sight of her. She had come to him, two nights ago, and they had had sex upon his mattress in the other half of the cellar. It had been a strange coupling, urgent but joyless, a fulfilling of an animal urge without any of the trappings of human grace which he remembered from a former life. It had brought no comfort to him and none, he fancied, to her. She had grunted urgently at the climax, then made to leave him, but he had held her in his arms for the remaining hours of the winter night.

The warmth they had given to each other had been a comfort. Indeed, when dawn clawed its way into the basement and the other denizens of this warren stirred themselves, that warmth was the only thing they could be certain that they had offered to each other.

His eyes were used to the dimness now. He gave her more bread, watching her eat with the same satisfaction he had derived from studying a puppy's urgent gobbling when he was a boy. She had dark hair and ears which were dirty and yet as delicate as porcelain; a well-shaped nose dominated an intense, thin face above a slim neck. She must have been elegant, even perhaps beautiful, once. He tried to picture her as she might have been before all this, but he could not do it.

She looked down at the injection marks on her arm, twitched her thin legs beneath the filthy blankets and said unexpectedly, 'You're good to me, you are, Jack Clark.'

He would like to save this girl-woman, if he could. Get her on to a rehabilitation course, before it was too late. But he had bigger fish to fry. He mustn't let himself become distracted by this strange, half-wild and almost ruined creature.

He levered himself up from the edge of the tea chest and went and looked at the decaying covers from garden chairs and the discarded cushions which served people as mattresses in the other half of the cellar.

There was no one else here at the moment, though he had heard the sound of movement in one of the upper storeys of the rambling house. Whoever supplied the changing population of this place with their drugs was going to have quite a turnover here alone, and there was plenty of other trade in the streets around, when you knew as much about the game as he did now. They were dangerous people, the ones who controlled the trade, but they had promised him the concession for this area. He was moving up the hierarchy in that lucrative and hazardous industry.

He went back to his own mattress and consumed the last two slices of the bread and marge. You could get stale loaves from the backs of the shops on a Monday, if you knew where to go. He hadn't yet been reduced to ferreting his way through the waste bins of the town, as the more desperate denizens of places like this did in search of food. You didn't last long, once you got to that stage.

With his belly full, he pulled the old feather eiderdown around him and lay down to doze for a little while.

He had no clear idea how long he had slept when a sudden shiver racked his whole body. He clasped his hands automatically across his chest beneath the cover for a few seconds. He had no watch; that had gone long since, to buy coke, when he had first come into the house. But it must be hours now since he had taken his early morning rock: good stuff, this latest batch, but you couldn't expect its effects to last for ever. You felt the cold, as the cocaine faded from your veins. But Jack Clark refused to consider the idea that the drugs became less effective as you became more addicted.

He wasn't going back to the girl. He spoke to no one in particular as he announced to the semi-darkness, 'I'm going out now. Going into the park. There's people there, expecting their supply.' You never knew who was listening to you in this place, or what kind of state they were in. Or how they would react: horse and coke and E and LSD made people unpredictable, given to wild reactions and sudden bouts of violence.

He went out of the house again, blinking a little as the pale sun lit up the drabness of the street. He turned north, in the direction he had indicated he would take before he left the house, and resumed his quick, short-paced shuffle towards the park.

He had almost reached the main road which ran past the entrance when he turned abruptly at right angles, moving, without looking to his left or his right, away from his original route. He was a mile from the park, moving along a lane with a high hedge at his side, when a silver-grey Ford Mondeo eased to a stop beside him. He neither looked at the driver nor exchanged any words with him. Instead, he glanced swiftly up and down the deserted lane, then slid swiftly and wordlessly into the back.

He prostrated himself along the back seat and was conveyed swiftly for several miles in this supine state, invisible to anyone outside the vehicle. Only when it turned through the wide gates and became hidden from public gaze behind the high walls of the police car park did Jack Clark cautiously sit up.

One or two of the uniformed men who were passing gazed curiously at the filthy and unkempt figure who slipped from the rear of the Mondeo. They watched him shamble in front of the driver and into the building. Another druggy arrested, another broken man helping the Drugs Squad with their enquiries, they concluded.

The driver did not enlighten them. It would be more than his job was worth to break the cover of Sergeant Jack Clark.

Two

There was an excellent view from the top storey of the new Brunton Police Station.

Crime being one of the indisputable growth industries of the twenty-first century, the station was eight times the size of the old nick, which had stood with its blue lamp in the centre of the town for almost eighty years. It was a charmless block of a building, its harshness emphasized by the raw newness of its orange brick. But it had six floors, and the rooms at the top were large, with penthouse views over the old town and the country which edged into its suburbs.

Chief Superintendent Thomas Bulstrode Tucker had made sure when the plans were on the table that he secured one of these large offices with a panoramic view of the town and the area to the north of it. That was only fitting for the Head of Brunton CID. The fact that the penthouse office isolated him from his team of officers, beavering away three floors below him, was another advantage, as far as he was concerned.

Tucker had long since divested himself of

any direct connection with the investigation of crime. That was much better left to the younger men and women in his ever-growing empire. Public Relations was his strength – it loomed so large in his calculations that he always invested it with capital letters. Tucker was a suave, smooth-featured man in his fifties, whose years and silvering temples gave him the necessary gravitas for the weighty and meaningless simplicities he delivered on public occasions.

At such times, he appeared without fail in an immaculately pressed and well-fitting uniform: the increasingly fearful men and women in the street were more easily reassured by a man in uniform than by one in plain clothes, he maintained. He was probably right. When he was wheeled on to make his grave statements to television cameras or radio microphones, Thomas Bulstrode Tucker was usually successful, whether in proclaiming the latest successes of his underlings or in assuring an impatient public that everything possible was being done and they must remain patient.

His equanimity was hardly affected by the fact that his colleagues regarded Chief Superintendent Thomas Bulstrode Tucker as a complete tosser. That was one of the more polite phrases for him which circulated on the busy floors beneath the chief's splendidly elevated office.

On Monday afternoon, Tucker gazed out

over the softly sunlit town and enjoyed the view for a few moments. From this height, you could appreciate the changing seasons. There were definite signs of spring today. The days were lengthening and the birds were nesting around his suburban home. Not too many springs now before he could contemplate a well-earned retirement and a splendid pension.

Just avoid banana skins and any serious cock-ups for another year or two, Thomas, and you'll be able to cement your position as a well-respected figure in the Lodge. Free-masonry had served him well; in retirement, he could see himself consolidating, perhaps even embellishing, what he saw as his bur-geoning reputation within the brotherhood.

Tucker sighed deeply after his contempla-tion of the extensive but unremarkable sprawl of the old cotton town. Then he turn-ed reluctantly away from the wide window of his private visions and back to the mundane business of self-preservation. He buzzed the number on the internal phone and said authoritatively into the mouthpiece, 'Come up here for a few minutes, please, Percy.'

Chief Inspector Denis Charles Scott Peach had been given the forenames of the most charismatic cricketer of his father's young days, Denis Compton, but was now univer-sally known as 'Percy' in a police service which loved the simple pleasures of allitera-tion. This was the man who succeeded in carrying the considerable burden of Thomas Bulstrode Tucker upon his broad shoulders. A man who worked at the coal-face of crime and relished it. A man who produced the clear-up figures for crime upon which Tucker sailed, but which he could never have produced for himself.

DCI Peach knew what happened in Brunton CID better than any other man. He was also more than any other officer the man responsible for the unit's successes and considerable reputation. Tucker might be a bumbling fool at everything except public relations. But he was not such a fool that he did not know the worth of Peach, did not recognize how vital the man was to his own reputation and progress.

Tucker detested Peach, detested the liberties the man took and the insolence he suspected but could not pin down. But he knew also how much he needed his DCI.

For his part, Peach regarded the man he had christened Tommy Bloody Tucker with cordial contempt for most of the time, and with a contempt which was not at all cordial when Tucker perpetrated his worst excesses. Cloaking his disdain under the thinnest veil of subservience, he taunted his superior officer relentlessly, knowing that the older man needed him more than he needed any other person to preserve the fiction of his efficiency.

Percy Peach now appeared in answer to

Tucker's summons, a squat, powerful figure, with gleaming black toecaps beneath an immaculate grey suit. He was only thirty-eight, but he looked at first sight a little older because of his shining bald head, the whiteness of which was emphasized by the jet-black fringe of hair around it and the equally black moustache and eyes in the round, alert face.

'You didn't give me your normal Monday briefing on the events of the weekend,' said Tucker. Start as you mean to go on, he told himself. Assert yourself to this presumptuous upstart.

'Written report was on your desk at nine forty this morning, sir,' said Peach stiffly. 'I hope someone hasn't purloined it whilst you were out and about on the tasks of your arduous day, sir. People are light-fingered everywhere now, sir. Even in police stations, it appears.' He was standing erect in the military 'Attention' position, his eyes rigidly fixed not upon Tucker's face but on the wall three inches above the chief's head, a pose he adopted for no other reason than that he knew that this stance of exaggerated deference irritated and disconcerted his chief.

Tucker said, 'I always prefer the informality of a verbal exchange when it's possible, you know.' He waved in exasperation towards the chair in front of his wide and uncluttered desk. 'Do sit down, Percy. We have things to discuss.'

Peach noted the use of his first name with dismay. Attempts at intimacy from Tucker were always a danger sign. He positioned the chair very carefully, as if its exact proximity to the figure in charge of Brunton CID was a matter of supreme importance in some unwritten but important ritual. Then he sat upon it as if it might at any moment explode beneath him.

'Yes, sir. Nothing remarkable this weekend. Bit of violence in the town centre on Saturday night. Routine stuff, I'm afraid to say.'

'We mustn't just accept these things, you know.' Tucker was suddenly at his most sententious. 'My policy is to charge these ruffians, if at all possible.'

'Yes, sir. Zero tolerance, sir. Like Mayor Giuliani, sir.'

'Pardon?' Tucker looked like a low-IQ rabbit stricken with incomprehension. His eyes contrived to be at once devoid of understanding and full of suspicion, a combination which his DCI found wholly intriguing.

'Late Mayor of New York, sir. Zero tolerance was one of his watchwords. The policy worked well there, apparently. Might work well in Brunton, if the individual-rights lobby would think of the victims instead of the criminals, for once in a while.'

'Ah!' For a moment, these two very different men found their enmity removed by the thought of a common foe. Tucker nodded his agreement and added a salvo against a second police *bête noire*. 'And even when we make out a good case against some young thug, the bloody Crown Prosecution Service won't take it on.'

'Indeed, sir. The CPS want a cast-iron case before they'll consider taking things to court.' Peach brightened a little. 'Which is what I'm trying to give them, with one of the toughs from the weekend.'

'That's the style, Percy. Give 'em hell, eh! Well, at least you know your Head of CID is right behind you.' Tucker jutted his chin aggressively and set his head in his 'leading the troops' position.

'Good to know that, sir. Wouldn't like to come downstairs and question Mr Atwal yourself, would you?' Percy Peach raised his eyebrows in optimistic encouragement, although he already knew the answer to his question.

Tucker's scalp prickled as Peach had known it would at the mention of the name. 'Atwal? Are you telling me that you are questioning a member of the immigrant community?'

Peach wrinkled his brow as if asked to deal with an extremely complex question. 'Difficult to pronounce on that, sir. No doubt the man he was hitting with the baseball bat regarded him as an immigrant, but Mr Atwal assures me that he was born here and has lived in this area for every one of his twenty-four years.'

'There are racial overtones to this, Peach.'

And you're wetting yourself again, thought Percy. He was glad to hear his forename removed from Tommy Bloody Tucker's address and enmity re-entering the chief's tones; you knew where you were when there was a little formality in the exchanges. 'You're on to it as usual, sir. Nothing slips past you, as I constantly emphasize to the lads and lasses downstairs. I was saying as much to the girl who had her head split open in making this arrest, only this morning.'

Tucker's concern was as usual not for his officer's welfare but for the PR aspect of the incident. 'You need to go easy here, Peach. We operate in a very difficult racial climate, in this area.'

Correction: *we* operate and *you* piss about up here, thought Percy. He sat very erect and addressed himself to a point on the wall behind the Chief Superintendent's head. 'I appreciate that, sir. And I am glad that you are counselling that we operate zero tolerance whenever there are incidents of racial violence like this. It is the quickest way of stamping them out, in my opinion. And the officers who have to deal with this escalating problem will be gratified to know that they have your support. They will be very happy to take a hard line: we have been waiting for a lead on this.'

He nodded his approval and half-rose to

his feet, as if anxious to rush away and announce this brave new world to the men and women straining at the leash on the floors below them.

Tucker was looking pleasingly pale. He was as usual not quite clear how he had arrived at a stance which was the very opposite of his inclination. 'You mustn't be headstrong, Peach. I have an overview of this situation which you cannot be expected to have when you are more closely involved in it.'

'Ah! Your overview, sir.' Peach recognized a familiar phenomenon, settled sadly back on his chair and shook his head with elaborate melancholy. He looked like a man who had been hit over the head with a sock full of wet sand.

'Indeed, Peach. My overview tells me that we have to be excessively cautious in this area. My advice – my reluctant advice, Peach – has to be that you should let this Atwal fellow go with a caution. To do otherwise might be to provoke resentment among our Asian community.'

'And to release him without charge would certainly fuel the resentment of the National Front and the British National Party and every other right-wing lunatic. They gather extra votes every time we do not act in cases like this.' For a moment, Peach found himself abandoning his baiting of his inadequate superior to speak with a real passion. 'The police service needs to be seen to be even-handed, sir.'

Tucker shook his head sadly. 'If you had to go into some of the meetings I have to attend, Peach, you wouldn't dismiss racial tensions so lightly.'

And if you had to pick your way through the blood on the streets and see your own officers at risk, you wouldn't be such a time-serving and contemptible disappointment to us, thought Percy. He found himself unexpectedly tight-lipped and staring for once straight into Tucker's face as he said, 'I'll question Atwal and his cronies myself, sir. Then I'll make a decision.'

Tucker looked uneasy in the face of this confrontation. But the only alternative to giving Peach his head was to get involved himself, which he was never going to do. 'Better come back to me for a final approval, if you decide to charge him. My advice is a caution.'

Advice which was being offered without knowledge of a single detail of the case, thought Percy grimly. But he knew that he was going to have difficulty in getting the witnesses he needed to convince the CPS that they should take on an assault case. He would probably have to let the arrogant young hoodlum downstairs go with a caution anyway. The matter would end with this silly sod in front of him thinking his wiser counsel had prevailed.

To make his disapproval manifest, Peach

spoke every syllable with elaborate slowness as he said, 'Was there anything else you wanted to say to me, sir?'

Tucker stared at him for a moment, a rabbit now caught in headlights. Then his memory clanked into gear and he said querulously, 'Yes, there was, Peach. If you hadn't distracted me with your inanities, you would have known about it by now.' He squirmed a little on his seat, feeling he needed a different pose for this portentous revelation. 'We are to be part of the most important police operation in the north-west this year. A major part, in fact. The Drugs Squad have been working on this one for months, and are now ready to make their move. They believe they can seize some of the really big boys: the drug barons.' Tucker paused to let Peach appreciate that portentous phrase. 'And I have decided to entrust the matter to you and the team you select. But I don't want any cock-ups. The prestige of Brunton CID is at stake.'

What you mean is that you don't want to be around when the shit's flying but you'll emerge to claim the glory if all goes well, thought Percy. He had worked with Tommy Bloody Tucker for too long to feel either surprise or resentment. It was the way of the world and the privilege of rank to do such things, but Tucker took it to extremes. Success was always his and his alone; failure was never remotely to be connected with him.

Peach looked at the wall beyond his chief and said modestly, 'You're far too ready to let us enjoy all the excitement, sir. I don't think you should deny yourself like this. I think you should take charge of this operation yourself. Let us have the benefit of your overview.' He dwelt on the last word just long enough to leave irony hanging in the air over the big desk.

Tucker stared at him suspiciously. 'It is not my policy to interfere with my staff. You know how I like to let you and the others take the glory.' It did not sound convincing, even to him, but he put all the conviction he could muster into the words.

'But it isn't fair for us to monopolize the action, sir. This would be an opportunity to bring your fabled experience back on to the streets and savour the full benefits of leading from the front. A rare opportunity.' Peach paused to give due weight to this last phrase.

'No. I shall liaise with senior officers in the Drugs Squad and the Serious Crime Unit over this. That is my function. That is what the system requires of me.'

'Well, there's no getting round the system, sir, is there? A pity, though: I can guess just how much you'd like to be sharing the dangers with us.'

Tucker looked at him sharply, but his DCI's face was as inscrutable as a warrior's mask. 'You'll have the Armed Response Unit to back you up.' He was sprinkling the capitals in each of his statements about the operation, as if by doing so he could stress its magnitude to this man who refused so steadfastly to be impressed.

Peach nodded, suddenly serious. Bullets flying about; trigger-happy young coppers on the one side and villains who were not bound by any rules on the other. People could get hurt. Despite his goading of Tommy Bloody Tucker, the last man he wanted around in such circumstances was this bumbling figurehead. 'Let's have the details, sir. The when and the where, to start with. I'll need to decide carefully who to deploy on this one, by the sound of it.'

Tucker smiled a superior smile. At last this insolent subordinate was recognizing the importance of this commission. The Chief Superintendent touched the side of his nose in the gesture of secrecy which Peach found the most irritating of all. 'I cannot tell you that at the moment, as you will appreciate, Peach. I don't even know the details myself, as yet.'

That was but one more drop in the vast pool of Tommy Bloody Tucker's ignorance, thought Percy Peach, as he went thoughtfully back down the stairs to rejoin the real world. But he was unusually quiet as he began to think about the personnel he would deploy on this. For all his wordplay with Tucker, this wasn't something to be taken lightly.

Three

Jack Clark was exhausted.

You would expect to be able to relax when you reached the haven of the police station. Instead, as an undercover officer coming here from the most dangerous of all situations, he knew that he would be put through a series of tests and interrogations, most of which he did not understand and did not want to understand.

They had put him in a room on his own, a blessedly warm room. He knew it was no more than an empty office, but it felt like a palace after the basement in the squat. He stood motionless for minutes before the single window, looking out at the lights of the town, at the sky darkening to navy in the early March twilight.

He did not recognize any of the people who attended to him. But that was all right: he found he did not want to recognize them, or to exchange any words which would make them colleagues. He had striven for months now to attune himself to the dangerous world of the squat and the strange companions of that house, some of them pathetic, some of them menacing. He had worked hard to make this place of friendly, unthreatening faces into an alien one; he could not afford to switch back to it now.

They took his order and brought him food from the police canteen. Having a choice of food was more than he could cope with: he opted for the steak pie and chips which was the first thing on offer, and scarcely heard the words of the rest. The female officer who brought the tray to him was scathing about the quality of the canteen cuisine, but he fell upon the food as soon as she was out of the room as if it had earned the highest Michelin rating.

It was the first really hot food he had consumed in weeks, and the syrup sponge and custard which followed formed a warm lining in his stomach for the cold night to which he knew he must return. He sipped the mug of hot, sweet tea as if it were a new and priceless beverage, noting with a shock how filthy and cracked his nails were, as he wrapped them around the diminishing warmth of the earthenware.

Then Jack Clark folded his arms, slid them on to the table in front of him and put his head sideways upon them, as he had not done since he was a small child in the nursery school. He was safe here, as he had not been for months: he curled up like an overfed animal to sleep off the meal.

They gave Sergeant Clark four minutes

before they came into the room. He seemed sound asleep, but he was awake in an instant as the door slid open, his deeply set eyes as narrow and watchful as those of a wild creature cornered in its lair, his lean body twisting on the chair to confront them.

The psychologist was swift, expert and impersonal, testing him without a change of expression, whatever his replies. If he felt sympathy for this debilitated, hunted figure, he gave no sign of it in his face. And he wasted no time: Clark had to be back in the squat in no more than two hours, or suspicions might be aroused about where he was and what he was doing.

The National Crime Squad pursues major criminals in drugs, in arms and people trafficking, in fraud and paedophilia. The fifteen hundred officers and five hundred civilian staff are based in covert locations throughout England and Wales. It is the people who work as undercover agents in the drug industry who take the maximum risks, disappearing for months on end without being able to contact their nearest and dearest, unable to assure them of their safety or even their continued existence.

Each year, a few of these officers disappear for ever, removed from the face of the earth without even remains to mourn. The surprising thing is that people still volunteer to undertake such work. Those who do are driven by a complex of motives which they do not always understand themselves, the chief of which are a lust for excitement and a need to explore the most secret parts of themselves.

Such personalities are by definition extraordinary. And the extraordinary is also unpredictable, especially when operating under the extremes of stress which undercover work demands. Officers who volunteer to work like this have to be checked as regularly as their perilous work allows. In order to make their cover convincing, they have to take illegal drugs. Usually they do as Jack Clark had done, and pretend to be injecting or swallowing more cocaine or heroin than is actually the case, but there is no way they can be convincing without being users.

Some of them become unpredictable junkies, no longer any use to themselves or to their employers, destined for early death from the drugs themselves or at the hands of the people they set out to expose, unless they can be swiftly pulled out and sent for rehabilitation. Others join the enemy. The sight of thousands of pounds passing between the bigger fish in this dark pool can be a real temptation to swim in it yourself, to drop your police contacts, supply information to the other side and begin your move up the sides of this lucrative criminal pyramid.

As often as it is possible, your mental balance and your continuing loyalty are checked, as Jack Clark's were now. He understood all that, but he was not interested in the details. He went through the tests as unthinkingly as a beast in the fields where he had worked as a boy, in that existence which seemed now to belong to another being altogether.

When it came to his debriefing and he stood for the first time in front of a man he recognized, his attitude was transformed. He had information to give. He wanted to convey what he had to offer as completely and as accurately as he could, but also to absorb whatever information these people at HQ had gathered and could relay to him, to make his own situation less hazardous. The success of the whole operation might depend on the exchanges of the next few minutes.

More pertinently for him, his own life might depend on any one of the scraps of information he could give, which the chief superintendent in front of him was assimilating and collating with what came in from elsewhere. That sounded melodramatic, but it was absolutely accurate; you grew used to melodrama, once you accepted the role he had adopted.

He gave names, watched the man nodding in front of him, gathered that he was offering confirmation of what had come in from other sources. The thought that there were others working on his side against the big battalions of the enemy was a consolation to him. When you were watching your back and playing out a lie for twenty-four hours a day in that squat and elsewhere, it often felt as if you were working alone against impossible odds.

Jack Clark had grown so used to secrecy that he found it difficult at first to release what he knew, to offer to this man who operated from behind a safe desk the snippets he had gathered at such danger to himself. But the officer was experienced in dealing with men like Jack, and his questions showed that he appreciated the dangers surrounding him. He did not offer praise or approbation, understanding that this mission had passed far beyond such simplicities, that reassurance to this hunted figure would come only with the successful conclusion of this enterprise. The senior man tried by his words and his reactions to convey the impression that success was now inevitable, even though both of them understood that there could be no certainties in this desperate conflict.

Eventually Jack said, 'There's a meet on. The big boys are flying in, I think. I don't know when.'

'Wednesday night.'

They had other information than his, then. Jack was lifted again by the thought. 'I've been asked to go there. They're going to put me into a bigger dealership, I think.' Not offer me one, put me in it. You don't have choices when you're playing with the big boys in drugs. These people moved you around like a piece on a chessboard. And sacrificed you in the same way, if it suited their game to do so.

The man questioning Clark understood that he had already been dealing, in a more minor way, but he deliberately avoided any mention of that. Undercover agents were not officially allowed to do anything which broke the laws of the land, which included dealing drugs, or even carrying them for supply. Yet you couldn't possibly acquire credibility and move closer to the big men in that odious trade without doing such things. In the perilous assignments of undercover work, you were supposed to fight with one hand behind your back.

Jack Clark's chief said, 'Play along with that. Get as many names as you can. We'll need all the evidence we can offer, when we bring this to court. And it will be easier to get you out if you're at that meeting.'

Jack noted without resentment that his own safety seemed to come almost as an afterthought. 'All right. I don't know where the meeting is yet. I don't think they'll tell me, until a couple of hours before it.'

If the senior man opposite him knew more about this, he didn't communicate it. Too much knowledge could be as dangerous as too little to an operative. 'If it's as big as we think it is, we'll move in. Take the lot of them. You could be out of this in a few more days, Jack.'

There was no smile from the grubby, hollow-cheeked man he was trying to encourage. He said dully, 'I'll need to get out without my cover being blown. I don't want some thick plod in uniform letting on to them that I'm playing on the other side.'

Jack Clark was already mentally back in the squat, where the police were the enemy and you snarled an automatic derision of them. The man opposite him understood that, even approved it. 'You'll be arrested with the others. Taken in to the nick with the rest of them. We'll release you later, whenever we know it's safe.'

It might soon be over, then. He might soon be back in this world of central heating and regular meals and frivolous talk of women and football and television. He wasn't sure he'd be able to cope with the banality of it, after the life on the edge he had lived for the last four months. He gave his first smile at the other man in this small and suddenly claustrophobic room, uttered his first attempt at rejoining the world of police bureaucracy. 'Don't let the bastards grind you down, eh?'

The chief superintendent gave him a grin, then reached out and put his hand on top of the grimy paw of his junior. 'See you soon, Jack.'

The four words and the simple gesture

were an attempt to convey a wealth of under-standing, of appreciation of the unspeakable dangers this man had lived with and was about to return to. The man who had placed him there had more sense than to suggest there might be a promotion for Clark in the work he had done. In that twilight world Clark was going back to now, such incentives had no meaning at all.

Clark lay prone on the back seat of a different car for his return, but slipped from it within half a mile of the spot where he had been picked up. He did not go directly back to his cellar, but shuffled instead to the edge of the park, so that if anyone met him he would be coming from the direction he had indicated. By the time he reached the squat, he was securely back in the persona he need-ed for the next fifty hours. It had dropped easily on to his stooping shoulders, feeling more natural than that stranger he had in-vented at the National Crime Squad centre.

'You sell your horse and your coke?' a voice asked him from the deep shadows at the far end of the basement.

He peered into the darkness, his eyes not yet accustomed to the gloom. He didn't recognize the voice, couldn't be certain whether the speaker had a high rating or no rating at all in this dangerous world he had infiltrated. 'Couldn't deal a single rock,' Jack Clark said bitterly. 'The place was alive with fucking pigs!'

At that moment, he felt genuinely resent-ful.

It didn't take DCI Peach long to select his team for the Wednesday night operation. One of the advantages of Tucker's ineffi-ciency was that Percy had been able to hand-pick the men and women who worked with him in CID. Over the last few years, he had built up a group of officers whom he trusted and who trusted him.

You got a fair deal, if you worked for Percy Peach, they said. You didn't get an easy ride, but you didn't expect one. You'd get the occasional fierce bollocking, but only if you didn't stick to Percy's strict rules. If you did, he'd support you, even when things went wrong. His loyalty and affection for his team were never expressed – DCI Peach would have considered that a weakness – but they were unswerving.

As his reputation as a thief-taker had grown over the years, it had become a mark of efficiency in CID work to be selected for Percy's team. You had a busy and occasion-ally a hazardous life, but an interesting one. The inevitably dull periods of boring routine which the police machine demands were reduced to a minimum under Percy Peach. Other people, usually uniformed officers and civilians, could do the computer trawls and the house-to-house enquiries, whilst Percy and his team got on with the business of detection.

There would be an Armed Response Unit involved in Wednesday's operation, ready to move in immediately when the order was shouted. Like most policemen, Peach did not want to carry arms himself and was uneasy whenever armed police were brought in, but he recognized that on this occasion their presence was necessary. The snatch would take place in darkness. That was always an advantage, if you knew exactly what you were doing, if every man and woman knew their own parts in the operation and didn't lose their discipline when the villains reacted like cornered tigers. If things went wrong, darkness could change sides in a flash and become the enemy.

Villains' reactions were never predictable, and from what Tommy Bloody Tucker had told him, Peach divined that these were to be very big villains indeed. There'd be some hard men in this house, wherever it was, all of them with a lot to lose if they were arrested and charged. Some of them would certainly have killed already and would have no hesitation in doing so again if they saw it as the only option. Unless everything went exactly as planned, there'd be bloodshed: Percy's only concern was to ensure that it was not on his side of the exchanges.

He had a discreet word with each of the officers he selected for this job, apprising them that they should be ready for a briefing

41

on Wednesday morning, when he would know more. He would not know everything, even as they went out on the operation: the nature of missions like this ensured that you could never know everything about the strength of the enemy and the disposition of his forces. Despite the air of confidence he brought to everything he did, the men he spoke to understood that this was a big one, that there would be danger as well as kudos on Wednesday night.

But each of Percy Peach's team knew that he had been selected for this, by the man who carried universal respect in the Brunton nick, and each of them was lifted by the thought of that selection. Peach himself was pleased by their reactions; he was delighted and secretly proud to see in each of his selections that strange combination of composure and eagerness which marked the good villain-taker.

There was only one omission from his team which gave him pause for thought as he fell asleep that night.

In the squat at the other end of the town, Jack Clark was almost asleep when he sensed rather than heard a movement at the foot of his mattress.

He was instantly awake and alert. You were even more vulnerable when you slept on the floor than when you were in a bed. You could get a good kicking and worse before you could make a move to protect yourself. He closed his fingers on the blade he had slipped beneath his cushion-pillow as he settled down for the night.

Someone was muttering an incomprehensible and seemingly unending litany of prayer in the other half of the basement, moving back in a drug-induced haze to some forgotten period of his life when religion had been important. Perhaps it was this ruined creature who had lit the candle which flickered on the other side of the dividing wall, perhaps twenty feet away, giving him a ghostly, vestigial illumination.

Jack saw the dim outline of feet standing astride the corner of his mattress, the vague shape of a figure magnified into a Colossus by the gloom and his own position of vulnerability on the flagged floor beneath it. The voice said, 'You're a user, Clark.'

'So what? I keep myself to myself, don't I? I don't—'

'You need to watch that habit, if you're going to be any use to us.' The speaker moved his boot, caressing the sole of Jack's foot under the blankets, letting the prone man know how helpless he was. Jack sensed with that movement that this was a man who enjoyed the feeling of physical domination, the knowledge that he had it in his power to cause serious injury.

Jack struggled into a sitting position, making sure that none of his movements was swift enough to cause any alarm to the man who stood over him in the darkness. The light from the flickering candle was pitifully small: he could still see nothing of the man's torso and head, could not even be certain whether he was black or white. Jack fancied he might be West Indian, from some tiny inflection in his words, but he could not concern himself with that now. He said, 'I'm not an addict. I use a bit of coke, to give myself a lift, but I'm not a junkie.'

'I know that. *We* know it.' The man couldn't refrain from asserting his position of trust in something larger. That vanity could be a weakness in him, thought Jack Clark. 'I wouldn't be here now if we thought you were anything more than a user.'

'I'm not. I could stop tomorrow, if I had to.' The old user's refrain, which Jack had heard so often from others, and seen to prove a delusion almost equally often. He thought he knew now why the man was here, but he wouldn't voice it. Men like this liked to feel that they were calling the shots.

'You're a lucky boy, Jack Clark. You've been picked out for bigger things. You're a very lucky boy indeed. You could be making real money, in a year or two, if you kick the habit and build up your trade.'

'You want me to deal.' It was safe enough to say that much, now. Jack knew that the man had been sent here by someone much more powerful, that this bruiser couldn't afford to damage him, unless he proved un-cooperative. But he kept his hand on the blade beneath the cushion. Men like this, heavies who dealt in violence, could be unpredictable.

'We might do. Might want you to do more than you do now. Might even want you to take charge of a section, if you prove yourself and things work out. Might get you out of this shithouse for a start, if you are found to be suitable for promotion.' The voice dwelt on each syllable of the last word; this was a man to whom sarcasm was an unfamiliar luxury.

'I'd like that.' Jack leant forward, nodding eagerly in the dim light, almost fawning. A gratitude which was almost pathetic was what this man expected, was what might be the best thing to make him abandon any suspicions. 'What do I have to do?'

'There's a meeting on Wednesday. They'll want to run the rule over you. See whether you come up to standard.' The big man made no attempt to conceal his contempt for the filthy figure huddling forward under the blankets.

'I'll be there. What time on Wednesday? And where should I go?'

'Not so fast, scumbag!' The messenger took a gentle kick at the feet beneath the blankets, just for the pleasure of it. 'You keep yourself out of trouble and off the sauce until Wednesday, and then we'll see about it.'

He turned and made for the steps and the way out of this foetid place. He was on the third step and completely invisible when he delivered his final words. 'No need for *you* to know the when and the where, Jack Clark. You'll be taken there under escort, if they decide to use you.'

Jack slid back beneath the blankets, but it was a long time before he could address himself again to sleep. It was on. The end to this part of his life, which he had thought sometimes would never come, would be on Wednesday. If he could preserve his cover until then, all might yet be well.

Four

Lucy Blake had that odd feeling that one sometimes experiences in those three or four seconds between sleep and consciousness.

It was a delicious moment, for she realized after that moment of alarm that she was not only safe but where she wanted to be. There were thick curtains at the long low window, but enough light was seeping in to tell her that a new day was beginning. She reached out and picked up her watch from the bed-side table. 7.01. Five, maybe ten, minutes before she needed to slide from beneath the duvet and begin her working day.

She snuggled back beneath her cover, rolling on her back to gaze at the ceiling she knew so well. She decided that there was something infinitely reassuring about waking from a deep and untroubled sleep and finding yourself in the room where you had spent your childhood. Returning to the womb, the psychologists would probably call it. But Lucy Blake had the police officer's habitual distrust of psychologists: they were people who complicated simple issues and protected vicious people from the consequences of their crimes. She preferred to call this feeling a pleasant nostalgia.

She could hear familiar sounds beyond the wall of her bedroom. Her mother was already up and in the kitchen downstairs. Lucy tried to picture Agnes Blake now, but found that instead she saw her twenty years ago, brisk and businesslike and infinitely knowledgeable, her mission for half an hour in the morning to get a lively eight-year-old off to the village primary school, with a good breakfast inside her and everything she needed for a busy and productive day there.

But at that moment all musings were rudely dispelled, as the door to the low-ceilinged room opened suddenly, pushed back by the knee of a woman who needed both hands to steady the china cup and saucer she carried before her like a votive offering, until she could set it down on the table beside her daughter's bed. 'Thought you'd like a cup of tea to start your day, our Lucy,' said Agnes Blake.

Lucy liked the old Lancashire form of address, and her mother knew it. There wasn't much that these two women did not understand in each other. She said, 'You shouldn't be running about after me, Mum. It's me who should be bringing you cups of tea in bed.'

'If you can't be spoiled at home, where can you be spoiled?' said Agnes Blake. She con-

48

sidered sitting down on the edge of her daughter's bed for an intimate little chat, then decided against it. You had to be careful how you approached young people nowadays, even when this one was your only and highly cherished child.

Lucy eased herself up and sat with her back against the headboard. She sipped her tea and said, 'Thanks, anyway, Mum. I'm glad I was able to stay.' She meant it; she enjoyed coming home to the old cottage at the base of Longridge Fell, even though she was very happy in her neat little purpose-built flat in Brunton. 'You're very snug in here, now that you've got the central heating.'

'Aye. You were right about that.' It was Lucy who had persuaded her to put a central-heating boiler and radiators into the cottage: Agnes had been the last one in the row to accept the improvement. She still kept coal for a fire in the bunker behind the cottage, but she lit it only on special occasions nowadays.

Most such occasions involved visits from Percy Peach, feared Detective Chief Inspector in the Brunton CID and recently retired star batsman in the Lancashire League. Agnes Blake was an unwavering cricket fan, and that had helped to cement her relationship with Denis Charles Scott Peach, the man named after the laughing cavalier of English cricket in the nineteen forties and

49

fifties. Lucy had been full of trepidation when she had taken home a bald, divorced man who was ten years older than her, but her mother and Peach had hit it off immediately, and so thoroughly that she sometimes felt quite resentful about their relationship.

Lucy and Percy were engaged now, to her mother's undisguised delight. They couldn't broadcast it at the police station, since couples with a close relationship were not allowed to work together: it was only someone as out of touch as Chief Superintendent Tommy Bloody Tucker who would not have realized that Percy and his favourite detective sergeant were an item. Lucy enjoyed her work, and enjoyed working with the local legend Percy Peach even more. For these reasons, she favoured a long engagement.

Her mother had other ideas. She was nearly seventy, and it was time she had grandchildren. Surely her Lucy could see the logic of that? She watched her daughter attacking the breakfast cereals, set a rack of toast in front of her and said, 'It was good to have you here for your day off, love. It's a shame you have to rush back into danger this morning.'

'No more danger than crossing the road, Mum. Think how worried you'd be if I'd ever made it as an air hostess, flying all over the world.' She harked back to when she had been thirteen and had wanted like every other girl in her class to become a stewardess with British Airways. Mums liked you to hark back. It was a useful diversionary tactic; very often, they took up your memories and threw in their own recollections of the days when their children had been young and foolish.

The tactic didn't work this time. Her mother banged the teapot on the table and said, 'Have you fixed a date for the wedding yet?'

Lucy suddenly found the back of the corn-flakes packet of surpassing interest. 'I told you, Mum. We're far too busy to think about that at the moment.'

'And is that what Percy thinks, our Lucy?'

'Yes. We haven't even discussed a date yet. I'm sure he's no more anxious to rush into anything than I am.'

'They'll be asking me at work, you know.' Agnes still worked for a few hours each week at the small local supermarket, despite her advancing years.

'You shouldn't be discussing our business with your friends at work. I told you we didn't want it broadcast.' Even as she spoke, Lucy realized how unfair that was. The doings of Detective Sergeant Lucy Blake filled her mother's life, and she loved to tell her friends and neighbours of the latest developments. You surely couldn't begrudge that to a widow who lived on her own. But Lucy Blake was on the back foot and she knew it. She said grudgingly, 'Perhaps we'll get round to thinking about it, when the summer comes.'

'The SUMMER!' Agnes sounded as if her daughter had uttered the foulest of obscenities over her breakfast table.

Lucy pushed her plate aside, snatched up her mug of tea, and said, 'I really must be off, Mum. I have to be in the station by half-past eight. Find out everything that's been going on on my day off, you see.' She disappeared up the narrow stairs and shut the bathroom door.

Her mother was neither diverted nor mollified. 'I'll have to speak to Percy!' she called up the stairs. 'I expect I'll get more sense out of him. I usually do.'

DS Lucy Blake drove away from the village with that threat still ringing in her ears. An alliance between the formidable Percy Peach and her mother had already been more than she could cope with on several occasions. She told herself that she must be firm, that the considerations of her career must come first.

Before the day was out, she was having harsh words with DCI Peach, over an entirely different matter.

At noon on this bright spring day, Jack Clark felt unnaturally exposed.

He had become a creature of the night since he had gone undercover, and he had grown used to having the cloak of darkness over most of his activities. Now not only were the days getting longer, but he had been summoned for the first time to meet his supplier in broad daylight.

He looked anxiously behind him as he approached the apparently deserted warehouse, first over one shoulder and then over the other. The street was empty. It was cold still, despite the sun; he was glad of the thick vest he wore beneath his ragged and filthy outer garments. He moved towards the high wooden doors in the rapid, shuffling gait which had now become part of his persona. He remembered hearing some actor say that getting the walk was the first part of any character you assumed. Jack Clark could scarcely now remember that he had walked in any other way.

He stood and looked at the high wooden doors, at the spot where heavy lorries had once moved in and out of the loading bays under huge bales of cotton. Then he raised his eyes from the cobbled yard to the windowless brick walls, which stretched like high cliffs above him towards the clear blue of the March sky. The place looked entirely deserted, but he knew that there was life inside it.

Sure enough, a small wooden door to the right of the padlocked ones opened at that moment. No one beckoned to him, but he forced his unwilling legs towards the dark oblong of the doorway and slipped into the icy interior of the building. There were sky-lights in the roof, but that seemed impossibly far above him. After the brightness of the day outside, the overwhelming sensations here were of cold, dampness and dark.

He caught a movement, twenty yards away to his right, and a voice he could not identify said simply, 'This way.'

He did not look at the man; menials were not important people. He took the way that was indicated to him, moved through an open door, heard the unwelcome sound of it being shut firmly behind him. He was firmly trapped, if that was what these people were about.

There was a single lamp on the table in what must years ago have been a busy office. It was the sort of lamp students use for study, with a flexible stand which allowed you to direct maximum light to the book were reading or the notes you were making. It was directed towards him, turned slightly upwards, so that it shone full into his un-shaven face as he stood before the table. The voice from the man who sat in the gloom on the other side of the table said, 'We've been watching you, Clark.'

Jack's heart lurched. Was he about to be exposed? Was this man about to tell him how pathetically inadequate his attempts at deception had been, before he felt the barrel of a gun at his temple as his last sensation upon this earth? He sensed that it was better to say nothing than to offer any proof of his assumed identity. He stood very still, nodding his head as if he took the man's statement as approval. He could see his white breath wreathing away from the harsh and brilliant light into the darkness; he wondered if the man could see the unevenness of his breathing from the patterns of this vapour.

'You've done well. So far.' He caught the contempt in the last two words, understood in that moment that contempt was habitual to this man, a means of asserting his position against those below him in the chain. Jack could see a little of him now, in the vestigial light which fell away from the lamp to the other side of the table. The man was sitting, enjoying the feeling of relaxed power his pose gave him against the frightened man on the other side of the table. He wore a dark anorak, which at this moment seemed too big for him. The only visible part of him was his face, and that was heavily shaded by the hood of his anorak.

Nevertheless, Jack recognized him. He had seen him only once before, but he would remember his name, given time. He did not trouble himself with that name now. He had long since trained himself to give absolute concentration to his own behaviour in situations like this, where any false move could be fatal. He measured the impact of each monosyllable before he said, 'I'm glad you think so. That I've done well, I mean.'

'So far.' The man enjoyed repeating his caveat. 'You've shifted what we've given to you, without using too much of it yourself. Junkies are no good to us, you know.'

'No, I know that.' Jack was tuning in to the rhythm of this. His part was to be craven, to pander to the prejudices of this man who thought he was so much cleverer than he actually was. Jack knew that this was why he had volunteered for this crazy assignment: to put animals like this behind bars. That unexpected thought gave him a lift, but also made him cautious. If he gave any hint of excitement now, he would be sounding the wrong note.

The voice from the gloom below him said, 'We've decided you're capable of a bigger round. That you're capable of shifting more.'

'Good.' He didn't trust himself with any more words: he was afraid of overplaying his Uriah Heep mode.

The man studied him for ten, fifteen, twenty seconds, which seemed to Jack to stretch into minutes, enjoying keeping the abject figure standing in the glare of the lamp while he sat in comfortable dimness on the other side of the table. 'If you do well in what we give you, you'll make money. The sky's the limit, Jack Clark. If you shift what you're given and please the big men, you might even be able to afford to shave and get out of that shithouse!' He leant back on his chair and allowed himself a little snort of amusement at his own humour. Then, as Jack began his mutter of thanks, he snarled, 'You'll be at the meeting tomorrow night. Someone will take you there. Now fuck off!'

Jack Clark scurried like a frightened mongrel from the room, from that baleful presence, from the warehouse, out into the blessed and dazzling open air. That was the conduct he knew was expected of him.

As he set off back towards the squat, he muttered to himself, 'I'll have you, Banham. Your days are numbered, mate.'

It seemed to him a good omen that the man's name had come back to him.

'Good day out in the country?' Percy Peach was at his most innocent.

Lucy Blake was still wondering how to play this. 'Not bad. I like my colleagues, but it's good to be somewhere with not a policeman in sight, occasionally.'

'Indeed. Even when your Chief Inspector thinks that the sun shines out of your dear little arse. Well, your substantial and beautifully rounded arse, to be strictly accurate, as all CID officers should train themselves to be.' Percy peered round his desk in an attempt to memorize the details of that particular section of his sergeant's anatomy, but as she was sitting firmly upon it, it was distressingly invisible.

'And what's been going on here in my absence?' Give the man the opportunity to confess whenever possible, she thought. That was one of Percy's own maxims.

If he detected any menace in her tone, he gave no sign of it. 'And how's my favourite mother-in-law?' Percy gave her his widest and most innocent beam.

'She's not your mother-in-law yet. And perhaps never likely to be, at this rate.'

'At what rate?' Percy contrived a look which combined bewilderment with hurt, an expression rarely if ever witnessed by the criminal fraternity of Brunton.

Lucy Blake realized that she would have to tackle this head-on. 'There's a big job on tomorrow.'

Peach nodded, allowing a slight frown to trouble his noble brow. 'Confidential, that's supposed to be.' But he knew the prospect of a major criminal snatch would have drifted through the section as rapidly as wind-blown smoke; that didn't mean anyone would have dared to breathe a word of it outside the station.

'Come off it, Percy. You know this is a big one.'

'Apparently it is, yes. But it hasn't been confirmed yet. And it's no use pressing me for details. I know not the time nor the place, my pretty flame-haired temptress.'

'It's not flame, it's chestnut. And you're trying to divert me with your compliments. You don't usually get this daft at work.'

'You're right.' Percy affected to look apprehensively at the door of his office, as if he feared hidden listeners. 'You're my Delilah, you are, threatening to undermine my position of trust.'

'You've already lost your hair. And I don't see you bringing the temple of Chief Superintendent Tucker crashing about our ears.'

Percy contemplated that happy vision for a moment, his face suffused with a dreamy bliss. Then he shook his head and his shoulders in turn, as if to dismiss this Utopia from his mind. 'If it comes off, we should have a couple of the major drug barons in our cells by tomorrow night. I can't tell you any more than that, because as of this minute I don't know any more myself, Detective Sergeant Blake.'

'You've been getting your team ready for this operation.'

'I've had an unofficial word with one or two of the boys, yes. They need to be aware that they might not be home for their evening meal tomorrow. I'm always the soul of consideration in these things, as you know.'

'Several of the boys, in fact. And there's one female detective sergeant who so far hasn't heard a word about this. I'm giving you the opportunity to remedy that omission, DCI Peach.'

Percy had known from the start that this was why she was in his office, though he had enjoyed exercising his rarely used diversionary skills in the elaborate verbal minuet which had delayed it. He said stiffly, 'I have to deploy my resources as I see fit. Chief Superintendent Tucker has directed me to do so.'

'And you always give the utmost attention to Tommy Bloody Tucker's directives.'

'Occasionally even the greatest idiots must be right. It's called the George Bush Law of Averages.'

Lucy decided that only directness would serve her now. 'I want to be on that team tomorrow night.'

Percy Peach decided, on the other hand, that this was a moment for an uncharacteristic retreat into officialese. 'It's possible that when I know more I shall be able to reconsider the matter.'

'You don't intend to use me tomorrow night, do you?'

Percy sighed. 'No, I don't. Lucy, this is one of those occasions when I want hard, reliable men around me.'

'But not hard, reliable women.'

Percy eyed her delicious curves, but decided that this was not a moment to comment upon her lack of hardness. 'We've already got the Armed Response Unit on standby. There'll likely be bullets flying about, tomorrow night.'

Lucy Blake's lips set into the thin, determined line he hadn't seen since the early days of their relationship. 'You're taking Gordon Pickering and Clyde Northcott and

Brendan Murphy in there. Three DCs: all three of them together haven't got the experience that I have.'

'Three men who can handle themselves when the fists are flying. Each of them stronger than you, even when you're fired up.'

'Like now, you mean? You're refusing to take me on an important assignment, just because I'm a woman.'

'And there are places where I'd take you and not them. Places I do take you, all the time. All right, I'm saying this isn't the place for a woman. I'm paid to use my judgement, amongst other things.'

'You're saying that a woman wouldn't be reliable like the men, in times of danger.'

'She might. But the men wouldn't be reliable if I had a woman like you around. They'd be watching out for you, when I want them to watch their own backs. Not to mention mine.'

She recognized a certain logic in this, though she wasn't going to admit it to Percy. Men were sentimental creatures, at the best of times. Despite their normal tendencies for lust and irresponsibility, they were prone to outbursts of chivalry at the most inopportune moments. Lucy Blake was driven to an irritated, 'This isn't equality, you know.'

'I have to go in there with the best team I can muster. I have to back my own judgement about the selection of that team. I'm considering my own safety, as well as that of everyone else involved in this.'

'And of course it wouldn't be the fact that you have a personal relationship with me that makes you want to make sure that I'm not in any danger.'

'Of course it wouldn't. You wouldn't be going in there tomorrow even if you were the ugliest and most objectionable female I can think of. Even if you were Barbara Tucker, for instance.' He threw in Tucker's Brünnhilde-like wife in an attempt to lower the tension. 'In fact especially not if it was Barbara Tucker. She'd present far too big a target.'

Lucy felt the corners of her mouth trying to crinkle. She knew now that she wasn't going to win this one. She repeated desperately, 'This isn't equality, and you know it.'

'You can always appeal to higher authority, if you don't approve of my decision.'

'To Tommy Bloody Tucker? He thinks women are only good for making tea and cleaning offices. He wouldn't put a woman within a mile of this action.'

'I told you, the George Bush Law of Averages. Even our much derided leader has to be right sometimes.'

'I still think you're wrong. I'm sure our Federation Representative would agree with me.'

'I doubt that, on this occasion. But as I'm telling you this project is still at this moment theoretical and highly confidential, you can hardly bring in the Fed. Rep., can you?' Percy, realizing he was sounding smug, tried to offer an olive branch. 'You'll be involved in the subsequent interviewing, where your skills will be much appreciated.'

'Except that the National Crime Squad or the Drugs Squad will take over all the really juicy interviews, as you well know.'

DS Blake was usually very clear-sighted about such matters. But on this occasion, as things would turn out, she was quite wrong.

Five

At ten o'clock on Wednesday night, there was no moon. But it was a cold, clear night, with just enough light from the stars to allow the long, low outline of the big house to be seen clearly against the night sky.

Peach usually felt himself irresistibly reminded of the house in *Psycho* on such occasions; he had met a few examples of the Anthony Perkins character in his career, some of them sinister, some of them no more than odd. But this house was clearly much bigger and grander than that decrepit motel in *Psycho*. It was much more like a National Trust mansion, both in its own dimensions and in the size of its grounds.

Marton Towers had never belonged to one of the nation's great landed families. It had been built in the heyday of neo-Gothic, when Victoria was still a young queen, and when labour was cheap, materials solid, and workmanship excellent. There were turrets, castellations and even the odd minaret, all executed with the exuberance of a Britain confident of its empire. In the days when King Cotton had ruled Lancashire, one of its magnates had enjoyed pouring his profits into this demonstration of his success.

Percy moved his small team into position at 22.05. Ultimately, they were to make some important arrests, whilst the Armed Response Unit covered them and every exit with their weapons. A piece of cake, Percy had told his team, in that cliché beloved of commanders. Well, it would be, wouldn't it? If things went to plan. If the element of surprise enabled them to keep the initiative. If...

Things rarely went exactly according to plan, when the police made a raid. Indeed, you couldn't plan every detail. Especially on a battlefield as big as this one.

Percy didn't like the size of the big house, feared the way that his resources might have to be spread too thinly over too wide an area. From three hundred yards away, he could already see many lights piercing the massive outline of the mansion against the navy sky. As well as the high block of the main house, there were servants' quarters, kitchens, old stables that had been converted into garages and workshops and God knew what else.

All of these were places where men could hide. Dangerous men, in an industry like this, where there were many millions of pounds available to employ muscle and guns. DCI Peach showed nothing to his team, but he was more on edge than he could remember being for years.

Somewhere behind him, a little further down the lane, members of the Armed Response Unit were probably peering over the seven-foot-high stone wall of the estate and thinking the same things he was thinking. Percy Peach hoped they were. It never paid to underestimate your enemy, or the dangers which were going to confront you in the next half an hour.

There was a solid stone gatehouse at the entrance to the Towers. A high arch framed the wrought-iron gates which screened the tarmac drive up to the front of the house. No one entered without passing the Cerberus who guarded it. A Cerberus which took the shape of Arnie Wright, a heavy who had done time for GBH and now controlled access to the man who owned Marton Towers.

If they were to retain the element of surprise on their side, Cerberus must remain toothless. Arnie Wright must not be allowed to warn his master and the drug barons who were meeting with him at this moment in the dining room of the big house of the imminent disruption of their feast.

Three men were plenty for this task. Percy glanced sideways, caught a glint of light from the gatehouse on a face which was blacker than the moonless night above them. DC Clyde Northcott, once a drug user himself, before he was recruited, first into the police and lately into the CID, by Percy Peach himself. Six feet three of bone and muscle. A hard bastard. A good man to have at your side on a night like this.

And on Peach's other side, the paler, fresher face of Brendan Murphy, who should have been Irish but who had spent all twenty-five years of his life in Lancashire. In that moment, Percy Peach was surer than ever of his decision to exclude DS Blake from this enterprise. It was simply not a suitable assignment for her. That was what he had told himself as well as Lucy, until now. It was only here, feeling the cold solidity of the estate wall against his fingertips, that he acknowledged to himself that he could never have faced Agnes Blake, if her daughter had come to any harm here.

A second later, they were at the gatehouse, slinking like predators out of the darkness and up to the thick stone walls of this huge sentry box. Arnie Wright was lounging back on his chair by the desk, turning the pages of the *Sun*, happy that he would be undisturbed for the rest of the evening now that all the expected guests had arrived. His unconscious assumption was that no one came to this isolated place on foot, that any strangers who came to disturb him would do so in a vehicle, whose engine noise would give him due notice of their arrival.

Peach studied him for a moment through the orange square of the gatehouse window. Wright's right hand was on the edge of his newspaper. It was perhaps five feet from the warning button which would give notice to the house that someone, some alien presence, was at the gatehouse and threatening to enter the main house.

Those could be the most important five feet of the evening. Peach nodded to each of the men beside him, felt them taking the same deep breath as he took, as they approached the door.

And then they were in, shouting instructions at the broad, startled face at the desk, telling it not to move. Wright did move, of course. As Peach flung himself into that five-foot gap between him and the electronic link to the house, he leapt up from his seat with a fierce, automatic oath.

But he had no chance. Clyde Northcott was on him, the force of his attack carrying Wright back against the wall, his ebony hand on the man's throat, bending his chin and his head backwards against the cold, unyielding plaster. 'Don't even think about it, sunshine!' he snarled into Wright's face from three inches.

And Wright's dilated eyes filled with fear as they saw the fierce determination in the dark pupils which were so close to his. He shook his head the minimal quarter of an inch which Northcott's grip allowed him, signifying that no, he wouldn't think about it, whatever 'it' might be. A hard bastard, this. Arnie Wright had met a few of them whilst he was

68

in Brixton. He knew when he was beaten.

Brendan Murphy cut the electronic link to the main house. Peach radioed to the uniformed men in the van a hundred yards down the lane to come and collect Wright, then gave the news of the first move in the battle to the Armed Response Unit who waited a little further away.

So far so good. The first phase was completed.

There were four nationalities among the group which sat around the big mahogany dining table in Marton Towers.

Jack Clark waited with two other men in an anteroom alongside the very grand panelled room, where Victorian industrialists had eaten huge meals and striven to achieve the transition from trade into the gentry. He could hear a low murmur of conversation from behind the huge panelled door of the dining room, but he could distinguish not a syllable of what was being said. He fancied that the conversation was in English, the new *lingua franca* of the twenty-first century, but he could not even be sure of that.

Jack wanted to hear laughter from behind that door, to hear voices raised in amusement and friendly exchange. Laughter meant that you were relaxed, and when you were relaxed you were vulnerable. He had long since ceased to wear a watch, but he knew that the strike must come soon, if it

69

came at all. He prayed that his friends when they came would be borne into that room on an irresistible tide of surprise.

His friends. He had come to terms with that now, but it had taken him a full day to switch sides again in his mind. He had worked so hard to submerge himself into his character in the squat that he had found it difficult to drag himself out of it, to change his mindset to accommodate what was going to happen here.

If things went according to plan. His brain framed again that condition, trying for the mindset which would ensure his safety, if tonight's raid failed and he had to live for a little longer with the armies of the night.

It was a long, narrow room where the three of them sat so nervously. Like people waiting to be interviewed for a job, Jack thought. But they did not talk nervously to each other, as candidates for a job might have done whilst they waited their turn. They sat on upright chairs a few yards from each other, with their backs against the wall.

The three of them had long since learned not to leave their backs unguarded, Jack decided. Since each of them had come into the room, he had made no eye contact with the others. The strange nervous trio sat quite still, gazing at the polished oak blocks of the parquet floor. And waited.

They heard the clink of crockery being removed from the big panelled room beside them, and knew that the time was coming when they would be called upon to speak, to make the right moves, which would enable them to move up to the next rank in this lucrative hierarchy of evil. With the knowledge that the moment was at hand, they did begin to move, massaging nervous hands together, scuffing the soles of trainers against the polished floor. But still they looked at that floor and never at each other.

Then the broad mahogany door of the dining room opened, and a figure stood for a moment silhouetted against the more brilliant light of that room behind him. All three pairs of eyes turned to the features they could not distinguish, each man wondered whether he was the one to be summoned into that dangerous group beyond the figure in the doorway.

It was at that moment that hell broke loose.

Even Jack Clark, the only one who should have been prepared for it, was shocked by the fury and the suddenness of the police arrival. The door at the other end of the big dining room, fully thirty yards from Jack, burst open as if a bomb had been detonated, and everywhere there was noise, crashing into their ears as if noise itself were a weapon. A harsh voice, impossibly loud, yelled from the other end of the room that armed police were surrounding the place, that every exit was covered, that no one should move.

No more than a second later, helmeted police with sub-machine guns poured through the door at the end of the anteroom where Jack and his companions stood petrified, screaming at them not to move, informing them in rapid, shouted words that they too were surrounded and that escape was impossible. A single shot went off in the dining room; it was followed by an almost simultaneous burst of police fire and a yell of anguish.

As always with a successful police raid, everything seemed to happen impossibly fast and at fortissimo volume. Jack heard the words of arrest being yelled in the dining room, the absurd instruction that the unseen men in there need not say anything, but it might harm their defence if they withheld information which they might later wish to use in court. The trappings of civilization, applied in a situation where no one could afford to be civilized.

And then Jack Clark found himself with his face against the wall, with a fiercely committed black officer holding his arm hard against the small of his back, so that he was squealing with agony and lifted almost off his feet as the words of arrest were shouted into his ear.

Behind him, DCI Peach glanced round the anteroom and permitted himself a brief moment of satisfaction. They'd got the undercover man safely in their clutches, and they hadn't blown his cover. Make sure it's Clyde Northcott who arrests our man, he'd said, then there'll be no suspicion among the enemy that he's one of ours.

Let the hard bastard do the job.

Twenty minutes later, it seemed to be all over.

On the broad gravelled area in front of the main house, an army of police vehicles was now visible in the white blaze of the arc lights they had turned upon the scene. There were five Armed Response Vehicles, four powerful saloons and one estate car. On an order from their chief, the ARU personnel were beginning to stow away their Heckler and Koch 9mm sub-machine guns and their Glock 9mm pistols in the double-locking safes, which were welded into the bodywork between the back seat and the boot. Procedure: that police watchword for all occasions.

The ARU men retained the backup side-arms which had been carried in the forward sections of the vehicles. But with the order to lock away the automatic weapons, they were beginning to relax. That order meant in effect that the mission was successfully concluded, that the divisional commander who was responsible for the overall strategy of this raid was happy that every dangerous person in this huge house had been arrested. In half an hour they would be back at base, removing their bullet-proof body armour, in that final divesting which signified that an operation was over.

There were five other police vehicles, their sirens silent but their blue lamps flashing steadily, which were now about to carry a variety of occupants away from Marton Towers. Some of them were the muscle with which the biggest criminals always seemed to surround themselves, as if a battery of thugs was a badge of success. But a great house of this size needed also a battalion of servants, many of whom were no doubt totally unconnected with the villainies which had financed the maintenance and prosperity of the Marton estate over the last few years. But everyone with even a random, peripheral connection with the owners would be questioned, every scrap of evidence assembled, to counteract the slick and articulate lawyers who would eventually appear for the defence in a high-profile court case.

The ambulance carrying the single casualty of the evening had already departed. The Turkish drug baron who had risen from the dining table and drawn a pistol, in defiance of the orders shouted at him, had been shot in the chest. Probably not fatal, the paramedics had volunteered, as they had slid the red-blanketed figure into the back of their vehicle and prepared to set the siren blaring for a swift passage to the hospital.

The chief of the Armed Response Unit was glad of that, for the sake of the man who had fired the burst from the Heckler and Koch. No one liked killing, even though it might be his job, even though the world might have been better off with this particular man removed from its surface.

DCI Peach was relieved that his part in this major operation had been successfully concluded. He was happy to see his own small team reassembling without injury at the conclusion of the raid. There was a strict discipline in the Armed Response Units, but with adrenaline and testosterone pulsing through the veins of young men, accidents could always happen.

His team were full of the happy excitement that is near to hysteria which comes with the successful conclusion of a tricky and dangerous enterprise. Once they had secured the gatehouse and access to the big house, their main duty had been to arrest the three men who had been waiting in the anteroom to be appointed as drug dealers, including their own undercover man, the Drugs Squad sergeant.

Jack Clark now sat in the back of the police van with his two companions, more dishevelled and unkempt than ever, and taking care to look thoroughly cowed and depressed by his arrest. It was not entirely a pose. With the knowledge that his months of deception were almost over, that his isolation in extreme danger was coming to an end, all energy had left him and exhaustion was taking over.

He sat on the bench at the side of the van, his shoulders hunched forward, his eyes on the floor of the vehicle. He roused himself only to continue the fiction of his arrest, as he felt DCI Peach studying him through the open doors at the back of the vehicle. 'That black bastard almost broke my arm!' he complained morosely.

Peach gave him a wicked grin, which he allowed to ripple round the other prisoners in the van. 'He's good, isn't he? Powerful lad, DC Northcott. And if I were you, son, I wouldn't add racial abuse to my other sins.' He slammed the doors cheerfully on the three men inside, banged on the metal to signal to the driver that he could drive his cargo to the nick. They would be separated for questioning, of course. That was when Jack Clark's long ordeal would finally come to an end.

Peach and his team were among the last to leave the scene, securing the doors of the mansion before they drove away. Property had to be secured, even when it belonged to the worst of villains. They drove between the high wrought-iron gates with the bronze crests upon them and past the empty gate-house. It seemed a long time since they had crept along its stone walls with such elaborate care to surprise Arnie Wright. A lot of drama had been crammed into the last ninety minutes.

It was no more than ten minutes after the last police vehicle had left that the first tiny orange glow appeared at the square window of the cottage. It was one of a terrace which had been formed from the former stables of Marton Towers. The light flickered, grew swiftly brighter, leapt with a crash through the glass and up the outside of the building.

And then there was smoke, whirling upwards into the night sky in a swift and hideous funnel, obscuring the thin sliver of moon which had now appeared low in the midnight sky. For a little while, there was no noise which could be heard from the gatehouse or the road. But the flames spread greedily sideways and upwards, until the first-storey windows in the long low block were as bright as those on the ground floor. It was not long before joists caught, and the ceilings began to fall with crashes like shellfire on to the old flagged floors where horses had once been groomed.

The conflagration was well advanced, rearing wildly and terribly against the blackness around it, before a motorist, driving along the lonely road which ran beside the long stone wall marking the boundary of the estate, caught the glare in the night sky. The fire station was seven miles away, but at that time of night, its machines made swift progress to the blaze.

For the second time on the same night, the normally invulnerable Marton Towers was invaded by a fleet of professional vehicles. This time they came not just with lights flashing but with bells ringing and sirens sounding to clear their passage, flinging the gravel behind them, as they swung across the front of the great mansion and away to the conflagration on its right.

The main house was safe. There was not much the firemen could do for the offices and mews cottages. They played their hoses on what was left of the roof and sprayed foam on whatever they could see of the interior. There wasn't much left in there that could be salvaged, by the looks of things. But even their powerful torches didn't reveal very much, amidst the smoke and steam which dominated the scene.

At least there was no need for heroics. There was no one screaming to be rescued, as the flames crept along the long, low building with such terrible speed. That was always the nightmare. It was a shame to see a building as venerable as this literally going up in smoke within an hour, but at least there seemed here to be no loss of life.

A fuller investigation would have to wait until the morning.

Six

On Thursday morning, Chief Superintendent Thomas Bulstrode Tucker was at his most benign.

'Good work last night, Peach. A straightforward assignment, once we'd planned it, but these things can always go wrong. Don't think I'm not aware of that. You and your men did well.'

'Thank you, sir. I shall convey your sentiments to them, in due course. They will no doubt show their usual appreciation.'

'We need all the good publicity we can get at present. You can leave all that to me, though, Percy. I've already called a media conference for two o'clock this afternoon. Nothing wrong with trumpeting our successes, you know.'

'Yes, sir. And there's certainly no one who surpasses you, when it comes to blowing the trumpet. I emphasize that to the lads and lasses downstairs, whenever I sense a rumble of discontent.'

Tucker noticed no irony. 'I thought I should take the opportunity to stress to the media just how successful we were last night.'

'Yes, sir. Blow your own trumpet, as you say.' Percy noticed that Tucker had made this into his DCI's enterprise before the event, in case it went wrong. With success, it had become 'ours'. No doubt by two o'clock this afternoon Tucker would be speaking of 'my' raid at Marton Towers.

'I understand there was one casualty.'

'Yes, sir. One of the big drugs men was shot. Turkish, I believe. He's had surgery in Brunton Royal Infirmary, I'm told: another unwelcome burden on the National Health Service. I think he's expected to survive; from what I hear, he'd be no loss to our society.'

Tucker frowned at such insensitivity. 'Casualties are never a good thing, even among villains, Peach. Casualties do our image no good at all.'

'Yes, sir. I think this chap was trying to blow one of the Armed Response Unit into kingdom come at the time.'

'That's as may be, Peach. I understand the difficulties. I just wish this hadn't happened, that's all. No doubt one of the newspaper men will wish to raise it this afternoon.' Chief Superintendent Tucker frowned at the thought of this blot upon a perfect day.

'Give you a chance to make your usual vigorous defence of the boys who were running the risks, won't it, sir?'

'One has to be diplomatic, Peach, on these occasions, whatever one's private feelings on such matters.'

You'll end up bloody apologizing before you've finished, you time-serving old windbag, thought Percy. But this fool was in charge of CID, and Percy Peach must do what he could for his team. 'DC Northcott did very well last night, sir. As did DCs Murphy and Pickering.'

Tucker looked puzzled, as if he could not put faces to the names of these men whose careers he should have been monitoring. Then recognition of one name dawned. His distaste sounded in every syllable as he said, 'Northcott? Isn't he the officer who had a drug problem himself at one time? The black officer you insisted on bringing into our team?'

'Indeed, sir. He was excellent during the raid last night. I gave him the responsibility of arresting the undercover man, and he carried it off most convincingly.'

'I'm glad to hear it. I should keep a close eye on Northcott, however, if I were you.'

'Indeed I will, sir. He should go far, in due course. Being black and reliable and good at his job. If he was only female and lesbian he'd go even further, but that would be a difficult transition for a six-foot-three hard bugger, wouldn't it, sir?'

Tucker, who seemed quite unconscious of his own prejudices against women and ethnic minorities, winced at such political incorrectness in his DCI. 'When I advised you to keep a close eye on DC Northcott, I meant that one of his background would need—'

'Good to know that you're aware of his progress and his potential, sir. Could be a candidate for the Masons, before he's finished, our Clyde!' Percy chortled delightedly at the notion.

Peach's chortle was a frightening thing. Tucker shuddered and decided to relinquish the subject of DC Northcott. 'Anyway, the main thing is that we did well last night. Our preliminary planning session was well worth while. That's the secret of success, you know, Peach. Forward planning.'

Percy was not aware that his chief had made any contribution at all to the planning of last night's activities, but he shrugged his broad shoulders philosophically. 'I'll make sure the CID section as a whole understands exactly how much your overview and your grasp of strategy contributed to last night's success, sir.'

Tommy Bloody Tucker tried to catch his man's eye with an admonitory glare, but found that Peach's glassy stare was now fixed as usual on the wall above his head. He searched his mind feverishly for something which would take this bantam cock of a chief inspector down a peg or two. 'I understand that the operation was not a complete success. That as well as the casualty we have already discussed, a fire occurred, despite the very substantial police presence.'

'No, sir.'

'What do you mean, "No, sir"? The report I have in front of me speaks of very substantial fire damage in a row of terraced dwellings at Marton Towers. Further details to follow, it says, but clearly very substantial damage. So it's really rather silly to try to pretend that—'

'Fire certainly occurred, sir. Substantial damage, as you say. But it wasn't part of our operation, sir. Very probably had no connection at all with it. The fire did not start, or at any rate was certainly not apparent, until some time after the last police officer had left the scene, sir.'

Tucker leaned forward and made a note on the pad in front of him, frowning as if he were digesting and recording a complex abstract idea. 'I'll make that clear if any of these journos try to raise the matter of the fire at my media conference. Good point that, Peach. No fire until after the last police officer had left the scene. I'll remember.'

'Yes, sir. Pity about the damage: it's the part of the house which used to be the stables, in Victorian and Edwardian days. No impairment of the main house where we snatched the drug villains, fortunately. I'll be able to let you know how extensive the destruction of the cottages and offices is, in due course.'

'Oh, there's no need for you to get

involved, Peach. Leave it to the fire-service boys: just make it clear that the fire was nothing to do with us, and keep away, is my advice.'

'Can't do that, sir.'

'Really, Peach, I think I must insist—'

'Further details have just come in, sir. As you said they would, when you mentioned the fire. I'll liaise with the fire-service personnel, but it seems there might be a need for police involvement, after all.'

'If this fire was nothing to do with the raid last night, there really seems little point in—'

'There's a body up there, sir.'

'A body?'

'A corpse, sir.' Peach chose monosyllables wherever possible, and spoke as if he was spelling out the idea to a slow-learning child. 'Found this morning, in one of the cottages, sir. Very little of it left, sir, it seems. I'm going out there to see exactly how much now.' He looked into the wide-eyed countenance of his superior officer and allowed himself a grim smile. 'Remains to be seen, as you might say, sir.'

Marton Towers had an estate of just under a hundred acres. That was modest by comparison with the great English estates, which had originated in medieval days and then been extended by judicious marriages and by supporting the winning sides in national upheavals. But it was large for the first half of the nineteenth century, when this impressive and rather grandiose residence had been built.

In modern east Lancashire, when twelve houses and more were crowded on to each precious acre, a hundred-acre estate was huge. It was enclosed by a seven-foot-high stone wall, which would in itself have cost as much as a small row of terraced houses to build. The lane which provided the only vehicular access to the Towers ran alongside the wall for a quarter of a mile before it reached the front gates. At the rear, where the boundary of the estate climbed gently up the lower slopes of a hill, the wall was just as well maintained, but rarely troubled by a human presence.

Sometimes the odd adventurous hiker would scale the low ridge behind the house, but no footpath was marked on even the large-scale Ordnance Survey maps, and the sheep who were pastured on this rolling and sparsely wooded ground were normally undisturbed.

On this Thursday morning, a solitary pair of eyes gazed down from the shelter of a group of beeches on to the rear view of Marton Towers. The pale March sun of the earlier part of the week had deserted Lancashire; the day was dank and chill, with the threat of a little drizzle or even sleet before nightfall. From behind the smooth trunk of a mature tree, the man watched the thin column of black smoke, which rose slow and straight into the still air. Then he took a small pair of binoculars from the pocket of his anorak and studied the site of the fire, which had so ravaged this particular section of the estate on the previous evening.

The single long line of what had been a pleasingly symmetrical appendage to the main house was now broken. There was an ugly gap towards one end, where thirty yards of what had originally been the slated roof of the stables had disappeared completely. On each side of this, partly ruined walls projected irregularly, like broken and blackened teeth.

On the other side of the scene, where there was access from the road, there were no doubt vehicles and activity, but from this man's viewpoint on the hill, the ravaged scene looked almost deserted. He had seen a red fire engine leave ten minutes ago. Even from eight hundred yards away he could catch the acrid smell that always hangs about a scene when ancient mortar and dampened wood have been consumed by fire and then doused by foam and water.

He knew where he was going to scale the wall. Stone walls weren't difficult, unless they had been exceptionally well maintained. Seven feet of smooth brick could give you problems, but in stone it was normally easy to find foot and hand holds.

He was over the wall in five seconds, dropping with simian agility to the grass within and moving swiftly to the cover of a clump of rhododendrons, which were heavy with buds. He moved cautiously nearer and nearer to the site of last night's conflagration, until he could see at first hand the blackened and splintered beams he had studied through the binoculars from half a mile away.

No one looked out to the rear of the ravaged masonry, even when he moved to within twenty yards of it, even when he could hear the sound of voices from within, even when he could catch the odd word of what was being said. And from here, he could see what he had not been able to see from the hillside.

There were long blue-and-white plastic strips stretched between newly erected posts at the front of the place, on the side of the gap which was nearer to the main house. They enclosed a rough rectangle which he thought was probably thirty yards by twenty, which began at the rear wall of the terrace which was now so near to him and extended for perhaps ten or fifteen yards out beyond the front wall.

The man knew what this denoted well enough. The police were here, as well as the firemen. These plastic strips were marking out a scene-of-crime area.

He moved swiftly but with no real haste

back to the rhododendrons. He had thought he would escape undetected from the scene, but when he was almost back at the spot where he had scaled the wall, there was a shout from behind him. He glanced over his shoulder and saw a uniformed constable, stepping over the blackened rubble and commanding him to stop. It was an order he was never going to heed.

He was back over the wall as swiftly and easily as he had entered, his trainers and his hands slipping swiftly into the crannies which gave him leverage. Then he was away up the hillside, gaining height efficiently over ground he knew well. The sheep started away in groups from the route chosen by this unfamiliar intruder, but no hunters pursued him.

When he looked back, the police constable had vanished. The man did not linger on the hillside. He had seen all that he needed to see.

Seven

DCI Peach felt entitled to a ritual police grumble as he settled himself into the passenger seat of the Mondeo. 'The police surgeon confirmed death at ten o'clock this morning. A formality, as usual. A waste of public money, when we're perpetually told how much policing costs.'

'You mean the local forensic physician. That's what we call them nowadays.' Lucy Blake corrected him with some satisfaction, whilst giving her full attention to the town-centre traffic.

'Clever little sod, aren't you, at times?' Peach glanced sideways at his driver, studying without embarrassment the dark-red hair, the faint freckling where it met the forehead, the clear aquamarine eyes studying the road ahead, the tilt of the small chin, the rounding of the left breast beneath the blue sweater, the thighs which moved so smoothly and efficiently as his DS changed gear.

'Finished your survey, have you?' said Lucy acidly. You couldn't do much about it when you were driving, but you might as well let him know that you were conscious of his appraisal.

'Just like to make sure that police personnel are in good working order. I don't get enough chances to study you in profile.' He observed the passing scene as they reached the suburbs of Brunton, waved cheerfully to an old lady coming out of the post office. You got to know a great number of the citizens, worthy and unworthy, when you worked for ten years in a town with a population of under a hundred thousand.

'I don't like being appraised like a prize pig,' DS Blake said primly.

'Like the Empress of Blandings,' said Percy, recalling a memory of P. G. Wodehouse from somewhere deep in his subconscious. He smiled, in fond reminiscence of a more innocent time in his own life, watched the hedgerows which were beginning to appear, and said, 'You're still resentful about last night's operation, aren't you?'

'It was a very efficiently conducted snatch, from what I hear. My only point is that I should have been involved.' Lucy was aware that she was beginning to sound petty, and was immediately annoyed with herself. 'But I've already made my views clear on that.'

'Indeed you have, DS Blake. Abundantly clear. But I'm sure your mum will be delighted that I didn't subject you to the danger of being shot to pieces. That the sweet body I've just been checking on is still in prime condition.' Percy smiled contentedly as they turned off the main road, on to the lane which would eventually take them to Marton Towers.

'Don't you dare discuss such things with my mum! She already thinks I should be stuck at home washing nappies.'

'Ah, the wisdom of age. If only our society would imitate others and acknowledge that the passing years bring a wisdom which is denied to the young!' Percy shook his head sadly. 'Anyway, there isn't much washing of nappies nowadays,' he pointed out in his mildest voice.

'I'm talking the way she talks,' said Lucy with irritation. 'Kindly leave the subject, please.'

'All right. Let's just point out that you may have missed last night's little excitements, but you're now on your way to the investigation of a suspicious death.'

'You think this is more than just a victim of the fire?'

Peach adopted an excruciatingly over-the-top Hollywood accent. 'I gotta hunch, doll. I gotta hunch, kid. And in this game, you gotta play your hunches, babe.'

Lucy shuddered histrionically. 'Don't give up the day job.'

The high gates of Marton Towers stood open and the gatehouse seemed to be untenanted. Peach gave it scarcely a glance as they passed, fearing obscurely that even an unspoken recollection of the previous night's action might provoke his DS into renewed recriminations.

They put on the paper suits, slipped the plastic bags over their feet and made their way cautiously between the plastic strips which denoted the designated path marked out by the scene-of-crime team. This one was still directed by a police officer rather than the civilian who was becoming increasingly common.

Sergeant Jack Chadwick was an old colleague of Peach's. He had been forced to leave CID for this job after a serious injury suffered whilst apprehending armed villains conducting a bank raid. He greeted Percy like the old friend he was, nodded at Lucy Blake and said, 'It's a grim one, this. But you'll have a better stomach for it than your boss.'

In the strange argot of the police service, this was a compliment. It meant not only that he knew Lucy Blake but that he rated her as a copper. She wasn't some shrinking violet of a woman who was likely to keel over at the sight of blood or a particularly horrid corpse, but a valued colleague. The notion was silly, out of date, understated and perfectly understood by all the parties involved.

Peach said, 'Where do we go, Jack?'

Chadwick gave him a grim smile. 'There are two scene-of-crime areas here. Overlapping and perhaps connected. There's the spot where the fire started, and there's a body, within a few yards or so of that spot. It's still quite possible, of course, that neither will be the scene of a crime. That we are investigating an accidental fire and an accidental death.' His tones indicated that he felt that unlikely.

Lucy Blake said sharply, 'You think this fire was started deliberately?'

Jack Chadwick shrugged his experienced shoulders. 'The fire-service boys do. All unofficial, as yet. Their expert is coming out here later this afternoon.'

They looked round at the blackened floors and the charred stumps of what had yesterday been desirable living accommodation. At that moment, a big Mercedes drew almost silently to a stop behind them. 'The pathologist,' explained Peach as he looked round. 'I arranged that he should meet me here at two thirty. As we both had to come here, I thought it might save a bit of time if I could get his initial reactions today straight away.'

The police preoccupation with speed was automatic; it stemmed from the knowledge that crimes which were not solved quickly were often not solved at all. The pathologist was a heavily built older man with sandy hair and thick-lensed glasses. Jack Chadwick wondered if he would ever meet one of the young and glamorous women pathologists who seemed to be so prominent among the crime series he saw on television.

The new arrival stood for a moment and

surveyed the scene of desolation around Jack Chadwick and his two CID colleagues. Serious fires always leave the area looking like a miniature war zone, so complete is the ruin they cause. All of them had experienced this smell before; it included charred wood, ancient mortar, dampness, decay, the chemicals of the firemen's sprays and other, unidentifiable, disturbing elements. The combination was not as strong or overwhelming here as in some instances, because the roof had gone and the place was open to the air. There was no need now for masks; the impact was more melancholy than disgusting. The prevailing effects were of destruction and decay.

Each of them felt the depression, the sense of one small piece of life lost for ever, but none of them voiced it. The pathologist allowed himself the unprofessional luxury of a sigh before he said simply, 'Where is it?' and then followed Jack Chadwick, the only one of the four who had so far seen the corpse, away to his right.

The thing was still an anonymous 'it'. Lucy pondered on how a death like this drained away all humanity. This thing did not even have a gender yet, let alone an age, or the complex network of human emotions and relationships with others which made a man or woman human. Yet not long ago it had probably been a lively human being, laughing, talking, raging, beset with all the complex intricacies of life.

They would need to bring as much as they could of that person back, through other people's memories, if this was indeed a suspicious death. She followed the three men through broken walls, stepping carefully over the detritus of bricks and charcoal, until all four of them stopped abruptly and instinctively.

It was so badly burned that it should have lost its humanity. It was totally black, with no hint of skin or flesh or blood in what they could see. Yet its shape told that it had been a person once. The appalled Lucy Blake distinguished first a trunk, and then the vestiges of what must have been arms and legs.

The corpse lay against the wall, in a position which no living human could have adopted and held for more than a second or two. 'We think she's fallen through from the room above when the ceiling collapsed with the fire,' said Jack Chadwick quietly.

Why did people, especially professionals, always assume that victims were female? For the same reason that they assumed that criminals were male, perhaps. Because of probabilities, because of the statistics they confronted every day, thought Lucy gloomily. She moved forward a little, to where the top of the remains lay in deepest shadow at the corner of the room, then recoiled with a gasp. The front of the head had retained what was clearly recognizable as a face, even with the hair, the eyes and almost all the flesh burned away. The lips had gone, but the teeth they had once concealed were twisted into an awful, incongruous grin, as if their revulsion and puzzlement were being mocked by the thing at the centre of them.

The pathologist set about restoring some professional detachment to what the four of them were staring at. He lowered himself ponderously on to one knee beside the corpse, as if genuflecting before some sacrificial altar. 'I won't be able to learn a lot here. I'll need this on the table at the mortuary before I can tell you much.' As the medical man began the preliminary examination which was all he could conduct on site, the other three turned away from him, as if to allow the thing which had once been human some last, vestigial dignity.

Jack Chadwick, who had discovered that dreadful object in the room beyond them many hours earlier, spoke to Peach and Blake as if they were grieving relatives rather than police officers who had seen worse than this. 'I'm sure she – if it is a she – died of suffocation from the smoke, long before the flames got at her. She'd have been able to get out, you see, otherwise: she wouldn't have been trapped, in the early stages of the fire. She probably didn't feel anything.'

Sergeant Chadwick found he suddenly needed to talk, after maintaining his detached front for many hours with the civilian photographers and junior policemen who made up his SOCO team. Jack found himself saying things you would say to relatives, rather than to fellow officers, just to relieve his own emotions. He had seen all sorts of corpses in his time, but he found that the blackened remnant next door was disturbing him more than any of them.

Peach walked to the other end of the crime scene site delineated by the plastic ribbons to what seemed to have been the source of the fire, and conducted a discussion with his colleague of many years about the possibilities that this fire had been started by a human hand rather than accidentally. Lucy Blake watched and listened, wondering whether Peach was deliberately distracting Chadwick's attention from the charred thing next door which seemed to be upsetting him. Percy would have ridiculed the notion of such sensitivity, but she had seen it in him before, and usually when she least expected it.

Such thoughts were abruptly dispelled by the news the pathologist brought when he emerged from beyond the shattered and blackened internal walls. Jack Chadwick had been wrong about both the gender of the corpse and the way it had died.

The pathologist tried to speak with the heavy, unemotional calm that would match his own bulk and his years of experience. But he knew the implications of what he had to communicate, and he could not keep the drama out of his voice as he said, 'Your body is male. And my first impression is that he didn't die in this fire. I hope there's enough of him left for me to confirm this and give you some more details when I get him on the table.'

Eight

Chief Superintendent Thomas Bulstrode Tucker was at his most affable with the TV make-up girl. 'Just cut out as many of the wrinkles as you can!' he said as she powdered him lightly. Modesty always impressed these young women, he thought. And his confidence would show her that he was now an old hand at this television and radio business.

His press-relations officer had not been able to arrange the media conference before five o'clock. No matter: that had given him more time to prepare and allowed him a covert visit to his hairdresser. He was at his best now, he felt, urbane and handsome in the perfectly tailored uniform he always adopted for these public occasions, his regular features groomed enough to suggest a man still full of energy, yet with the gravitas a senior officer needed. He looked like a man fitted to weigh and respond to the most serious crimes visited upon the citizens of Brunton and its surrounding areas.

He smiled benignly at the collection of four microphones which he would once have

99

found daunting. 'I am happy to announce a major victory in our unceasing war against crime and those who practise it,' he began. 'Last night a raid was conducted under my direction at Marton Towers.'

The young interviewer from Granada had been carefully briefed by him on the questions she should put. 'Our understanding is that you succeeded in apprehending some very significant criminal figures, Chief Superintendent Tucker.'

He nodded sagely during a calculated pause, which allowed him a slight, benign smile at his questioner and the wider world beyond the cameras. 'You will understand better than most that there are limits to what I can say at this moment, Carol. Under our splendid English legal system, even the worst of villains are innocent until proved guilty.' He snorted with amused derision at the thought of that. A swipe at the law and a sense of humour always went down well with the viewers.

Then Tucker leaned forward, as if imparting a significant confidence which was designed for his interviewer alone, but which his audience might be permitted to catch. 'My own view is that we arrested some very big villains indeed last night. I don't mind volunteering that thought to you, because I am quite certain that my opinions will be borne out whenever we bring these people to trial.'

'Would I be right in assuming that the major fish you netted in last night's raid were drug barons?'

He smiled benignly, a man in control of the situation and happy to encourage youthful enthusiasm. He said impishly, 'I think that will prove to be correct. "Drug barons" is indeed the popular phrase, though some of us working coppers are sometimes tempted towards more industrial language. Your sources of information are very sound, Carol.' As indeed they should be, since he had planted the question with her only ten minutes earlier.

'And you were present yourself at this highly successful raid, Superintendent Tucker?'

He frowned a little, despite his determined panache: he hadn't planted that one. 'On this occasion, I could regrettably not be present in person to make the actual arrests. I wanted to be, of course, but I was prevailed upon to take a more complete and overall view of our strategy. It is one of the penalties of office that one cannot be directly involved in the action and feel as many collars as one used to do. However, I think you would agree that on this occasion the strategy proved to be faultless.'

He had been waffling there, and his interviewer was intelligent enough to sense it. But it wasn't her brief to be controversial. This was a news item, and the man wasn't a politician. She offered him a few more of the questions he had asked for, and elicited the information that eleven people had been arrested at Marton Towers, that three of them had flown into Ringway on the previous day, that he was confident that these and two other men were very big scalps indeed for the relatively small Brunton CID section. Then her director gave the signal to cut and the cameras ceased recording.

Television presenters are always at least as much concerned with their own performance as with that of the interviewee. When the press took over the questioning, there were some among them who had no such concerns. Alf Houldsworth, the one-eyed and aged reporter for the local *Evening Dispatch*, had for many years been the crime correspondent of the *Daily Express*; as a young man, he had experienced the last great days of Fleet Street and its legendary drinkers, corruption in the Metropolitan Police and the mayhem of the Krays.

Alf Houldsworth had a keen eye for pretension, a keen ear for evasions and a keen nose for bullshit. He had detected all of these in Superintendent Tommy Bloody Tucker a long time ago. He now said, 'The public will indeed be gratified to hear of the apprehension of major figures in an evil trade. But was this not in fact a Serious Crime Squad operation?'

Tucker knew immediately that he had

overplayed his hand. But at least the television cameras had ceased to roll, and he was pretty sure that the radio mikes were off as well. He could afford to give this tiresome man short shrift. 'The Serious Crime Squad was indeed involved. But surely—'

'As were the Drugs Squad, I'm sure.'

Tucker wondered where this irritant in the smoothly running wheel of his world got his information. Houldsworth had been known to drink pints with Percy Peach, on occasion, but there surely hadn't been time for that here. He gave Houldsworth a benign and tolerant smile. 'I'm sure that the public are not concerned with the petty details of who did what. The important thing for them and for any right-thinking person is that serious criminals are now safely under lock and key.'

'Were the Armed Response Unit involved last night?'

Tucker looked round the room, inviting others to come in, but saw only busily scribbling ball-pens. The reporters recognized in Houldsworth a man who knew his stuff; they were quite prepared to make full notes on any casualties which fell under his rain of bullets. The Chief Superintendent said stiffly, 'The Armed Response Unit was indeed present last night; it may even have been reinforced with trained personnel from neighbouring areas. That is standard practice when one is conducting an important operation like this. And I think I may say that—'

'So the Brunton CID section was in fact a very small part of a big operation.'

'Look, Mr Houldsworth, you seem very concerned to denigrate what was in fact a very—'

'Just anxious to get the facts correct, Superintendent Tucker. We newspaper men are so often accused of getting them wrong, you see.' A small ripple of approving laughter moved through the bent heads of Alf Houldsworth's fellow hacks as they scribbled. 'So how many Brunton CID officers were actually involved?'

'That is scarcely your business, and hardly a matter of public interest, I'd have thought.'

'It's confidential information?' Houldsworth's disbelief was apparent in every syllable.

Tucker scowled the scowl which television had never seen. 'I believe there were five of my officers involved.'

'Amongst a total of how many?' Alf Houldsworth made no secret of the fact that he was enjoying himself. That was easier because he was plainly giving much enjoyment to his fellow journalists.

'This really is not relevant, you know.' Tucker managed a sickly smile, looked desperately around the room for a more friendly questioner, saw only ranks of happy, expectant faces and accepted defeat. 'I believe

104

there were forty or fifty police personnel involved altogether. As I told you at the outset, this was a very important and a very successful operation.'

'And your CID section made the arrests?'

Tucker saw rescue at last: this bitter, beaten-up journo had surely overplayed his hand. 'That was indeed our function. The key phase of the whole operation, if I may say so.' He gave his audience a beam, hoping for answering and congratulatory smiles. It was the wrong audience.

'At which you chose to be absent.' Houldsworth nodded seriously and made a note.

Tucker threw a patronizing smile at the bent grey head. 'Mr Houldsworth obviously does not understand police procedures. My duties as Head of CID were to provide the strategy for success, to select the best team, to maintain an overview of the situation.'

'So the tactics for this very successful series of arrests were yours, not DCI Peach's?' Houldsworth's watery but experienced blue eyes were now lifted, wide and innocent, towards the man on the dais.

Tucker wondered if his involuntary wince at the mention of Peach's name had been apparent in the crowded room. 'Detective Chief Inspector Peach is an able and experienced officer. I always give such men room for manoeuvre. They need to be able to react to swiftly changing events.' The familiar phrases which should have slipped smoothly from his tongue felt dry in his mouth. 'I really cannot reveal any more of the detail, you know. It might prejudice the success of future operations of this kind.'

Houldsworth nodded an unexpected acceptance. Then the forty-year-old woman at his side, a former protégée of Alf's at the *Daily Express*, looked up for the first time from her notes and said, 'There was a serious fire at Marton Towers last night.'

It was a statement, not a question, leaving Tucker no room for evasion. 'I believe there was. It had nothing to do with our very successful capture of the drugs barons.'

'You're convinced of that, are you? Our latest information is that the origin of the fire may not be accidental.'

Tucker regretted once again that he had not taken the latest briefing before going into the TV make-up room. Perhaps his visit to his hairdresser hadn't been such a good idea, after all. It was no use asking this un-smiling, hatchet-faced woman where she had heard this; he'd get the usual stuff about protecting her sources. The most direct of which was no doubt in this case the deplorable Alf Houldsworth. Tucker said stiffly, 'That is the first suggestion I have heard that arson might be involved. However, I repeat that, as far as I am aware, the fire was totally unconnected with our very successful raid.'

'As far as you are aware.' Her brief nod over her notebook conveyed that this man did not seem to be aware of very much. She kept her voice studiously low-key as she put her final question. 'And can you give us any further news on the body found at the scene of the fire?'

Tucker was disconcerted that she should know of this, dismayed to see the looks he was getting from the television and radio teams, to whom he had said nothing of either the fire or the death. He said testily, 'We do not yet know whether this is a suspicious death or not. I shall authorize a press release tomorrow, when we are fully acquainted with the facts.'

But the buzz as the correspondents hurried from the room to file their stories was all about these last two questions and his non-answers, not about his calm and urbane television performance.

Not for the first time, Thomas Bulstrode Tucker wondered quite how things could have gone so wrong.

The radio and television broadcasts on that Thursday evening carried Tucker's interview about the arrests of the major drugs criminals in the splendid but isolated setting at Marton Towers. It was news, good news, and stressed as such by the newsreader who introduced it.

But the successful attack on a drugs empire might not have been the lead item on the national news without the two simple facts which gave it an electrifying postscript. There had been a major fire at the big house in Lancashire during the hours following these important arrests, with a speculation that arson might be involved. And the charred remnants of a human corpse had been found among the debris. A stark statement, with no further details. But a sensational statement: the newsreader's satisfaction in that thought seeped into his professionally neutral tones.

Tucker had gone home to lick his wounds after the chastening conclusion to his media conference, but at eight o'clock that night, DCI Peach and DS Blake and most of the CID section were still at the station, setting up the elaborate machinery of a murder enquiry.

This one was more than usually complex. They would need to interview the people who had been arrested on serious but very different charges on the previous night, to find out whether they knew anything about either the fire or the body. They would need to interview the resident staff of the Towers, who had nothing to do with the drugs trafficking but who had been evacuated because of the fire danger on the previous night. They would need to identify and interview whatever other dubious characters had been in and out of the large estate in the period before the fire.

At present, they had no idea how far back

into the past their researches would have to extend. Because at present they had no accurate idea of when this as yet unidentified man had died.

The man in charge of all the permanent employees at Marton Towers had been overseeing the meal and its aftermath when the police intervened so dramatically on Wednesday night. As a result of this involvement, he had been arrested, along with everyone else close to the men at that meeting.

Now, almost twenty-four hours later, after some intensive questioning of him and others, the officers of the National Crime Squad had satisfied themselves that this man of fifty-seven was not involved in any but the most peripheral way in the drugs traffic. It was almost nine o'clock when a weary inspector came into the Brunton CID section and signified that they were prepared to release him.

Peach nodded. 'We'll have to let him go soon, if we're not prepared to charge him with anything. But I'd like a word with him first. We have what may well prove to be a murder investigation to conduct. If he's in charge of the staff up there, he'll be able to tell us things about the other people who live there. Until we can eliminate him, he's a murder suspect himself. I'd like to see him whilst he's still officially under arrest, still feeling under threat from the law and brutal policemen like me.'

After last night's operation and the very full day which had followed it, the Detective Chief Inspector was feeling unusually tired. But he took a deep breath outside the inter-view-room door, then bounced into the room as if he had just come on duty, fresh and full of energy. 'I'm DCI Peach and this radiant creature is DS Blake. And you are Mr Neville Holloway. I'm sure you won't have any objections to our recording what we have to say to each other in here, Mr Holloway. These machines save a lot of com-plications, when people remember things differently later on.'

The silver-haired man in front of him looked balefully at the cassette recorder Peach had set turning, then up into the cheerful, almost boyish, round face beneath the fringe of black hair and the bald head. 'I've said all I have to say. I know nothing about any of this drugs stuff.'

'I heard you'd been saying that. Repeat-edly, apparently.' Peach nodded casually, as if to indicate that he himself was still unconvinced. 'Still under arrest, though, at the moment.' He smiled cheerfully, as if that was a most happy state of affairs. 'And no doubt still, as a responsible and innocent citizen, anxious to help the police with their enquiries in any way you can.'

'I've already been interviewed for hours.

You should either charge me with something or let me out of here.'

'Know a little about the law, do you, Mr Holloway? I suppose I should have expected that.'

'What do you mean. I'm not a lawyer, and I've no knowledge of—'

'Been in trouble with the law in the past, though, haven't you? So I'd expect you to know a little bit about your rights.'

Neville Holloway glared at him, then shrugged wearily. 'All right, I've got a record. It's a long time ago, and I did my time, but it's once a villain always a villain, isn't it, with you lot?'

Peach nodded his head happily. 'A lot of us are what you might call unenlightened in our attitudes, yes. Perhaps it's because statistics so often support the view you've just expressed. Recidivism, I believe they call it, the people who claim to know about such things. Serious crime, fraud. On the increase, nowadays, unfortunately.'

'I did my two years.'

'Paid your debt to society, as they say. Seventeen years ago. No further record of offences, the computer says.'

'That's because there haven't been any. And I didn't have any connection with these drugs offences that people have been pressing me about all day.'

'Do you know, I'm almost inclined to believe that, Mr Holloway? But then, I always see the best in people. Bit of a soft touch – I expect that's my reputation among the local criminal fraternity. You've developed a different career for yourself now. You're the butler at Marton Towers.'

Neville Holloway smiled for the first time since Peach had mounted his challenge. 'Not the butler, Chief Inspector. Mr Crouch doesn't go in for such old-fashioned terms. And you could say my remit is a little wider than that. I'm in charge of the day-to-day running of Marton Towers – responsible for all the staff, not just those in the house, but those employed throughout the estate.'

'Pity you're not a butler: I've always fancied arresting one of them. But then no corpse was found skewered to the floor in the library. I'm charged with investigating an even more serious crime than trafficking in illegal drugs, you see, Mr Holloway. That's why we're still closeted together in this rather unpleasant little room at quarter past nine on a cold March night.'

'More serious?' Neville Holloway had told himself a moment ago that he was not going to give this annoying little turkey-cock of an inspector any more reactions, but this one was prised from him by his surprise.

'Murder, Mr Holloway.' Despite the calculated levity of his approach, which was designed to irritate a man fatigued by hours of questioning, Peach was watching his man closely. Holloway seemed to be genuinely surprised. But if he had any involvement in this death, it would have been good policy to feign ignorance. 'You are no doubt aware of the serious fire which damaged the former stable block at Marton Towers last night. One of the things found amongst the debris this morning was a body.'

Holloway looked suitably impressed. He thought for a moment and said, 'I was arrested along with the visitors to the house last night, and I have been in custody since that moment. Plainly I had no connection with that fire, which began after we had been taken away from Marton Towers.'

Peach smiled at such naivety. 'If only things were so simple, Mr Holloway! You could have set a device to ignite when you were off the premises. Or you could have paid someone else to start the blaze when you were safely elsewhere. But I'm a bit of a soft touch, as I told you, so let's assume for the moment that you had nothing to do with the fire. It doesn't let you off the murder hook, I'm afraid. This person didn't die in the fire. This person died some time before it started.'

'Who is it? And when did she die?'

Peach, having carefully left the gender of the corpse out of his information, was delighted with this. 'Now why should you assume that the body was female? Did you have some reason to expect a female victim? That's what I have to ask myself. It's a natural question, wouldn't you say, DS Blake?'

'Indeed it is, sir. Can you explain your reaction to us, sir?'

Holloway found himself more shaken by this studiously polite question from a pretty young woman than by Peach's truculent ironies. You expected policemen to be nasty and aggressive: he felt he could cope with that. He said, 'I can't explain it, no. I suppose that numerically, we have twice as many women as men employed at the Towers, so it was perhaps logical for me to assume this was a woman.'

More logical than it was for the SOCO officer to assume the same thing, Lucy thought wryly. She glanced at Peach, then said, 'The victim was a man, sir. The body was so badly damaged that it has not been possible to identify it yet. Have you any idea who this man might be?'

His first impulse was to protest complete ignorance immediately. Instead, he paused for a moment, as if to give the matter serious thought, before he said, 'Probably someone who worked on the estate, you'd think, wouldn't you? I'm not aware that any of our current employees has gone missing, but if we include the people who come in daily, quite large numbers are involved.'

'And you can no doubt give us those numbers.' She poised a small gold ball-pen over the pad in front of her.

114

'There are currently seven staff who live on the premises and eight more who come in each day. That does not include cleaners who come in for a few hours a week as required.' Despite his exhaustion, a little pride crept into his tone with the precision which came so effortlessly.

Peach's heart sank at the thought of the number of people who would need to be eliminated. He said with a grim little smile, 'You're obviously in touch with most things which happen at the Towers. We shall no doubt need to speak to you again, when we know more of the details of this death. You'll be released in the next half an hour, Mr Holloway.'

He switched the cassette recorder off and sat looking thoughtfully at the machine after the tall, erect man had left the room. 'It would be nice, wouldn't it? But it's too much to hope for, I'm sure.'

Nice wasn't a word DS Blake associated with Percy Peach. She said cautiously, 'What would be too much to hope for?'

'To be able to go upstairs to Tommy Bloody Tucker and tell him that it was the butler what did it!'

Nine

The post-mortem report was a mixture of disappointment and usefulness for the team who eagerly awaited it.

There was still nothing to identify the body. The fire had destroyed all the clothing; even the shoes, so often a clue to identification, had almost entirely fused with what was left of the feet within them. Certain fragments had been sent to forensic, but all that could be said with any certainty was that the shoes had probably been trainers, the most common of all footwear in the Britain of the twenty-first century. There were no rings and no watch. It was quite possible, of course, that these had been removed after death by whoever had placed the body in the old stable block, but too little of the fingers and flesh remained to indicate whether a ring or a watch had been regularly worn by the deceased.

But certain significant facts had nevertheless emerged. The corpse was that of a man in early middle age, most likely in his early forties, in the pathologist's opinion, though he warned that under questioning in court he might have to give a wider age band. If local questioning failed and they had to resort to combing the Missing Persons register in a search for identity, that would be some kind of help. The overwhelming majority of what the police call MISPAs are young people: this information would at least make for a more manageable field.

The man had died between not more than four and not less than two days before the fire. Again this opinion was hedged with the qualifications about the boundaries which could be asserted in a legal situation, but the pathologist had worked with Peach before and was prepared to give an 'informed opinion' which pinned the time of death down a little more. This man had probably died on the Sunday before the fire. It was not as exact a time of death as the police would have liked, but it was far more precise than Peach and Blake had feared, when they had looked at that blackened shape against the wall of the ruined building.

Most significantly of all, there was an indication of how the man had died. Peach had feared when he saw that gross cinder among the charred remains of the stable block that they might never know how he had met his end, but pathology and forensic medicine make great strides with each passing decade. In the view of the man who had conducted the post-mortem examination, this unknown victim had died from asphyxiation. There was more than that: he had not been manually strangled, but despatched by means of a cord or cable tightened about his neck. No trace of this remained upon the body, and the finger ends and finger nails where they would have looked for signs of a struggle and material from a killer were completely destroyed. But there was enough of the throat and of the lung cavities in the torso for the pathologist to be certain that this is how the man had died.

Murder, then. What they had all suspected from the start was now scientifically confirmed for them.

The bare facts went out on Radio Lancashire at one o'clock. An unknown male body had been discovered in the aftermath of the fire on Wednesday night at Marton Towers. Foul play was suspected. The victim was probably a man in good health at the time of his death, and almost certainly aged between thirty-five and fifty. Police were anxious to speak to relatives or friends of any local person of that age who had disappeared without explanation in the week before the dramatic events of Wednesday evening.

Peach put DC Brendan Murphy beside a phone for the afternoon to deal with the plethora of calls which would inevitably result from this. Wives whose husbands had disappeared with younger models. The bitter spouses of husbands who had disappeared rather than pay the maintenance which had been allotted to their wives and families. Sons who found the increasing pressures of life with an Alzheimer's or physically disabled parent too much on top of a full-time job. The myriad other casualties of stress in what is asserted to be the most advanced state of civilization the world has seen.

Brendan Murphy was both sensitive and patient, the ideal man to deal sympathetically with calls which had to be listened to, but which you knew within ten seconds were going to be a waste of police time. He was also shrewd and intelligent: if the one call in a hundred came through which was vital, he wouldn't miss out on the importance of it.

The radio news item brought a swifter response than Percy Peach had dared to hope for. As it happened, Brendan Murphy's skills of diplomacy were not involved. The woman did not pick up a phone. She came into the town, sought out the raw brick of the huge new police station, and asked for the man in charge of the case.

Murder opens doors more quickly than any other crime. The desk sergeant knew his job, and the woman was ushered into DCI Peach's office within five minutes of her arrival.

Policemen are very good at assessing ages: it is part of their early training, part of the precision about detail which makes for accurate descriptions of suspects and witnesses, and it quickly becomes second nature to

119

them. Peach put this woman at around seventy, or possibly a little younger. She appeared to be very disturbed at the moment, and distress always put years upon people's ages.

He took one look at her and ordered tea, without asking his visitor whether she wanted it. She was too full of emotion to engage in any of the social preliminaries of conversation. She said abruptly, 'It's this body you've found. The one it talked about on the radio at lunchtime. I think it might be my Neil. Please God it isn't, but I think it might be.'

Peach gave her his understanding, sympathetic smile: the one in his considerable range which the criminal fraternity of the area never saw. 'Please God it isn't, as you say, but you've done the right thing to come in here straight away, Mrs...?'

'Simmons. Brenda Simmons. And my son is Neil. And in good health, as it said in the news. And he's forty-three. Well within the range you specified on the radio.'

'I see. Well, you'd be surprised how many men in that age range have disappeared in the last week, Mrs Simmons. I have an officer who's been taking calls all afternoon about them. What makes you think that your missing son is the man we're trying to identify? Were you expecting to see him at some time during the last five days?'

'No. He never comes home.' She stopped

abruptly, wondering if she was correct still to be speaking in the present tense, and with that thought the fingers of her right hand flew suddenly to her mouth. 'It's Norman, you see. He doesn't get on with Norman.'

'Your partner?'

She looked at him as if she did not quite comprehend the word. 'My husband. My second husband. Not Neil's dad. The two of them have never got on. I've tried to make them like each other, but they never have, and there it is.' It came out with scarcely a breath between the phrases, as if she had somehow to apologize for her part in this common modern phenomenon. When he thought she had finished, she added bleakly, 'He won't come into the house at all, now, Neil. Not as long as Norman's there, he says.' She put both hands up to the hair at the sides of her head and felt around it carefully, as if she felt she could bring these two feuding men back together by maintaining the neatness of her coiffure.

Peach said, 'But you were expecting Neil to contact you in some way.' His heart was already sinking: she hadn't even been expecting to see her son during the important days. The tea had arrived. He poured her a cup, tried not to look at his watch as precious minutes slipped away.

'He phones me. Every Saturday or Sunday night, when he knows Norman is down at the snooker club. Failing that, some time on

Monday. He never misses. He's a good son to me, really, though he's never stopped missing his dad. That's why he can't stand Norman, you see. But Norman's good to me – I can never make Neil see that.'

A forty-three-year-old man who'd omitted to ring his mother. It wasn't promising; Percy thought sadly of his own failings in such matters. He said, 'He's probably just been busy, Mrs Simmons. Have you tried to contact him yourself since Sunday?'

'I've tried, yes. He has one of those mobile things. But he hasn't answered me. It's ringing out of order.' She sipped her tea absently; her features twisted into a small, involuntary moue of distaste at its strength. Then, as if aware of the need for manners even at this time of suffering, she said, 'It's nice and hot, though.'

Peach sighed and pulled his pad towards him. 'I'll record your son as missing, Mrs Simmons. Get him put on our computer with the others. You'll let us know when he makes contact with you again, won't you? It's Neil, isn't it?'

'Neil Cartwright. He kept his father's name when I married again.' That simple fact suddenly brought her close to the tears she had restrained. She said, 'He had a good job at the Towers, you know. He worked hard, but he liked it up there.'

Peach was irritated. With himself, not with this confused and distressed woman: it was

122

he who was at fault for not eliciting this important fact much earlier. He tried not to sound too eager as he said, 'Your son worked at Marton Towers?'

'Yes, didn't I tell you? He's a skilled carpenter. Does other things in the house as well; he even helps in the kitchen when it's necessary. But he's become more interested in gardening and outdoor things – he's been given responsibility for the estate at Marton Towers now. He's been there for the last four years.'

'He lives on the site?' Peach was careful to keep to the present tense, but he had a feeling that he had found their victim.

Perhaps Mrs Simmons picked up a little of the excitement he felt. 'You think it's my Neil, don't you?'

'It's far too early to say that, Mrs Simmons. We shall have to check things out. As soon as we know anything at all, someone will be in touch with you.'

She finished her tea, put the cup and saucer carefully back on to the tray on Peach's desk, and said awkwardly, 'There are things to do, aren't there? Things to confirm whether this is Neil or not.'

He realized that she was referring to the formal identification of a body, thought again of that blackened cinder with all the flesh burned away from it, resisted a shudder and realized that the only acceptable identification here must be by a DNA match. 'One of my female officers will take what we call a DNA saliva sample from you, Mrs Simmons. It's quite painless, and will only take a few seconds.'

If she understood the reason for this, she gave no sign of it. He led her unresisting to the little room at the end of the CID section which they had optimistically dubbed the lab and left her as he had promised with a young DC, assuring her as he left that she would be the first to know when the corpse proved not to be that of her son.

But when he got back to his office he found that he had written the name NEIL CARTWRIGHT in capitals upon his pad.

'There's nothing like a murder to get the sexual juices running freely. It's a well-known police fact, that.'

Lucy Blake could say nothing for at least half a minute because of the strength of her lover's embrace and the enthusiasm of his kiss. When she was allowed up for air, she said breathlessly, 'I haven't noticed that your hormones need any encouragement, Percy Peach.'

'Exciting word, that. Hormones, I mean. Reminds me of a joke which ran round the station in my early days. "When the whore moans, you know that you're—"'

'We don't wish to know that, CDI Peach! Kindly leave the stage!' She detached herself from what seemed like multiple tentacles with a skill which came from much practice. 'This room needs decorating.'

'Now you're beginning to talk like a wife, not a fiancée.' He stared glumly at the offending decor. 'I'll get round to it, one of these days. I don't seem to have much time, since you arrived, with your full and varied sexual activities.'

'I'm going into that freezing kitchen of yours to make some coffee. Just bear that devotion in mind, next time you're thinking of excluding me from a police raid.'

'Complain to your mum, if you're still moaning about that. See what she thinks of me keeping you out of the trenches.'

Lucy, who knew exactly how appreciative her mother would be of any protection offered to her beloved daughter, decided to let it go. She'd made her point, and she knew she wasn't actually being fair. The snatch of those dangerous men at Marton Towers had been far more suited to strong and aggressive males than to what she liked to think of as her subtler strengths. She brought in the coffee, then was unwise enough to let Percy see her glancing at the time on his mantelpiece clock.

Her fiancé said delightedly, 'You're thinking of an early night, aren't you? And quite right, too! We shall need all our strength tomorrow for another long day. I'll just sip my coffee slowly, and brace myself for my partner's complex sexual demands.' He stared dreamily through the steam of his beverage at the wall which had so recently given her offence.

'There's nothing complex about my demands. All I really need now is a good night's—'

Percy's finger was suddenly firmly upon her lips, preventing further speech. 'Don't let that coarse word sully your beautiful mouth, my darling. Or at least save it for the warm darkness beneath the bedclothes. I'm a broadminded man, but a bit of a traditionalist in these things, and I don't mind admitting to you that some of your—'

'I was going to say a good night's *sleep*, you wozzock!' said Lucy, flinging away his hand and trying hard not to laugh: the last thing this man needed was encouragement.

'And that is what you shall have, my dear! And so shall I! A man of my advanced years will need several hours of unbroken rest after the prodigious sexual performance which you are about to demand from me.' He downed his coffee and let out a long, histrionic sigh of anticipatory pleasure.

Lucy decided to ignore this. 'I'm going to get to bed before you. I don't want to have to endure your hideous gasps and grunts whilst I undress in your frozen bedroom. I can't see why you can't just bleed that radiator to get it working properly and cut out the shivers.'

'Seeing you shiver is one of the great pleasures of my life, Lucy,' he assured her earnestly. 'Your splendid curves are in a class of their own, but when one sees them trembling, one is transported to a Shangri-la of sophisticated sexual pleasure!' Percy Peach was on his feet and making for the stairs.

'There's nothing sophisticated about it, you wozzock. I'm just freezing to death!' she yelled at him from the bottom of the stairs, as he disappeared into the bathroom.

His voice, muffled but persistent, came to her through the sounds of running water. 'Wozzock? Is that a Lancashire term of sexual endearment? I suppose it must be, because you seem to use it more as your randiness increases. But I'll be a match for you, Lascivious Lucy, just you see if I'm not!'

Despite her resolution, he was in bed before her, as she had somehow known all along that he would be. She could never understand how his clothes were neatly folded on the chair beside his bed rather than flung in abandon round the room, when she considered the enthusiasm with which he discarded them. 'Signs of spring, now we're well into March,' he offered from between the smooth cotton sheets. 'Hope this room's not too warm for a hot-blooded woman like you.'

Lucy Blake was determined to undress and get into bed quickly, to avoid the childish peep-show which seemed to give her fiancé

127

such pleasure. But 'More haste, less speed' is one of the more accurate of proverbial admonitions. She had more sense than to sit on the bed as she normally did, for that would have put her within range of Percy's all-too-predictable clutches. But as she tried to divest herself of her tights while standing, she caught her toe in them and was left hopping drunkenly around the room, to an accompaniment of increasingly excited exhortations.

'Oh, you're so good to me!' he assured her breathlessly when he could muster sensible words. 'I only have to confess how your quivering flesh excites me for you to put on a show like that. Oh, you're so good to me, Lubricious Lucy Blake!'

'WOZZOCK!' she shouted at him, as she finally divested herself of the offending tights and flung them at the sparkling eyes above the white sheet.

'A trophy! Excalibur!' yelled Percy triumphantly. His head disappeared beneath the sheets and a white arm was held aloft, clutching the innocent nylon, mystic and wonderful.

Lucy took advantage of this performance to divest herself quickly of bra and pants, a process which usually produced some high notes in Percy Peach's accompaniment to the performance, and arrived precipitately in the bed beside him, shivering despite herself in reaction to the crisp coolness of the cotton sheets.

'There's no need to go on exciting me. Can lead to premature ejaculation, in a man of my advanced years, that. It was very nearly touch and go then, you know.'

'Why you can't join the others of this century and get yourself a duvet, I don't know!' grumbled Lucy, as she gave up the unequal struggle and succumbed to the tentacles.

'Because I can have the pleasure of warming you up. And stilling the tremulous beating of your flesh and your heart. I may very well let you have your way with me, when you're warm enough.'

It was twenty minutes before Lucy Blake, warm and exquisitely contented, murmured sleepily, 'I don't know why you go on about your advanced years, Percy Peach. You've the sexual energy of a man of eighteen, not thirty-eight.'

'It's no use trying to talk me into a repeat performance, you insatiable siren of a sergeant! And please don't think of me as younger than my years. I have the invention that only comes with the years. I'll demonstrate it, if you only give me a little recovery time.'

But she was happily asleep in his arms, breathing deeply and silently, her breasts soft under his protective arm, her bottom snuggling into the hollow of his crotch.

Percy Peach wished as he fell asleep that the moment could last for ever.

Ten

Neville Holloway was back in post at Marton Towers. With his employer in prison and awaiting trial, the future was uncertain for all of the house and estate staff, but no one would have guessed that from the man's manner.

As he emerged from his office and moved across the wide reception hall of the mansion, the General Manager of Marton Towers seemed to CDI Peach more like a butler than ever. Peach managed not to refer to that office as the butler's pantry, but this silver-haired, elegant man of fifty-seven, in his dark suit, stiff-collared white shirt and grey tie, looked as if he would at any minute summon a parlour maid and send her to work in the silver room. With his immaculate cuffs and grave, bloodless face he seemed a man framed for the indoor life, a man who was completely at his ease here, but who might be acutely uncomfortable if he had to operate outdoors under the wide skies of east Lancashire.

Holloway did not seem to walk like a normal man as he came across the polished oak blocks to meet them, but rather to glide, as if he had been schooled in his youth to eliminate any suggestion of the rolling gait of the outdoor worker. It seemed inconceivable that this immaculate figure had once served years in prison for a serious crime. He spoke as if their interview thirty-six hours earlier had never occurred. 'Detective Chief Inspector Peach? I believe you wish to speak to me about my staff. I am at your service. We can speak in private, if you will follow me.'

Peach tried not to mime the smoothness of the older man's gait as he and Lucy Blake followed the upright figure into his office. When they were seated in comfortable, rather old-fashioned round-backed leather chairs, Peach said, 'You have probably already heard that we are now officially involved in a murder investigation. In such circumstances, there can be no information that is confidential. We need you to be completely frank with us.'

Holloway inclined his head with the slightest of smiles. 'I understand that. I shall tell you whatever I can.'

'There is one person in particular whom I should like to hear about. A forty-three-year-old man named Neil Cartwright.'

'He isn't here at the moment, I'm afraid. He's on a week's leave. He's due back at work on Monday.'

'And where would you expect him to be now?'

A slight frown, as if the holiday preferences

of junior staff were beneath his concern. But maybe the frown was just an aid to thought, for Holloway said, 'I believe he intended to spend at least part of the time visiting his sister in Scotland.'

'He told you that himself?'

A deeper frown, this time definitely of concentration. 'I think he did. But I can't be sure of that. I may simply have picked it up in passing from one of the other staff. There is quite a lot of gossip among the resident staff as we go about our business.'

'Do you know the address of this sister?'

'No. But I'm sure his wife would be able to give it to you. As you would expect, Mrs Cartwright also lives on the site. She was one of the ones made homeless by Wednesday's fire. Fortunately, we have been able to provide all the residents who were affected with alternative accommodation, though some of the furnishings are a little rudimentary.'

Peach nodded. 'I'm glad about that, because we shall need to speak to all of them, in due course. Thank you for your assistance in providing us with a murder room, next to the scene of the fire.'

Holloway nodded gravely. 'It was office accommodation which was not much used. In Mr Crouch's continuing absence, I cannot see that it will be required in the foreseeable future.' He spoke in the formal manner of an actor playing a part; clearly he had immersed himself in the new career he had made for himself after his release from prison. This was the first acknowledgement the General Manager had made to anyone that his employer was unlikely to return to the Towers.

As if accepting his own part in this formal verbal minuet, Peach now volunteered to him a piece of information. 'Mr Cartwright will not be returning to work on Monday. It is probable that he never left the site during his leave period. Neil Cartwright is our murder victim, Mr Holloway.'

If Neville Holloway was trying to look surprised, he did not succeed. But he had probably concentrated for years now on not looking surprised, since the persona he had adopted demanded that he should be permanently unruffled. He eventually nodded slowly and said, 'I feared the body you found would be that of a resident. This is a bad business for us, coming on top of the arrest of our employer.'

Peach made no secret of watching him closely, but it was DS Blake who now said, 'You must have some thoughts on who killed Neil Cartwright. You should share them with us now.'

Neville Holloway had ignored the younger woman beside Peach completely until now. He said immediately, perhaps a little too quickly, 'I have no idea who might have done this. The news of this death is as much a surprise to me as it no doubt was to you.'

He was distancing himself from the death, making as clear as possible his own non-involvement in it. But that was as natural a reaction for the innocent as the guilty, and could certainly be taken as normal behaviour in anyone with a prison sentence behind him. Lucy Blake said, 'In that case, we shall need a list of the resident staff, as well as the names of those who come in daily.'

Holloway rose unhurriedly and strode across to a filing cabinet in the corner of the room. He flicked through the files in the top drawer of the cabinet, methodically extracting the ones he wanted. It was systematic but unhurried. Lucy wondered whether such a well-organized man really needed the files to assist him, or whether he was giving himself thinking time for what he was going to say, deciding just how much information he wished to give them.

He gave them two lists of names, which looked as if they might have been typed out in anticipation of exactly this request. Then he resumed his seat, allowed himself a small, grave smile and said, 'As it's Saturday, most people are not on duty and will not necessarily be around for you to interview immediately.' He seemed as though he was trying not to look too happy about that. 'The employment files will jog my memory about the detail, if I should need that.' Without looking at any paperwork, he said, 'I suppose we should start with the wife. Sally Cart-wright is forty-one. A little younger than her husband. There are no children. She is also employed here. She's never been given the formal title, but I suppose you'd call her the housekeeper.'

'Why not formally?' Peach regarded it as his mission to investigate anything which was a deviation from the norm at this stage.

Neville Holloway allowed himself the slightly patronizing smile of the only man who understood exactly how these things worked. 'The original lady with that title left. Mrs Cartwright was originally quite a junior employee, but she had gradually taken on more responsibilities. However, at the Towers we have periods of intense activity, when the owner is in residence, and other times when the requirements of the house are rather different. We have a relatively small staff, for such a large house, and I have rather resisted formal titles of late; I have found that if you give some people too detailed a job description, you can have job-delineation disputes. We like our staff here to be both willing and adaptable.'

It was a long, even verbose, account, and, judging by the smoothness of its delivery, one he had no doubt given before. It made Peach wonder anew whether this man was more concerned with obfuscation than information. 'It sounds as if Mrs Cartwright is a competent woman. You're telling me that she has, in effect, been promoted.'

'She is very competent in what she had been asked to do.' If he thought he was damning her with faint praise, he gave no sign of it. 'As indeed was her husband.'

Peach was striving not to let his irritation with this bland practitioner show. They needed his cooperation to cut a few corners at the outset of a murder investigation which was beginning some five days after the death. 'According to his mother, whose DNA match has confirmed the identity of the victim, Neil Cartwright was a skilled carpenter.'

Holloway again allowed himself that slightly patronizing smile. 'Neil did not have formal qualifications to support his expertise. And latterly, we have chosen to employ him on other concerns: without having a formal title, he has for the last two or three years been in charge of the estate. But I would not argue with the description of him as a skilled carpenter; I was certainly satisfied with the work he occasionally did in the mansion and elsewhere for us. He knew what he was doing, but he had acquired his skills in what I suppose we could call an unconventional manner.'

Peach looked at him impatiently, then divined what he was hinting at. 'You mean he learnt to be a carpenter in prison, don't you?'

Holloway was for the first time discomforted. He hadn't expected this sharp-eyed policeman to guess what he meant without further questioning. 'That is so, yes. I don't know what degree of skill Mr Cartwright possessed before he—'

'So have all your colleagues on the staff been in trouble with the law before they were appointed here? You preside over a gang of jailbirds, do you?' Peach was enjoying disturbing the waters through which this stately ship of state had been sailing so serenely.

Holloway said with distaste, 'Not all of them are "jailbirds", Chief Inspector Peach. You have been kind enough to point out that I endured a spell of incarceration myself, many years ago. And it is true that the majority of our staff here have either undergone prison sentences or suffered fines or cautions, at some time in their pasts.'

'All of 'em, I should think.' Peach nodded his satisfaction in the discovery.

Holloway looked at him with distaste and said unctuously, 'Mr Crouch was of a philanthropic disposition.'

'I'll bet he was.'

'He liked to give people who had gone wrong in their lives a second chance.'

'Come off it, Mr Holloway! Tell it like it is. Crouch employed people like that so that he could have a hold over them. So that they wouldn't ask any awkward questions about what he was up to and what went on here. So that they wouldn't talk to inquisitive policemen if they came enquiring.'

'Mr Crouch gave me a second chance and I took it with both hands. I'm grateful to him. And I haven't let him down.'

Peach looked at him balefully. He knew that even though he disliked this man, he was probably both shrewd and intelligent. He sensed also that he wasn't going to get much help from him in this investigation. 'I believe that you haven't broken the law again yourself. Unless we count turning a blind eye to what you must have suspected was going on here. What about the people you supervise?'

Neville Holloway took his time, picking his words as carefully as the lawyer he often felt he might have been. 'As far as I know, everyone here is going straight. They'd be foolish if they weren't. They've been offered gainful employment, at wages which are in most cases a little above the going rate. They're sensible people, or we wouldn't have taken them on. They aren't going to step out of line again.'

Peach weighed these words as carefully as the man had selected them, nodding a little at the logic of the argument. Then he said, 'And yet one of them may be a murderer.'

'You've no proof of that.'

'No. Not as yet, I haven't. But the probability is that Neil Cartwright was killed by someone who knew him well. Someone who worked with him, perhaps. Maybe even someone who directed his working life here.'

DCI Peach knew he should be dispassionate, but he quite enjoyed delivering that thought.

Michelle Naylor was not looking at her best. She was surprised how pale her face looked when she glanced in the mirror in the small hall of the cottage. Her usually animated features looked small, still, almost doll-like, beneath the tight curls of her black hair.

But then no one would expect her to look at her best, after what had happened during the week. She had initially been quite excited by the police raid, with all the shouts and all the vehicles racing about the place. When you did not feel threatened yourself, it was quite thrilling to be on the fringe of the drama, almost involved in it and yet quite safe. It had felt almost as if the big house was being attacked by an army.

Michelle was only thirty, and her experience of armies and armaments was confined to television reports from Iraq and Israel, though she did know a little about uniformed police.

The fire had been a different matter altogether. Losing your home, even when you didn't own it, even when there was time for you to rescue all your precious individual items before the flames took over, was a disturbing thing. This was her first, and she now hoped her last, experience of a destructive fire. Even though she had never been in physical danger, she was amazed how terrifying she had found the intense heat, and the great orange flames leaping out of control towards the night sky, and the noise of wood and masonry crashing amid smoke and red-hot cinders.

And then to learn the next day of the body, and how it had been so horribly burned, with no one even knowing it was there. No one had known about it until Thursday, when the firemen had brought the blaze under control and dared to venture into the stables – they all still called it that, though it was a long time since there had been horses there.

And last of all the news, running round the residents like wildfire this morning, that this charred, half-vanished black thing had been the body of Neil Cartwright. No wonder she had been shocked when she glanced at the mirror: you could only expect to look like a wild, half-mad thing, when you had been through what she had been through this week.

At least it was Saturday. No one would ask her where she was going, or question why she wasn't busily engaged upon some household task. She'd seen Neville Holloway take a man and a woman into his office earlier on: the couple had looked like plainclothes police to her. But you couldn't be sure; all kinds of people had been in and out of the mansion in the last few months.

There didn't seem to be anyone about as Michelle started her car, which was still parked behind the main house, in front of the damaged stable block. One of the disadvantages of living at Marton Towers was that there was only one way out of the place for vehicles. You had to drive down the long, straight ribbon of tarmac to the gatehouse and the exit. You felt as you did so that everyone in the place was aware of your movements, wondering where you were going and what you were about.

She had never had that feeling so strongly as on this quiet Saturday morning, when neither the owner nor any of his visitors were occupying those bedrooms which overlooked the drive. Her apprehension must be because of what she was about, the secret mission which she had determined upon during a sleepless night.

Michelle felt the blood pounding in her temples as she drove those three hundred yards to the gatehouse, felt panic threatening her; she knew she would not be able to frame coherent words if anyone stopped her.

But no one did. She snatched a glance at the deserted gatehouse as she passed it, confirming that it was still locked up and unoccupied. Then she was on the lane outside, moving swiftly towards the bend, where the familiar clump of trees shaded the road and would provide concealment. She made her hands and arms relax on the steering wheel, pressed herself back against her seat in an attempt to dismiss her tension, forced a small, private smile. It had been easy really, hadn't it? She had got the difficulties and the dangers wildly out of proportion.

Very probably no one had seen her.

Michelle knew what she was going to do. Hell, she'd been over it enough times, during the long hours when she had waited for the dawn. She had no idea whether the refuse collectors worked on a Saturday, and there would be too many people around the council disposal dump for her to go there; she didn't want to risk meeting anyone who knew her. If necessary, she'd go into the centre of the town, slip down the alley behind the shops and restaurants, where she knew there were huge, cylindrical refuse bins. Surely what she had in the boot of the little black Ford Fiesta could disappear into one of these without the fear of discovery?

All the same, she would rather not run that risk. She drove through areas of Brunton where she couldn't remember ever going before, old, narrow streets where the terraced houses were crammed close together. Asian faces looked out from the doorways at her. The brown eyes of men who stood talking at the street corners looked curiously at the slim young woman with the white face in the small black car. But none of them interfered with her erratic progress; no one stopped her to ask where she wanted to go or to offer her help with the local geography.

Then, just when her head was beginning to ache anew with the strain, and she was deciding she would have to settle for those waste bins in the town centre, Michelle Naylor found what she was searching for.

She saw the pile of black plastic bags on the corner of the road first. Then, as she turned the little Ford into a gently curving road where the houses had long front gardens, she caught sight of the yellow lorry. The big, ugly vehicle was a hundred and fifty yards away; she could see the big circle of its grinder mechanism turning, long before she heard the sound of those powerful blades.

She stopped the Fiesta for a moment, watched as two of the workers flung a score of the plastic bags accurately into the lorry's destructive jaws. Then they moved away, and the vehicle crawled forward a hundred yards to its next stopping point. All its attendants disappeared to collect individual bags from the gateways of the houses and gather them together at spots agreed for their assembly and despatch into the refuse lorry.

For the moment, the rear of the big wagon, with its grinding mechanism still steadily turning, was deserted. Michelle eased her car forward, its engine note unheard beneath the harsh noise from the big vehicle in front of her. When she stopped, she found her limbs suddenly petrified, and she had a moment of panic when she thought she would not be able to get out of the car and do this after all.

It lasted for no more than two seconds at most. Then she was through the door, burrowing into the Fiesta's boot, producing her own mouthful of food for the voracious monster in front of her. She paused for a moment, assessing her aim, then tossed her own plastic bag into the exact middle of the dark hole at the centre of those powerfully destructive blades.

She knew she should turn and depart immediately, but she found she had to watch the final disappearance of her guilt into that obliterating machine.

In seconds, it had disappeared for ever, soundlessly dispatched into oblivion with the kitchen waste of hundreds of houses. She had a sudden moment of searing pain at the finality of what she had done, at the irrevocability of this closure. She had not been prepared for the feeling, and her eyes filled with tears as she turned away from the raucous grating of the machinery.

A slim young black man with a collection of plastic sacks over his shoulder appeared suddenly round the side of the vehicle. She had thought he would be curious about her presence there, but he called a cheerful greeting and gave her a smile which said he was near the end of his shift.

Five minutes later, Michelle Naylor was

back in her car and driving out of the town, with her mission accomplished. She should have felt an immense relief. Perhaps that would come later.

At the moment, she felt numbed and curiously empty.

You could not possibly have any idea what the wife of a murder victim should look like. At thirty-eight, with fifteen years' CID work behind him, Percy Peach had years of experience of meeting such women, and they had come in all shapes, sizes and ages.

And yet this one was a surprise. Sally Cartwright looked a little older than her forty-one years. She was not unattractive, but she had the blonde hair and fair-skinned, blue-eyed face which usually seem to age a little more quickly than darker beauty. She was moving towards a comfortable plumpness, carrying a few extra pounds round her waist and thighs, but was certainly not obese, that favourite contemporary word.

In the wedding photograph on top of the television which was set in the corner of the room, she looked quite stunning, a willowy, smiling young woman at the peak of her beauty, whose curves the long white wedding dress noticeably failed to conceal. She was smiling happily at the camera; people always said the bride looked radiant, but on this occasion the epithet had certainly been justified.

Police officers are trained to observe, and both of them took in the detail of the room as well as that of the woman at the centre of it. It was comfortably as well as tastefully furnished. The dark-red sofas sat well on the near-white carpet, which like the walls seemed to have just a hint of red in it. The pictures were Victorian or Edwardian water-colours, and the heavy frame of the mirror over the fireplace was surely from a similar period. There was a single light on a low table, as if its occupant acknowledged that, in the middle of a cloudy March day, this low-ceilinged, north-facing room needed a little extra illumination.

She said, 'It's a little late for coffee, but I don't suppose Mr Holloway thought of offering it to you. Would you like some now? I have it ready, if you would.'

That was what was unusual about this widow, Percy decided. Her composure, in the hour of her bereavement, in the face of this awful and shocking death. Without looking at Lucy Blake, he said, 'That would be very welcome. Thank you.'

Within sixty seconds, Sally Cartwright brought in a tray with a cafetière, china cups and saucers and a plate of what looked like home-made biscuits. If she was conscious of their scrutiny, as she surely must have been, she gave no sign of it. She poured coffee with a supremely steady hand, set a small table beside each of them, then proffered small

146

plates and biscuits.

Then, as if to show them without resentment that she was aware of their taking in of these things, she nodded at the plates and the cups and said, 'They're Royal Doulton. Not mine, unfortunately. They came over from the main house, where there is a surfeit of fine things.'

'You're the housekeeper there?'

She smiled at DCI Peach. Just as coolly as he had assessed her, she took in the suppressed energy of his squat frame, the keenness of his black-eyed scrutiny, the precision of his small moustache and the neatly trimmed fringe of black hair beneath his bald dome, the neatness of his light grey suit and shining black shoes. Then the full lips broke into a small smile as she said, 'We don't deal much in formal job titles at Marton Towers; Mr Holloway once took pains to explain to me that it might stop us operating outside the boundaries of our job descriptions.'

'You don't agree with that view?'

A shrug of the shoulders. 'He's the boss. He's much older than anyone else here, and he has set ideas about how the house should be run. But it works well enough. Everyone seems to do whatever is asked of them, without making too many complaints.'

'You like working here?'

She took a sip of her own coffee, offered the plate of biscuits around again. 'Is it relevant whether those of us who work at

Marton Towers are happy or not?'

He was ready for that, even welcomed it, as a lead-in to more important questions. 'Indeed it is, Mrs Cartwright. If we are to find out who killed your husband, we need to begin by getting as clear a picture as possible of the life he lived here.'

She nodded coolly. The first mention of her husband and the reason why they were here had not unsettled her. Peach would not conclude yet that she was not grieving over his death, for he had seen grief take many forms. Shock has strange physical effects: it can destroy all forms of control, or it can atrophy normal reactions for a time, so that people move through the period after the death of someone close to them almost as if in a trance.

Peach said, 'Would you say that "housekeeper" was an accurate description of what you do here?'

'I would. So long as you don't consider me another Mrs Danvers.' She allowed herself a small, sardonic smile at the absurdity of that image. 'Mr Holloway is definitely the one in charge of things, both inside and outside the mansion. But after coming here as a general domestic worker, I have taken on more and more responsibility for the smooth running of the house over the last three or four years, and he has looked to me to do so. He's wrong about us being afraid to cross job-delineation lines, of course. We were all glad to be employed here. The work isn't generally over-taxing, and the conditions of service are good.'

Peach asked the question she had almost invited. 'Why do you say that most of you were glad of the work in the first place?'

'We have what you might charitably call chequered pasts. Most of us would have had difficulty in being appointed to the sort of posts we have here, if we had sought them elsewhere.'

'Thank you for being so frank about that.'

'You're police officers. You could find out about these things, if you chose to.'

'Most of them, yes. But where there are no convictions, they do not always show up on police computers.' He wouldn't volunteer to her how patchy some of the earlier computer files were, in a service that had been tardy and amateur in recognizing the value of electronics. 'What is your own skeleton in the cupboard?'

Sally had known it would come out, eventually. But now, when she was invited to produce it herself for this polite, insistent man, she had to conquer a moment of diffidence. 'Nothing too dramatic. I was dismissed from a secretarial post, for stealing office supplies. I had broken off an association with one of the partners, and he was looking for something to hit me with. The police were involved, but eventually the charges were dropped and it never came to court. As I say, the man was looking for something to hit me with, and the police recognized that. But I left without a reference, and it made it difficult to get work, for quite a long time. I had never done domestic work, until I came here. Now I like it, and enjoy the responsibilities I have.'

She told it as calmly as she had delivered everything else so far; only when she had mentioned the aborted affair had there been a touch of acid in her tone. Peach said, 'All the other people who work here have something similar in their backgrounds, haven't they?'

She looked at him evenly, weighing him as an opponent, wondering exactly how much he knew. 'I expect so. We don't enquire too much into each other's backgrounds. When you've been in trouble, you know when to leave things alone.'

Peach grinned. 'Unlike policemen, who pry into anything which takes their fancy and claim they're only doing their duty.'

She gave him a wan smile. 'And who have a very large machinery behind them to ensure we tell them the truth.'

DS Blake had so far been quite content to study the reactions of the newly bereaved woman under Peach's polite but insistent interrogation. Now she said quietly, 'Have you any children, Mrs Cartwright?'

'No. There are no children resident on site.'

Lucy had expected that from the tasteful, uncluttered decor of this room. 'Another part of the employment policy, is that? Like employing people who will be grateful for the work and not ask too many questions about what their employer is up to?'

It was the first time they had stated these ideas openly to her. Sally Cartwright decided not to contest them. 'I think now that it might be deliberate policy not to have young children around, yes. It was only when I found that no one else on the site had them that I considered the notion.'

'And why would that be?'

'I've no idea.' The answer came a little too quickly and curtly, signifying that she was shutting the door on any further speculations in the area.

Lucy Blake made a note, allowing the moment to stretch, before she looked round the elegant, established room and said, 'You didn't need to be rehoused, after the fire?'

'No. I was evacuated, along with everyone else, but this end cottage wasn't damaged at all. I've had the windows open for two days, trying to get rid of the smells of the smoke and the firemen's foam. But we were very lucky.'

It was the first time she had spoken in the plural, as if her husband was still alive, as newly bereaved people often did. Lucy Blake rose from her seat and walked across to the wedding photograph on top of the television. 'I presume this is your husband.'

'Yes. It was taken sixteen years ago. As you would no doubt have deduced, from the look of the woman standing beside him.'

Lucy had never met a woman who could make wry jokes against herself in such tragic circumstances. She found herself admiring Sally Cartwright's self-control, but feeling that they had so far peeled away only her surface layers. She examined the man in the photograph. He was a slim, erect figure of around six feet tall; dark-haired; holding himself straight but a little self-conscious for this formal picture; handsome, in a thin-faced, diffident way; sporting one of the droopy Edwardian-style moustaches which had been fashionable for a brief period around the time of this wedding. She found herself totally unable to relate this good-looking, uncertain-looking young man to the blackened remains they had looked at eighty yards from here two days earlier.

She tried to keep her voice steady as she said, 'Do you have a more recent likeness?'

'I expect so, yes. I'll unearth a later picture before you go, if you like.' Sally Cartwright enjoyed the feeling of being more in control of herself than the pretty young woman with the striking chestnut hair who was question-ing her.

'What exactly did your husband do at Marton Towers?'

'He was in charge of the estate. I suppose

in the old days he'd have been called the head gardener. He did more than that, though, he looked after the woodlands as well. He called in outsiders for major jobs: things like tree surgery and drainage work. Mr Holloway says it always pays to use specialists for things like that.'

'Even so, Neil couldn't run the whole estate on his own.' It was the first time Lucy Blake had used the dead man's first name; she could discern no reaction in his widow.

'No. Neil was the only resident outdoor worker on the site, but he had one man who worked full-time for him. Ben Freeman. He comes in on a bike from the village down the road, about three miles away, though I haven't seen him this week. There are two older men who come in part-time. Their hours vary; they work about twice as long in the summer as in the winter.'

'Head gardener is quite a responsible job in a place like this, even if he didn't have the title.'

'Yes, it is. Neil's job rather evolved over the years, the way mine has. He was a good carpenter, and he did a lot of work in the main house when we came here. But he had always been interested in gardening, and he went on a couple of courses to learn more. Mr Holloway is good at spotting potential and rewarding it. Sorry, that doesn't sound very modest, does it?' For the first time since they had come into her house, she looked a little embarrassed. But it was for herself, not because of anything concerning her husband.

Peach was by now a little nettled by her composure. He had been grateful for it, at first. But he had come here prepared to be full of consideration for a woman riven by grief, and now felt that there was a danger that she rather than he was controlling their exchanges. He said abruptly, 'It seems probable that your husband never left Marton Towers before he was killed.'

'He did.' Sally found that she felt curiously calm, now that the moment she had waited for had come.

'You know that?'

'Yes. He drove out of here last Sunday at about one o'clock. Almost exactly six days ago.' She looked at her watch as she spoke, as if the confirmation of this symmetry appealed to her.

'You saw him go?'

'Yes. I watched him put his case on to the back seat of the car, then waved him off as he drove away.'

'So at some time after that, he came back here.'

'Possibly. But his car never came back, as far as I'm aware. It's possible that he was killed somewhere else, and his body brought back to be dumped here and destroyed in the fire.'

Peach smiled grimly. 'Perhaps you should

have been a detective rather than a house-keeper, Mrs Cartwright. We have to be careful to take all possibilities into account.'

She allowed herself a faint smile. 'I've had a lot of time to think about these possibilities, since we heard on Thursday about the discovery of the body.'

'But you didn't know it was Neil then.'

She was not at all discomforted. 'I suspected it. I rang his sister in Dundee. Neil had never arrived there, and she hadn't heard anything from him.'

For the first time, she seemed a little on edge, but that was understandable enough. Peach said, 'You will understand that in the case of a suspicious death, we have to ask some embarrassing questions. How would you describe your own relationship with Neil?'

Despite his brief preamble, the question she had been waiting for hit her like a stone. 'We had the normal ups and downs that most married couples have. But not serious ones. We'd have liked children, but we'd got used to being without them years ago. We hadn't any financial worries: we were both doing well here. I think both of us had doubled the monthly wage we had when we were first appointed. I'd say that on balance we got on at least as well as the average married couple – perhaps even rather better than that.'

He'd let her deliver all the phrases she'd

rehearsed, when she'd expected him to punctuate them with his questions. She wondered if it now sounded too much like a statement she had prepared. She said impulsively, 'The wife is always a suspect, in cases like this, isn't she? Well, I didn't kill Neil!' and then wished that she hadn't made that assertion.

Peach studied her for a moment, with his head tilted a little to one side, like an intelligent but not necessarily friendly dog. 'And who else do you think might have killed him, Mrs Cartwright?'

'I've no idea.' She wondered again if her denial had come a little too quickly, right on the heels of his question, as if she had given it no thought. She said, 'I've considered the matter over the last forty-eight hours, and I can't think of anyone. Certainly no one on the site.'

'Had Neil no enemies?'

'No. None who would want to kill him, anyway. He was a popular man. Everyone seemed to like him. It's inconceivable to me that anyone would want to kill him.' She looked down into the empty coffee cup beside her, and seemed for the first time to be near tears.

'Nevertheless, someone did kill him, Mrs Cartwright. Maybe in cold blood, maybe in a sudden fit of anger. You say you can't think of anyone who would have wished him dead. Can you tell us of anyone who stood to gain by his death?'

'No. No one. Except me, I suppose, and I've already told you that I didn't kill him.'

'Indeed you have. Well, please do go on thinking about it, and contact me immediately at this number if anything occurs to you. I'll remind you once again that no one should try to keep secrets during the course of a murder enquiry.'

They took down the details and registration number of his car, then waited a moment whilst she found the more recent photograph she had promised them. It had been taken a year earlier, on the estate, Sally Cartwright said. It showed a smiling man leaning upon a small tractor. He looked if anything more handsome than in the wedding photograph, with the confidence which maturity had brought to his face. The years were often kinder to men than to women, Lucy Blake reflected, as she put the picture carefully into her document case.

Sally Cartwright stood in the doorway of the cottage to watch them climb into the police car. Lucy Blake looked back as Peach turned the car carefully over the gravel at the corner of the big house, a hundred and fifty yards from the far end of the stable block. The widow was still standing motionless in the open doorway of her cottage.

Eleven

'They say they can't release the body for burial yet. We'll have to wait for the funeral. Doesn't seem natural, somehow. They tried to explain the reasons to me, but I wasn't really listening.' Brenda Simmons stared steadily ahead of her as she sat at the table, but she saw nothing.

'It's because of the suspicious circumstances, love. When they eventually arrest someone for killing Neil, the solicitors for the defence may ask for a second, independent, post-mortem examination, in case they want to contest the findings of the original one.'

Derek Simmons wondered whether he should have volunteered this detail to her. He'd been glad to find anything to say, but perhaps it was insensitive. It couldn't be easy, when your son had been burnt beyond all recognition. At least he'd managed to avoid mention of the word murder.

Nothing had been easy over the last few days. Brenda had been devastated by grief for the son who had been so cruelly and unnaturally snatched away from her. Derek had offered her what comfort he could. But all the time a still, steady voice within him had been telling him that he was a hypocrite, that a man whose heart was shouting with relief over the death of Neil Cartwright should not be uttering the platitudes of consolation to a suffering woman.

Perhaps in time Brenda would understand a little of his relief, but it was far too early for that. He must be sure to conceal it for a long time yet, but it wasn't going to be easy. He had grown used to sharing confidences with this woman who was his second and much more suitable wife. They hadn't had secrets from each other over the last few years. They hadn't had many differences at all, in fact.

Apart, that is, from Neil. The son who had held resolutely to his departed father's name, who had never tried either to modify or to conceal his contempt for his stepfather.

He was sorry for Brenda: he understood her grief, was even pained a little on her behalf, when he saw her suffering. But he couldn't disguise from himself the fact that he was delighted to be rid of that sullen, hostile presence, that steady irritant in the peaceful world that he had set up for himself in his second marriage. Despite all Brenda's efforts, he and Neil had never got on with each other, never would have got on. He was delighted that his difficult stepson was gone, whatever the circumstances of that going: his only difficulty was concealing that delight from his wife.

He went into the kitchen and checked on the progress of the new potatoes he had bought to try to tempt Brenda into eating a proper meal. Almost ready. He put on the sprouts and gave the sausages a final turn as they spat quietly under the grill. He wasn't a great cook, and he hadn't done much in the kitchen in the years with Brenda, but he could get by. You didn't reach the age of sixty-six and live the varied kind of life Derek Simmons had lived without being able to get by.

'Varied'. He liked that word. Covered a multitude of sins, 'varied' did. He put the plates to warm and called through to his wife that the meal would be ready in eight minutes. Might prise a smile out of Brenda, the idea that he could be as precise as that in his culinary skills.

She tried to eat, to please him, tried to keep up her end of the conversation he struggled so conscientiously to create. But it was no good. She eventually pushed her plate aside and said, 'I'm sorry, Derek. I know you've worked hard with the meal, and it's really very nice, but I just can't eat at the moment. Leave the washing up to me and go and watch the football. I'll be better doing something.'

At seven o'clock on a Saturday evening, there was no football on the television, of course. That just showed how out of touch

Brenda was at the moment. There was the usual Saturday night drivel, but he did not switch the set off. Silence would put yet more strain on his conversational skills and his powers of dissimulation.

Brenda came in after twenty minutes or so, glanced at the television set, and sat down with the paper. Derek watched her staring at the crossword; twenty minutes later, she had put in but a single answer. He said tentatively, 'I know this is very hard for you, love, but you need to pull yourself together, somehow. You're going to be ill, at this rate.'

Brenda Simmons said with a sudden touch of venom in her voice, 'Whereas you're going to be fine. You never liked Neil. You must be glad he's gone. I expect it's made your week.'

He tried to reassure her that it wasn't so, but he couldn't find the words to be convincing, and he shut up after a couple of sentences. Another ten minutes went by with them stealing surreptitious glances at each other whilst pretending to be involved with their own concerns. Then Brenda Simmons sighed and said, 'I'm no company for anyone, at the moment, Derek, am I? Why don't you go down to the club and get yourself a game and a bit of cheerful company?'

He tried to conceal the way that his heart leapt at the suggestion. She couldn't know that he had been wondering how to propose just this. And she surely couldn't know that he had other reasons than a bit of banter with his friends to take him there.

Derek said carefully, 'I don't want to leave you, at a time like this.'

'You're serving no purpose here, are you? We'll only get irritated with each other, eventually. And I'll be all right – I'll probably be better on my own for a bit, in fact. I might have a little weep, when I don't feel the need to keep up appearances for your sake. And you need a change. That's if you're not too tired, after everything you've been doing in the house.'

'No. No, I'm all right. I've not done much, you know. Been round with the vacuum and made a simple meal: just the sort of thing you dash off in a couple of hours without noticing.'

She smiled at him, trying to show that she appreciated his efforts, trying to conceal the fact that at this moment he was an irritant, that she wanted him out of the way, so that she could have the house to herself and her sorrow. 'Get off with you, Derek Simmons. And remember you're driving home, and don't drink too many pints!'

She knew that he wouldn't risk being caught over the limit; it was just her way of dismissing him, and both of them understood it. He said, 'I'll go for an hour or two, then. Give myself a change, and you a bit of space.'

He tried not to sound too eager, and yet he found himself out of the house and in the driving seat of the car in three minutes. He reversed the car carefully out of the garage, looked hard at the light behind the curtains as he drove away into the cool March darkness. She wasn't watching. He turned left rather than right at the end of the road, away from the snooker club, towards the other end of the town.

At the same time that Derek was escaping from the Simmons house, Percy Peach was feeling at a bit of a loss. He did not see Derek Simmons' car drive past him in the opposite direction as he drove along the Preston road, but there was no reason why he should. Percy had no knowledge as yet of what the stepfather of Neil Cartwright looked like, let alone whether he had any connection with the crime.

Percy was at a loss because Lucy Blake, who nowadays kept him company on most of his Saturday nights, had gone to a school reunion, despite all his frivolous suggestions that she'd be kept in detention or made to write essays. The devil finds work for idle hands, moralizers say. Percy wouldn't have put it as strongly as that. But as he passed the end of Tommy Bloody Tucker's road, he scented a little harmless mischief.

DCI Peach's definition of 'harmless' was not quite the same as that of other and kinder people. He turned the silver Mondeo round at the next junction and drove thoughtfully back towards the residence of the Head of Brunton CID.

It was an impressive house, Edwardian and detached, with rhododendrons arching over the gates and a magnolia heavy with buds near the front door. Barbara Tucker opened the door when he rang and peered down two steps at the cheerful round face of her husband's *bête noire*. 'Oh, it's you!' she said. Her disapproval was deafening.

With the light behind her, Barbara's formidable bulk at the top of the steps made her an even more impressive Brünnhilde. 'You're looking radiant tonight, Mrs T!' Percy said. 'Regrettably, though, it's your husband that I need to see.'

'It's not convenient. We're going out. It's Saturday night, you know, and he's off duty.'

Percy decided that Tommy Bloody Tucker's talent for the blindin' bleedin' obvious had probably been refined by marriage. 'We policemen are never off duty, Mrs Tucker. Your husband has often had occasion to remind me of that.'

She said with unconcealed distaste, 'I suppose you'd better come in.' Then she went to the bottom of the staircase and yelled into the upper regions of the house, 'Thomas! That Chief Inspector of yours is here to see you. On Saturday night.'

He's going to get a bollocking for this, when I'm gone, thought Percy happily.

Thomas Bulstrode Tucker had been trying

and failing to tie on a black bow tie, so he was already irritated. He took Peach into a dining room without heat and said, 'You'll have to be quick. We're going out. We're off to a dinner with the Chairman of the Brunton Police Authority,' he said self-importantly. He couldn't resist the opportunity to impress, despite his impatience to be rid of this annoying subordinate.

Peach was not a man easily impressed. 'Be careful about the company you keep, sir. Do you want me to help you with that tie?'

'No, I don't! Just tell me why you've come disturbing my weekend and then get on your way.'

'Your orders, sir.'

'My orders?' Tucker hoped fervently that Barbara was not listening outside the heavy dining-room door.

'You said that I was to keep you fully briefed on the situation, sir. That this was a high-profile case and you wanted the latest information to be relayed to you at all times.'

'I didn't mean at seven twenty on a Saturday night.'

'Yes, sir. I'll make a note of that for future reference. Put it in writing for myself, later in the evening.'

'Well, what is it?' Chief Superintendent Tucker had discerned a silver lining. He might be able to impress the Chairman of the Police Authority and other luminaries with the latest news on the case; he would make it clear to them that he had been working on this crime until the very moment he had to come to dinner with them.

'There's still a chance that the butler did it,' said Peach portentously.

'The butler?'

Peach thought that Tucker in a white shirt with a string of bow tie in his hand could still look appealingly like a distressed fish. 'Doesn't call himself that, sir. But he's something similar. Thought you might like to stretch a point for your friends when you're holding them rapt with your account of the mysterious affair at Marton Towers. I'm told that in Agatha Christie the butler was often a leading suspect.'

'Look! Get on with it and get out!'

'Yes, sir. Admirably succinct, as is your wont. Well, Mr Neville Holloway is still in the frame. That's the butler, sir, though he calls himself something different. So is the victim's wife, sir. Rather a voluptuous lady, I think you'd find her.' He glanced thoughtfully towards the door and the Brünnhilde beyond it, beside whom Sally Cartwright was certainly sylph-like. 'She didn't seem unduly distressed by having her husband burnt to a rather large cinder. Interesting, we thought.'

'This could have waited until Monday.'

'Your orders, though, sir. Too conscientious for your own good. Never really away from the job. And there is one thing that I needed to warn you about.'

'And what would that be?' Tucker's voice was ominously steady now.

'All the employees up there seem to have been in trouble with us boys in blue, sir. Several of them have done time, and all of them seem to have been questioned in connection with previous offences.'

'And why do I need to know this, at the moment when I am preparing to attend an important function on a Saturday evening?'

'Didn't want you embarrassing yourself, sir. Didn't want you unwittingly suggesting that any of these people might make sturdy members of your Lodge.'

'Don't be ridiculous. The only man who might even be considered for the brotherhood is the man in overall charge at Marton Towers, the man you so witlessly refer to as the butler, and even he—'

'Neville Holloway, sir.'

'Well, it's just possible that a man like him might be—'

'Fraudster, sir.'

'He is?'

You'd know that, if you'd kept in touch with the case. If you weren't such an old fraud yourself. 'Done years inside for it, sir. Came out seventeen years ago. Been going straight since then. So he says.'

'If this is all you've come to say, then you can be on your way. We're just about to—'

'About to go out junketing with the Chairman of the Police Authority, yes, sir. Well, I shan't detain you any longer. Just thought you'd like to let the big man know that we're ceaselessly in pursuit of criminals, even on Saturday nights.'

Tucker said, 'I shall certainly let Henry Rawcliffe know that. I'll tell him all about your efforts in this high-profile case.'

Percy knew that he wouldn't do anything of the sort. The only person mentioned favourably to Henry Rawcliffe would be Chief Superintendent Tommy Bloody Tucker himself. But if the rumour he had heard that morning about the Chairman of the Police Authority had anything in it, that suited Percy down to the ground.

Barbara Tucker was checking the string of pearls on her ample neck when he emerged into the hall with his chief. Someone should surely tell her that orange wasn't the right colour for an evening dress on one of her splendid proportions. It would take a much bigger man than Tommy Bloody Tucker to do that; a latter-day Siegfried would be required.

'Enjoy your evening!' Percy Peach called from the darkness, as Brünnhilde shut the front door firmly upon him.

There was no one in at the house when Derek Simmons got there. He waited out-side the shabby front door in the car for twenty minutes, in the faint hope that the man he wanted to see would come back. Then he saw the woman who lived next door peering out at him suspiciously for the second time, and knew it was time to go. The last thing he wanted was to have her ringing the police. He would have to hope he could buttonhole his friend in the more public setting of the snooker club, after all.

The club was crowded on Saturday night, but he got a game within twenty minutes. 'Don't usually see you on a Saturday,' said his opponent, as he potted the first black of the frame.

Derek said a little too loudly, 'No. Sunday's my night. I'm here every Sunday. Quieter than Saturdays. I'm invariably here for most of the evening, on a Sunday.' The more people around here who were made aware of that, the better.

It was a scrappy game. Derek was quite a skilled player, and his opponent, knowing he wasn't up to the same standard, played a cagey safety game and waited for his chances. As he left the cue ball near the bottom cushion for the third time in a row, he said, 'You fully retired now, Derek?'

'Yes. I do a bit of part-time, though, when people want plans drawn for extensions and the like.'

'Consultancy.'

Derek grinned. 'That's what you'd call it, if you'd retired from a high-powered job in industry. It means I do the odd small job, to bring in a bit of beer money and keep me out of mischief.'

He tried to focus on the game, but he couldn't concentrate when he wanted to. He was watching the door all the time to see if the man he wanted to see would come into the club; it was so crowded that he was afraid of missing him. The decibel level was rising with each passing minute. The Rovers had won that afternoon, and there was much lively discussion of the merits of various players.

Derek eventually missed a crucial brown, which he would normally have potted without difficulty, and his opponent gleefully finished off the frame on the pink. He was happy enough to go back to his friends and relate the details of his triumph over the formidable Derek Simmons.

And Derek was happy enough to be rid of him, for he had spotted the man he had come here to speak with. Harry Barnard was a lean man, with an even leaner head and a pencil-thin moustache of the sort sported by Hollywood stars in the nineteen fifties and sixties. He was one of those men who had never moved on from the fashions of their youth. At this moment, Derek Simmons found such permanence quite appealing. A man who did not change his appearance might be solid and reliable, once he had given his word.

He bought two pints of bitter and shepherded Harry away from the group beseeching him to play dominoes and into the far corner of the huge room. They sat down together on the bench which overlooked the snooker tables. They would not be disturbed here. Those who were playing snooker were immersed in their game, and all those who were not playing snooker were busy drinking and exchanging insults and cheerful laughter at the other end of the club.

Harry Barnard's watery grey eyes looked curiously at the man who had bought him beer and waylaid him before he could even remove his coat. He said, 'Don't usually see you here on a Saturday night, Derek.'

Derek Simmons tried not to show his impatience. 'The wife sent me out. Told me to come and enjoy myself.'

Harry gave him the roguish smile he had borrowed from a young David Niven and never returned. 'There won't be many people in here who can say that.' He peered across the snooker tables at the noisy concourse beyond, wanting to light the cigarette he had lit for many years at this point, before enlightenment had changed the law and forbidden it.

'I'm lucky with Brenda. She's a good woman.' Derek meant it. He wondered why in Lancashire you had to be ashamed of confessing that you loved your wife, that she had made a difference to your life. 'She's devastated by the death of her son. But she sent me out to enjoy myself. I think she really wanted to have the house to herself.'

'Rotten business, that. I can understand what she's going through.' He couldn't, of course, and he wasn't at all affected by this death himself, but it seemed the right thing to say. Harry Barnard was a conventional man, so he sought out the right things to say.

'It's hit me hard, as well.' Derek wanted to assert that: it was important to him that as many people as possible should think it.

'You weren't the lad's dad, though, were you? It wasn't as bad for you as for Brenda.'

'No, it wasn't the same at all. Still, I don't mind admitting it to you, Neil's death's hit me quite hard.' Derek glanced up over the two pint tankards: Harry seemed to be taking that at face value.

'They found out who did it yet?' Harry couldn't conceal his curiosity. A murder mystery excites most people, especially when it happens on your doorstep, and when you know people who were near to the victim it gives it an added piquancy.

'Don't think so.' Derek decided to pretend that he had only a marginal interest in the investigation, lest his companion should think he had either any connection with it or any anxiety about it. 'They didn't even let Brenda see the body. Said that they could identify it from a DNA match. She had to give them a saliva sample.'

Harry Barnard was silent for a moment,

digesting the implications of this, savouring the details of police procedure. 'There couldn't have been much of him left, then.'

'I don't suppose there was, after a fire like that.'

'Not a nice way to go.'

'He didn't die in the fire.' Derek Simmons was wondering how he could get his man away from the grisly details of the death and on to what he wanted from him. 'He was dead before the fire. Brenda reckons he could have got out, if he'd been alive.'

'So how did he die?'

'I don't know. Don't reckon anyone knows, yet. If they do, they're not saying.'

'Police will know more than they're telling us.' Harry Barnard spoke from the safe citadel of invincible ignorance.

'Yes, I expect so. Harry, you remember we played snooker last Sunday night?'

The thin man nodded. 'Play most Sundays, don't we?'

They were about the same standard, and both of them useful players, who played in the league team for the club. Derek tried hard to sound casual as he said, 'If anyone asks you, I was here for the whole of Sunday night. Say from seven to half-past ten.'

'Course you were. Same as usual.'

'That's the idea. Just in case anyone should come asking you. I don't suppose they will, but just in case.'

'Right you are. I'll have another pint with

you, then show my face at dominoes. We'll have a frame of snooker later, Derek, if you put our name down for a table.'

Harry Barnard wouldn't even have thought about the matter, if Derek hadn't come asking him. But while he was playing dominoes, he remembered that his old friend hadn't come into the club until about eight thirty last Sunday night.

Twelve

James Naylor would have preferred to be interviewed with his wife. He had said so, told them that it would save time for the CID people, as the two of them could only tell the same story. But the cool female voice on the phone had told him that that wasn't usual in murder cases, that CID officers liked to listen to what people had to say individually and then check to see whether there were any significant discrepancies.

She'd made it sound quite sinister on the phone, as if she was issuing a warning that there would be trouble in store for him unless he was completely honest. Lucy Blake hadn't been Percy Peach's detective sergeant for three years without learning to play even the meanest card in her hand to maximum effect.

They'd arranged to see Naylor in the main house, away from the familiar furnishings of his home as well as the wife who was better with words than he was. He told himself that he had nothing to fear, if he told his story boldly and answered their questions as briefly as he could. Perhaps, indeed, it was better to see them without Michelle at his side, if the subject was going to be Neil Cartwright.

James Naylor would have liked them to sit with him in his kitchen, where he could have had the utensils of his trade all round him and felt in control. But Neville Holloway said it wasn't really a suitable place for a formal interview with the police, and James couldn't argue with that. There were plenty of other rooms available in the mansion, on this quiet Sunday morning. So the two officers sat down with him in the little ante-room outside the boss's office, where James couldn't remember going since he had been interviewed for his job over four years ago.

The woman who had spoken to him on the phone turned out to be quite a stunner. The dark green sweater, which made a nonsense of the term 'plain clothes', did nothing to disguise the curve of her breasts, as well as accentuating the colour of her striking dark-red hair and her unusual green-blue eyes. She said, 'You know that we wish to speak to you about the murder of Neil Cartwright. I'd like to clear up a few personal details first.'

He told them in answer to her quietly spoken questions that he was now thirty-one; that he had come to Marton Towers four years and four months ago, initially as assistant chef and general domestic help; that he enjoyed working here; that, like the wife of the deceased man, he had been successful, and had been promoted to take more responsibility.

He was now officially Head Chef. He couldn't help giving the title capital letters as he delivered it to them. The post was occasionally very demanding, when the owner was in residence and brought guests to stay at the Towers, but there were also long periods when James Naylor cooked only for the residential staff of the estate. Mr Holloway had sent him on courses during the slack periods, and he now felt confident that he could handle the job.

'Which you may not have for much longer,' said the man with the bald head and the piercing black eyes, who had been silent whilst DS Blake recorded the details of his background.

James detected a new note of aggression. 'Why do you say that?'

'Because the man who pays your wages is in clink, and likely to remain there for several years, unless the lawyers make an even bigger cock-up of things than usual,' said Percy Peach. He looked at that moment as if he would like to deposit Richard Crouch's chef behind bars as well.

'Mr Crouch is innocent until proved guilty,' said James Naylor, more sturdily than he felt.

'I see,' said Peach, nodding as though it gave him satisfaction to have this man confirmed as an enemy. He weighed up the stocky, powerful physique, looked hard into the brown eyes of the unlined face and found in them a pleasing apprehension. 'And I suppose you knew nothing about what was going on here? Nothing about what these important visitors you cooked for were up to?'

'It wasn't my business to ask about that.'

'Not an answer to my question, that wasn't. Still, I suppose I shouldn't expect an honest answer from someone who'd been involved in causing an affray.'

'I wasn't a leading light in that.' James searched his mind frantically for other phrases his lawyer had used in court. 'I was young and easily led at the time of the offence. The judge said the sentence should reflect that. I was bound over to keep the peace for two years.'

'Aye. As I said, the lawyers often come up with a load of crap.'

'I've got a clean record since then. I was warned to go straight, and I've done that.'

'And ended up working for a major criminal. Who's innocent until proved guilty, but who you know and I know is going down for years.' Peach decided that the softening-up process was now complete. 'Mr Naylor, we're not here to discuss either Richard Crouch or your past misdemeanours. Which is no doubt a relief to you. Or would be, if we weren't here in connection with something much more serious. Murder, Mr Naylor. Murder most foul. By a person or persons unknown. For the moment, that is. Did you kill Neil Cartwright?'

The question came so bluntly on the end of the invective that it took James by surprise. 'No. No, I didn't. Of course I didn't!' He struggled to make his denial as emphatic as he wished it to be. The trouble with having a light skin was that the blood always rushed into your face and made you look guilty; he'd had to struggle with that when he was a child.

Peach looked immensely disappointed. 'Hmm. Who did kill him, then?'

'I don't know.' James made an ill-advised attempt at defiance. 'That's your job, not mine, isn't it?'

Peach gave him the grin of a tiger which has discovered a helpless goat. 'My job is to find a murderer and put him behind bars, yes. In our grandfather's day, I'd have been able to say "string him up".' He shook his head sadly over this decline in rigour. 'Must have been a lot more satisfying, to be able to say that to a villain. But then, you tell me that you're not a villain any more. In which case, despite your record, you are a responsible citizen. And it is the duty of a responsible citizen to offer the police every assistance in the detection of crime. So who do you think killed Neil Cartwright, if you didn't, Mr Naylor?'

'I don't know.' James looked desperately for relief at the radiant female face to his tormentor's left, but she was busy recording his replies. 'If I did, I'd tell you, wouldn't I?'

'I sincerely hope you would, yes. To conceal any of your thoughts from us would be most unwise. That includes even those thoughts you regard as most secret. Murder leaves no room for secrets. Did you lose your home in the fire?'

Another question tacked on like an afterthought at the end of the dire warnings James found so unsettling. 'Yes, I did. That is, we did. My wife Michelle and I, I mean. We had time to get our personal possessions out. We spent Wednesday and Thursday night in a hotel, but we've been given rooms in the main house, for the time being. It's a suite on the first floor.' He allowed them an inappropriate glimpse of his pride in the higher status which he felt this conferred upon him.

'But the Cartwrights didn't lose their home.'

'No. Sally lives at the end of the stable block. Her cottage wasn't affected by the fire.'

'Get on well with Neil Cartwright, did you?'

He should have been used to the technique now, which involved the key questions coming at him like missiles rather than enquiries. James told himself that he had known all along that this one would come. 'Well enough.'

'You'll need to enlarge on that.' Peach had stopped smiling some time ago.

'We weren't bosom pals, but we got on well enough.'

'You lived very close to each other on the site. You must have seen a lot of each other.'

'Not that much. I worked in the mansion. I spent almost all of my time in the kitchen. Neil was out on the estate. When there weren't visitors to cater for, he came in with the rest of the staff for a midday meal. Otherwise we scarcely saw him in the main house. Our paths didn't cross very much.'

'You don't spend all your time working. You said yourself that there were slack periods, when the mansion didn't have visitors to demand your attention.'

'Neil worked in the gardens and around the estate. The slack periods didn't make much difference to him.'

There was something here, but Peach had as yet no idea what. He thought of Sally Cartwright's apparent detachment about her husband's death. Had the buxom Mrs Cartwright been having a fling – or something more – with this fresh-faced, vigorous younger man? Peach had never had a residential post himself, but he imagined there could be a hothouse atmosphere when people were living as well as working very close to each other. 'You may not have seen much of him during your working day, but you lived very close to each other.'

James looked at the patch of blue sky outside the window, and fervently wished he was out of this small room and in the fresh air. 'We weren't bosom pals. We didn't go out drinking together. We got on well enough. I don't know what more I can say.'

'Did you meet much socially? Did you go in and out of each other's houses?'

'A little, in the early days. Not much, in the last year or two.' He wished he hadn't said even as much as that. But they'd already spoken to Sally Cartwright, and they'd be talking to his wife in due course. Looking for discrepancies and following them up, as they'd already warned him. He wondered what Michelle would say when they got on to this. 'We had different interests. Sometimes, when you're living close to each other, you find you don't want to live in each other's pockets.' He had thought of that on the spur of the moment, and he was cautiously pleased with it.

'I see.' Peach pursed his lips and nodded slowly. 'What were you doing last Sunday, Mr Naylor?'

James wondered if everyone looked and felt guilty when the man flung questions like this at them so abruptly. He hoped they did. Thank goodness he had his answer ready for this one. 'I went into Tesco's to get a few things in the morning. With my wife, that was. I think I was on the site for the rest of the day. I went across to the main house at

182

about midday, to find out from Mr Holloway just when Mr Crouch and his guests were arriving, and to discuss menus with him.'

'And you were in your stables cottage for the rest of the day?'

'I think so, yes.'

'So your wife could confirm that.'

'I expect so. We might not have been together for the whole of the day. I really can't remember every detail.'

'No, I don't expect you can. Even though it's only seven days ago.' Peach contrived to make that sound like an accusation. 'Who do you think killed Neil Cartwright?'

'I don't know. I'd have told you at the beginning if I did.'

'I see. Well, give some thought to the matter, will you? We'll no doubt be back to speak to you again during the next few days.'

The pretty woman who had taken the notes gave him a quick smile as they left. But Peach's final words rang in his ears like an accusation, long after they had gone.

Thomas Bulstrode Tucker was not a good golfer.

In view of his modest skills, he would have been better advised to wear more muted and less individual colours, but he had an unfortunate taste for garish golfing attire. His plus-twos were in a combination of canary yellow and bright red which reflected no known Scottish tartan. The turquoise socks below them sat uneasily above the scarred white shoes, which bore the evidence of his many visits to brambles and blackthorn. His lemon cap bore the badge of the La Manga club in Spain, where he had once taken a hundred and thirteen shots to complete a round on the South Course. That was one of many personal golfing statistics which Superintendent Tucker kept entirely to himself.

After the dismal prelude of Percy Peach's visit, last night's dinner had really gone rather well. The Chief Superintendent had been able to enlarge at length upon his successes to Henry Rawcliffe, the Chairman of the local Police Authority. Admittedly, the grey-haired, adipose sexagenarian had listened to him with a rather distracted air, with only the most minimal conversational responses.

But that had allowed Thomas Tucker to enlarge upon his key role of direction of the Brunton CID section, and to show how he was right on top of the investigation of the sensational events at Marton Towers. He had managed to get Henry on his own for ten minutes at the end of the dinner. The man had not said much in response, but Rawcliffe must surely have been impressed, for he had accepted Tucker's invitation to be his guest and play a round with him at Brunton Golf Club.

When he arrived to play, Henry Rawcliffe

was not attired in Tucker's peacock splendour. He apparently preferred the low-key anonymity of greys and the darker blues. But Tucker was delighted to find that the Chairman of Brunton Police Authority was almost as bad a golfer as the man who had invited him to play. Rawcliffe took rather less time to play a bad shot, because he did not go through Tucker's elaborate preparations for disaster. He also seemed to find his failures less of a surprise. But Henry Rawcliffe topped the ball just as savagely along the ground, or hit the ground two inches behind that small and elusive white sphere, almost as regularly as did Chief Superintendent T. B. Tucker.

Rawcliffe's language in reaction to these trials was less virulent and colourful than Tucker's, so that his demeanour and indeed his whole presence on the course were less eye-catching than that of his opponent. But Sunday was a busy day, and on an afternoon of gentle winds and high-flying white clouds the members of Brunton Golf Club were out in force. They followed the erratic progress of this muted stranger and the familiar garish figure of Thomas Bulstrode Tucker round the course with increasing impatience.

Another, non-golfing spectator watched with interest from the edge of the course. The man who three days ago had climbed the wall at the back of Marton Towers, then fled when the constable in charge of the crime scene came out of the stable block, stood motionless beside a bunker, with a rake in his hand.

He studied the actions of the luridly clad Tucker and his companion without a smile. If this was the man in charge of the investigation up at the Towers, then there surely couldn't be too much danger for him.

Sunday tea in the old cottage at the base of Longridge Fell was a nostalgic ritual for Lucy Blake.

She was always reminded of teas twenty years ago, when she was a wide-eyed girl at primary school who believed that her father could do absolutely anything. This time of year had always seemed the best to her, when the days were growing longer and the sun was rising higher over Pendle Hill and her dad was showing her the first buds on the daffodils in the front garden, and teasing her about Easter eggs.

Her father had been dead for ten years now, though his memory was still bright in this house. His picture stood in pride of place on the mantelpiece, its silver frame bright with diligent cleaning, the neat writing in Agnes Blake's hand beneath it giving the information that this was Bill Blake after taking six for thirty-four. In the black and white picture, a smiling, exhausted man in cricket whites, with a sweater over his arm, looked at once pleased and embarrassed by the attention, as his team-mates applauded him up the steps of the pavilion.

One of the more surprising changes in a room which changed little had been the appearance a year or so earlier of another photograph alongside that of the dead man whose presence was still strong in this room. A colour photograph of a smiling Percy Peach, looking much younger because his bald pate was covered by a blue cap at a rakish angle. The same neat hand beneath the picture proclaimed that this was Denis Charles Scott Peach, coming back to the pavilion after 'yet another fifty' for East Lancs.

Agnes Blake caught Percy looking at the pictures as she came into the room. 'You gave up the game much too early, Percy. With your dancing footwork, you'd a lot of runs left in you,' she said with authority.

'I think I did, sometimes,' agreed Percy. 'Then I look at people ducking and diving with the ball flying round their heads and think perhaps thirty-six was old enough. You don't get that sort of thing at golf.'

'GOLF!'

Percy was still surprised by the depth of the contempt a seventy-year-old lady could compress into a single syllable, though he had experienced the phenomenon many times now. He said impishly, 'I think your daughter's thinking of taking up golf, Mrs B.'

The snort of derision might have come from the most mettlesome of stallions. Percy and his future mother-in-law not only understood each other perfectly but took an undisguised pleasure in each other's company. It was the only time when Lucy felt the stirring of a little jealousy. She had indeed toyed with the idea of golf. She'd never tried it, but it surely couldn't be so difficult, when you approached a dead ball in your own time and didn't hit it until you were quite ready to do so.

She'd said as much to Percy Peach, and he'd told her that her naivety was one of her most touching qualities.

One of the things which hadn't changed over the years was the excellence of Agnes Blake's baking. And with the advent of Percy Peach, she had a man to feed again, a man to pay her compliments about her scones and her trifles and her sponge cakes. Agnes had been born at the end of the nineteen-thirties depression, which had hit the cotton mills of Brunton and the Ribble Valley hardest of all. The men had been the breadwinners then, and young Agnes had been brought up on the precept that it was good to see a man eat.

Percy Peach did not disappoint her. He polished off the delicious roast-ham salad which constituted the traditional high tea in these parts, and moved on with zest to Agnes Blake's baking. And the woman who lived there alone was delighted. 'Good to have a sensible man to feed at last, instead of a vain young woman watching her figure,' she said, with an accusing glance at her daughter.

'I'd be like a house side, Mum, if I ate everything you set before me,' protested Lucy.

Percy graciously accepted a slice of fruit cake. 'I like to see a little flesh upon a lass, as you do, Mrs B,' he said magisterially, studying the flesh on his fiancée appreciatively as she stooped at his side to replenish his cup, ignoring the baleful glare which Lucy visited upon him in response to this sentiment. 'I expect she wants to look slim on the wedding photographs, but for my money, she's—Ouch! What did you do that for?' He gazed up in wide-eyed innocence into the angry blue-green eyes of Lucy, who had pinched his arm viciously with the mention of the wedding.

Agnes beamed delightedly. 'I'm glad you brought that up, Percy. I can't get our Lucy to talk about it. It's time we were fixing a date.'

'You could well be right, Mrs B. I'm always ready to bow to your superior experience of life, in this as in so many other things.' He intoned the words sententiously, then directed his widest and most innocent smile first at Agnes and then at her daughter.

'I've told her, I've a career to think of,' said Lucy furiously.

'Oh, the modern police service is very

enlightened in these things,' said Percy airily. 'Marriage is no hindrance to a woman nowadays – perhaps, indeed, rather the reverse, sometimes. And I'm sure your mother wouldn't be averse to the idea of grandchildren.'

He knew of course that nothing would give the lady greater pleasure. Lucy had not been born until her mother was forty-one, and Agnes was anxious to have grandchildren while she still had the energy to enjoy them. But he and the vigorous septuagenarian were as usual on exactly the same wavelength, one which Lucy found it difficult to tune herself in to. Her mother now came in with her usual spiel about wanting to romp with toddlers before the old man with the sickle came to carry her off, whilst Percy nodded sage agreement and interjected the odd well-chosen phrase of encouragement.

Percy, who had once objected to the idea of a woman DS at his side with every weapon at his disposal, now came through as the most enlightened of men. 'And should you wish to return to police work at a later stage, such as when your children reached school age, your rank would be safeguarded and your re-entry into the service warmly welcomed, I'm sure. We appreciate the value of family experience in a modern police officer.'

Lucy Blake thought she had never seen her man so sanctimonious; Agnes thought Percy a pillar of common sense.

Lucy resisted all attempts to pin her down to a date for the wedding. But by the time they left the cosy old cottage that night, the conspirators, their heads bent together over a calendar at the other side of the cheerful fire, had agreed on a series of possible dates in the summer and autumn.

'Sensible woman, your mum,' said Percy, as he drove down the lane after waving an extravagant farewell to his devotee.

'Judas!' his partner hissed at him through the darkness.

Thirteen

It was an impressive room. The tall stone-framed neo-Gothic window looked out over the gravelled forecourt of Marton Towers and the twin lakes which fringed the driveway as it ran down to the gatehouse.

Percy Peach was enjoying building up the tension in the woman to whom he had just introduced Blake and himself. He walked over to the window and took an unhurried look at this scene, which had changed so little since the grounds of the house were laid out over a hundred and fifty years ago. 'Did themselves well, the toffs, didn't they?' he said without rancour.

Michelle Naylor said, 'We're only here as a temporary measure. One of the disused cottages in the stable block is being cleaned up and heated for us. I expect we'll be in there by the end of this week.' She wondered why she was apologizing to this man for occupying this splendid suite in the mansion. She had planned many things to say during the intervals of a restless night, but this hadn't been one of them.

'Near Sally Cartwright, are they, your new quarters?'

192

'No. This cottage is at the other end of the stable block, actually. But only about a hundred yards away from Sally, I suppose.'

'Pity you're not going to be next door. I expect Mrs Cartwright could do with a little company and support, after what's happened.'

'Yes. Well, she'll get that from the residents generally. You become quite a tightly knit group when you live on the site as well as working together.'

'That's what I thought. Get on well with both of the Cartwrights, did you?'

'Well enough.'

'I'm particularly interested in the months immediately before Neil's death, for obvious reasons.'

'They're a little older than us. I suppose I should say they were a little older, in view of what's happened to poor Neil. But we got on well enough, as I said. There's always a danger of getting too close, when you are together all the time. We didn't want to live in each other's pockets.'

Michelle produced the phrase which James had told her he'd used to them on the previous day, and glanced up at Peach to see if he noticed the echo. She learned nothing from his impassive, watchful face.

'What was it that made you fall out with the Cartwrights?'

He spoke as if it were an established fact, as if he now expected her to account for herself. James had said that he hadn't given anything away when they'd spoken to him on the previous day, but perhaps he'd under-estimated them. Or overestimated his own powers of deception. Or perhaps someone else had been talking.

Michelle fought for calmness. 'We didn't fall out. Relations between us and the Cart-wrights might have cooled a little, that's all.'

'And why was that?'

Michelle was surprised at the tension in her shoulders as she forced a shrug. 'Who knows? Perhaps you should ask Sally Cart-wright.'

'Oh, we shall, Mrs Naylor. But at the moment, I'm asking you.'

'In that case, I should have to say that I don't really know. Sally's my boss, now. She's been promoted, if you like, though we're all expected to muck in together as required here and people don't have official job des-criptions. But Sally's really the housekeeper here now, with responsibility for all the other domestic staff in the main house. Not in the kitchen, or outside the mansion, but in all the reception rooms and the bedrooms. It's a responsible job, when there are visitors. The whole place has to look attractive and run smoothly.'

Peach looked at Michelle Naylor thought-fully, assessing her in the cool, detached way that CID officers cultivate, which the sub-jects of that assessment usually find disconcerting. This one apparently did not. She was small-boned and delicate, with tightly packed black curls and small bright eyes which were as dark as his own. She was pale, alert, observant; her movements were naturally quick. She was very pretty, in a reserved, feline sort of way. Mrs Naylor reminded him of a feral cat, which appears vulnerable but which is in fact very difficult to capture.

Peach had a feeling she had just delivered herself of a speech she had prepared in advance. He looked round at the high-ceilinged room, with its elegant chaise longue and its oil paintings on the wall, before he smiled at her and said, 'Are you admitting that you are a little jealous of Mrs Cartwright's new and superior status? You seem to be suggesting that it has led to a cooling of relations between the two of you.'

'Nothing has happened as far as I'm concerned. I'm suggesting that Sally might be conscious of her new status, not me. As I say, we are not encouraged to take account of such distinctions at Marton Towers. But it has sometimes seemed to me over the last year or so that Sally Cartwright – and possibly her husband as well, for all I know – were a little conscious of the position she had acquired here. That perhaps she thought it necessary to put a little distance between herself and people like me whom she sometimes had to direct during the day.'

'Your husband didn't mention this to us

when we spoke to him yesterday.'

Michelle found to her surprise that she was now quite enjoying this exchange. It was like a rally at table tennis, where your opponent played a good shot and you tried a return which was as good or better. Careful, girl, she told herself. Don't get too excited: remember that in this game you're playing against the fuzz.

She forced herself to take her time, then gave them a fond, indulgent smile at the mention of her husband. 'James is an innocent, Detective Chief Inspector Peach.' She relished her control as she rolled out his full title. 'My husband probably wouldn't be very conscious of the subtle nuances of status which some women feel. And he's shut away in his kitchen for most of the time. So long as things are going well in there, he hardly notices anyone else. Perhaps that's why he's a good chef: I've noticed before that chefs are often only conscious of their immediate surroundings.'

She was a cool one, this. Peach, irritated by her control, gave an almost imperceptible nod to the woman at his side, and Lucy Blake said quietly, 'Did you find this new attitude in Mrs Cartwright exasperating?'

Michelle transferred her attention to this woman whose beauty was almost the opposite of hers. She eyed the striking chestnut, the wide green eyes beneath the forehead which had a suggestion of freckles left over from adolescence, the curves of the body which were such a contrast to her own slender grace. If you're going to try the 'soft cop after the hard cop' routine, it won't work with me, my girl, she vowed.

Michelle said sharply, 'I didn't find Sally's attitude to me exasperating, no. I'm not even sure this notion of her new status existed. That is what I said in the first place about it. If you're going to follow it up, I'd rather you didn't tell her that the thought came from me.'

'We treat everything we are told as confidential, Mrs Naylor. We shall make our own minds up about Mrs Cartwright, in due course. Did you lose much in the fire?'

Michelle was shocked by the sudden switch of ground, but she did not show it. 'No. We were told to get out and leave things to the professionals, but we had a few minutes to rescue whatever we wanted. I was sorry to see the furniture go: there was some good stuff, from the heyday of the house, but it wasn't ours. And I try not to be sentimental about objects.'

Lucy Blake could believe that. This didn't seem like a woman who would be sentimental about anything. She looked into the small-featured, pretty face beneath the frame of tight black curls. 'And Mrs Cartwright was evacuated with you to the hotel?'

'Yes. There was great confusion, as you'd expect. We were completely thrown by the police raid on the house and the arrests, to start with. We were all in the main house discussing what had happened to Mr Crouch when the news of the fire came.'

'And how do you think that started?'

'I've no idea. There's some pretty old wiring in the stabling block. Much of it dated from about the nineteen fifties, Neil Cartwright thought. I think he was planning to do some re-wiring, next winter, when things were quiet on the estate. He was away from the place last Wednesday, of course: or so we thought at the time. But I expect the fire-service people will come up with some ideas about how the blaze started.'

'When did you last see Neil Cartwright?'

Michelle took her time, pretended to think, as if the question had come as a surprise to her. 'I think it must have been on the Friday before he went off on leave. He came in for lunch in the main house. I remember it because he had a twig in his hair from a tree he'd been working on at the back of the grounds, and the men teased him about it.' She paused, her small, sharp-featured face grave with concentration. 'I don't think I saw him again after that. He had a week off from the Saturday, you know. He was going off to see his sister, somewhere in Scotland, I think.'

Lucy wondered how much of the vagueness was genuine and how much was calculated. 'Where were you last Sunday, Mrs

Naylor?'

'You're asking me to account for myself?' Michelle Naylor wrinkled her nose in amusement at the idea, looking more feline than ever.

'We shall be asking everyone to account for themselves, unless we have a confession.'

'And we shall give special attention to those with criminal records, of course.' This woman was far too calm: Peach was glad to come back in to the interrogation with a barb.

'A conviction for shoplifting when I was a kid? It's a long step from that to murder.'

'True. But you weren't really such a kid: you were nineteen at the time, and it was an expensive piece of jewellery you attempted to steal. Perhaps you were lucky not to get a custodial sentence, in view of your previous record of thefts.'

She was stung, and for the first time she let it show. 'That's what the magistrate said at the time, and I took notice of him. I've gone eleven years without even being questioned by you lot since then.'

'Until now, that is, when you find yourself involved in a murder investigation. So would you answer DS Blake's question, please: where were you last Sunday?'

'That all you've got for a time of death? A whole day to cover? It's not going to be easy for you, is it?' Michelle couldn't resist letting her derision show, in a little twist of the conversational knife which she knew she should have resisted. 'But of course I'll account for myself. As an innocent party, I'm only too anxious to assist the police to find the culprit, you see. I went to Tesco's with my husband on Sunday morning. I visited my mother and father in Bolton on Sunday afternoon. I was back in our cottage in the stable block by around seven o'clock, I'd say, and I was there for the rest of the evening. With James, of course. I'm sure my husband will confirm that for you, if you need it.'

Alibis provided by spouses were always suspect, but they were often also the most difficult ones to shake. Peach said, 'Who do you think killed Neil Cartwright, Mrs Naylor?'

'I've no idea. Someone from outside this place, I should think. I can't think that anyone working at the Towers would have done it. We're not murderers here, whatever you might think about people with minor criminal records.'

She was almost truculent with them, as the adrenaline coursed through her veins. They seemed to be watching for a reaction when they told her that they'd probably need to speak to her again, which she took as a confession of failure on their part. Then they took their leave of her.

Michelle went out of the suite with them and watched them walk down the wide staircase into the panelled reception hall of the mansion. From the long window in the huge first floor room, she watched the police car move sedately down the drive and disappear at the gatehouse.

The interview had gone well, she decided. She was surprised how well, and how when she had expected to be nervous she had taken them on and held her own. There would be some kind of reaction in her body now. After all that tension, she was sure she could actually feel her pulse slowing. She went and looked in the heavily framed antique mirror in the next room of the suite, noting how much colour and animation there was now in her normally pale face.

And then, quite unexpectedly, she burst into tears.

Fourteen

Monday morning. Sergeant Jack Clark of the Drugs Squad was not yet back at work. He'd been debriefed and had a short, unproductive session with the police psychiatrist. Then he'd been told to take at least two weeks off, after his intensive period of undercover work in the squat, to take things easy and have a complete rest.

Go off abroad, they'd said, if you fancy it. Rehabilitation, that was the word. Do anything you liked to cut yourself off from that strange life you had compelled yourself to lead for the last few months.

But it wasn't as easy as that.

He'd been all right at home for the first twenty-four hours. He'd slept the clock round, on the first night in his own bed. And he'd enjoyed just lazing about the place for the first day. He'd strolled down to the corner shop for a newspaper, where he'd been greeted like a long-lost friend by the Asian proprietor. He'd explained that he'd been away 'working in the south' for the last couple of months. Then he'd walked through the park on a crisp March morning, breathing deeply on the cool, clear air, watching the mothers and toddlers feeding the ducks, listening to the birdsong which was the herald of spring. Jack Clark had spent an hour savouring the innocence which surrounded him here, after the weeks of not daring to relax.

He'd even enjoyed resurrecting the ambience of a flat which had been empty for months. He'd lounged in the chair with his paper, made himself coffee at eleven, worked the microwave back into life for his lunchtime snack, created a small, deliberate untidiness upon the sterile surfaces of a home which had been unoccupied for so long.

It was four years since Jack's divorce. He was used to living alone by this time, he told himself. He made a cool, detached phone call to his ex-wife, who had another man now, to tell her that he was back in the land of the living. The call ended flatly, with him telling her what they had told each other a score of times before, that it was a blessing that there had been no children from their union.

By sundown, Jack Clark was bored. Worse than bored, if he was honest. He was beset by the relentless, gnawing knowledge that whatever he turned his hand to was no more than a diversion, an attempt to distract himself from more important concerns. And yet at the moment he had no important concerns: he was enjoying what his superintendent had called a well-earned rest. Except that he wasn't enjoying it at all.

By seven o'clock that night, Jack Clark knew that he was missing the danger which had driven his life for the last ten weeks. Knew that his life was incomplete without it. He despised himself for this strand in his personality, tried to convince himself that it was not in fact so, that this was a temporary, passing malaise. He had been warned that it would be an inevitable psychological consequence of the work he had undertaken as an undercover instrument in the necessary fight against an evil trade.

But Jack knew that his problems came from within, not from without. The super had told him that the squad needed people like him, that the unending war against the dangerous men who directed the illegal drugs trade could only be won with his help. But Jack knew that he needed that work even more than it needed him. He could never again take on a close relationship with a partner, because he was a loner who needed danger, who craved it as strongly as any addict craved his chosen drug.

He told himself that he had known this for some time now, that there was nothing new in this sombre recognition. But he was over-taken by a bleak and chilling loneliness.

He switched off the television which had flickered unseen in the corner of the room and picked up the *Evening Dispatch*. There had been a fire after the raid on Marton

Towers which had been the triumphant con-summation of his undercover mission. And amidst the desolation of the ruins, there had been the incinerated remains of a corpse. He read the bald details of the latest police press officer's handout, which confirmed that both arson and murder were suspected, though the two serious crimes were not necessarily connected. There were dangerous people up at the Towers, probably beyond the circle of the drugs barons he had helped to trap.

He felt a stirring of envy at the notion of danger. And he knew things: things which might just be helpful to the man looking for a killer. Jack spent ten minutes convincing himself of that. Then he rang Brunton CID section, and was told that the man in charge of the investigation was a Detective Chief Inspector Peach. Percy Peach, the station sergeant told him, as if it was a name every-one would know. Jack thought it was a ridiculous name for a detective, but he knew how people in the police service loved the simple pleasures of alliteration.

Jack Clark arranged to see DCI Percy Peach at nine o'clock the next morning.

Whilst Jack Clark was living through his edgy Monday, Percy Peach was enduring trials of another sort. Working undercover was the most dangerous assignment in the land, but at least men like Clark never had to deal with a Tommy Bloody Tucker.

'Hope you enjoyed your Saturday night junket, sir,' said Peach.

Chief Superintendent Tucker said testily, 'It wasn't a junket. It was a social occasion undertaken in the line of duty. I wouldn't expect you to understand that, Peach.'

'No, sir, I probably wouldn't. I was trying to find a murderer, myself.'

'And I was able to brief Henry Rawcliffe about our efforts. It's highly important that we make a friend of the Chairman of the Police Authority, you know.'

'I see, sir. And did you succeed in doing that?'

'I did indeed.' Tucker leaned forward confidentially over his big desk, unable to resist the temptation to confess his triumph. 'We had a game of golf at my club yesterday. That's how well we got on on Saturday night. That's how close we are.'

'Really, sir. You're sure that was wise, are you?'

Tucker glared at this irritant in his comfortable world. 'Of course I'm sure. If you're trying to cast aspersions on my golf, to imply that I wouldn't be able to give the man a good game, then I must tell you that you haven't seen the best of my game. You have an unfortunate tendency to—'

'Nothing to do with your golf, sir. I would not dream of commenting on anything so sensitive. I was thinking that a man in your position needed to be more careful than most about his choice of friends.'

Tucker gave the underling his most conde-scending smile. 'I think you can safely leave the nuances of social intercourse to me, Peach. It's hardly your forte, is it? And I could hardly make a better friend than the Chairman of the Police Authority, could I?'

Peach decided that the patronizing sod intended this as a rhetorical question, so he didn't venture an opinion. 'I thought I'd better brief you on the latest position at Marton Towers, sir.'

'And I agree with you. Leave my choice of friends to me and get on with what you should be doing.'

'Well, sir, as of this moment, it still seems possible that the butler did it.'

'The butler?'

It reassured Peach to find his chief back in goggle-eyed, dead-fish mode. 'Yes, sir. Mr Neville Holloway. General Manager at Marton Towers, he calls himself. Still in the frame, at the moment.'

'You're telling me you've still made no pro-gress in this matter, after all this time?'

'Four days, sir, since the remains were dis-covered. Including a weekend when my only junket was to have tea with a seventy-year-old lady. I can now tell you that there are others in the frame, as well as the butler. The wife, sir, for a start.'

'The spouse is always a suspect, you know, in a suspicious death.'

'Yes, sir. I'll try to remember that.' Peach shut his eyes and was silent for three seconds. 'This one didn't seem to be unduly affected by her old man's departure. It's possible that she was being knocked off by someone else, sir, but that hasn't been confirmed as yet.'

'That would explain why she wasn't too upset by her husband's death, wouldn't it?'

'It would indeed, sir. That was a line of enquiry we thought worth pursuing, sir.'

'She might even have killed him herself, you know, or partnered someone else in the crime.'

'That had occurred to us, sir. It's good to have it confirmed by your overview.'

Irony was wasted on Tucker. He said, 'Well, who else do you have to offer for this?'

'Mrs Cartwright is forty-one, sir. There's a younger couple, also living on site: James and Margaret Naylor. He's thirty-one and she's thirty, sir.' Tucker had a reporter's attitude to suspects: the first thing he always wanted to know was their ages.

'The wife, Tucker. Is she voluptuous?'

Tucker pursed his lips at this politically incorrect but highly relevant question. 'Eminently bedworthy, sir, I'd say. Of course, I'd always defer to your superior expertise in these matters, but that's—'

'Then you must consider the possibility that this younger man was conducting an affair with her. Very likely a highly passionate

208

affair. The attractions of the voluptuous older woman must never be underestimated, Peach.'

'I see, sir.' Peach frowned in concentration, as if striving to etch this precious insight into his memory. 'Well, we're checking out the non-resident staff at the Towers, the ones who come in to work there each day, and the other relatives of the deceased; they include a stepfather who didn't get on with him at all and has a past history of violence. So far my money's on either him or one of the four residents for this.'

'One of the women seems likely, if adultery's involved. But keep an open mind, Peach.' Chief Superintendent Tucker waved a lordly arm towards the door of his office.

Peach went back downstairs and made a call to an inspector friend of his in the Lancashire County Police. The information about Henry Rawcliffe, Head of the Brunton Police Authority, was most satisfactory.

After this moment of self-indulgence, he turned his mind to the people he had mentioned to Tommy Bloody Tucker as being in the frame for this one. Each of the five was concealing something, he was sure, but he relished the challenge of that: he'd break them down, in the next day or two. He would have been altogether less pleased with himself had he realized that his five main suspects were about to become six.

No one who saw the erect figure striding into DCI Peach's office would have recognized the furtive creature of the underworld who had lived from hand to mouth in the squat a week earlier.

Only a certain restlessness, an inability to settle in one position for longer than a minute at a time, remained from the being who had lived with incessant danger over those perilous months. Jack Clark's hair had been cut, his shirt was clean, dark trousers had replaced the torn and filthy jeans which had clung to his slim legs for so long. He even wore a tie; you might have mistaken this brave and reckless man for a banker.

Peach, of course, knew otherwise. The Detective Chief Inspector would have protested that he was a born coward, with a healthy consciousness of the vulnerability of his own skin. His colleagues, on the other hand, would have told you that Percy Peach was in fact a man who had never flinched from danger, whenever his work led him into it. But Peach knew that he could never have done what Clark had done, never have lived the necessary lie that he had lived over weeks of almost unbearable tension and vigilance.

Clark in his turn had been made aware as he chatted to the station sergeant of the iconic reputation as an aggressive taker of villains which Peach had built up for himself over the last few years in Brunton. For a few minutes, the two men circled each other respectfully in conversation, two very different creatures who were each slightly in awe of the other's strengths.

Rank was soon dispensed with; the pair spoke as two men playing very different parts in the same war against evil. They discussed the success of the raid at Marton Towers on the previous Wednesday night, with Peach paying fulsome and uncharacteristic tribute to the accuracy of the information Clark had provided to set it up, and Jack making more conventional noises about the swiftness and efficiency of the police swoop.

Then Peach said, 'But you didn't come in here to review past triumphs, Jack Clark.'

Jack was glad that Peach had taken the initiative: he had been wondering how to cut through the conversational pleasantries, without knowing when or how to do it. Polite conversation was not his strength. He said, 'You're right. I've been a bit restless, since last Wednesday night.'

Peach smiled wryly at him. 'Wish I could say the same. But I collected an investigation into arson and murder at the Towers, after the successful conclusion of the raid.'

'I know that. I was hoping I might be able to help you.'

For a moment, Peach thought the man was asking to join his team. But then he knew that it couldn't be that: this man lived and worked in a very different world from that of normal detection. 'You think you may have information?'

Jack nodded. Now that he was here, what he had to say seemed more vague and ephemeral than it had when he had paced the narrow confines of his flat. 'It won't give you an arrest. It will add to the sum of your knowledge.' He gave a grim little smile at the formality of that phrase.

Peach's smile was equally grim, but also encouraging. 'Any information will be welcome, Jack. We're nowhere near an arrest at present.'

'It's a bit vague, because what we were concerned with was trapping the big boys. But some of the people who worked at the Towers were dealing. I thought you'd like to be aware of that.'

'I can't say I'm surprised. But it's valuable information, because no one up there's told me a thing about it. I'm sure Holloway, the man in charge, was aware of it, even if he wasn't involved himself, but he's said nothing. Do you know who was dealing?'

'No. At least, the only name I can give you won't be of much use. It's Neil Cartwright, your murder victim. He'd been dealing for some time. I think he had the type of job they were planning to offer me, where you supply and direct your own small ring of dealers.'

'So he might have been using other domestic employees at the Towers to deal for him?'

'He might, or he might have recruited

completely different people from outside. People like Cartwright are small fry, when you consider the big picture, so they were of no real concern to us in the build-up to last Wednesday's arrests. And of course, Cartwright's dealing may have no connection at all with either the fire which followed the raid or the murder which preceded it.'

'But until we know that's the case, we need to give special attention to anyone who worked with or close to Cartwright.' Peach's mind was already on the sheet of paper he had been looking at before Clark came into the room.

'What was his job at Marton Towers?'

'He was Head Gardener. But that title wouldn't cover the full range of his duties. He was also in charge of the estate. And he had staff who worked for him. At least one of them was full time.'

'If it was an older man, it's unlikely that he'd have been recruited to sell drugs.'

Peach smiled at the earnest, neatly clad officer opposite him, who looked so unlike a man who would willingly put his life into extreme danger. 'This was a young man, Jack. A young man who seems to have made himself very scarce since the events of last week.'

Fifteen

Ben Freeman kept his eye on the Head Greenkeeper, who was planting a young tree in the rough beside the adjoining fairway. When you were on probation, it paid you to take extreme care over your work, to make sure that you understood exactly what the boss wanted and then deliver it to the best of your ability. He'd been warned about that when they took him on, and he was doing his best to perform.

It was the first time they had allowed him to drive the gang mowers which cut the fairways at Brunton Golf Club. There wasn't a great growth of grass so early in the year, but there was enough for him to be able to survey the appealing swathes he had just cut across the second and third fairways. He was pleased with what he saw. The pattern was regular and the lines were straight. With the neatening effect that mowing always has on growing grass, the two fairways looked a hundred per cent better for his efforts.

He glanced at his watch. Twenty to twelve already. The time went quickly when you were concentrating on the work. Lunch break in twenty minutes, and the rest of the day fine and bright, if the forecast they'd been given that morning was correct. A couple of the members gave him a cheery good morning and complimented him on the look of his work. It was a good life; he'd made the right decision in coming here.

He drove the tractor across to the Head Greenkeeper to ask if he should now move on to mowing another fairway. His boss was a powerful, grizzled man of fifty, with the dark, healthy skin which came from much work out of doors. 'You done well there, young Ben,' he said.

He'd been watching, then, estimating the skills of the newest member of his staff. Ben said, 'I've done a lot of mowing before. Mostly fine grasses, though. Smaller mowers than this, to give a fine cut. Lawns and the like.' He didn't know quite what he meant by 'the like', but he wanted to get in the line about lawns, because they might let him on to the greens, if they were satisfied with his other work. The more experienced lads who worked with him had said that that was the elite job at a golf course: when the boss trusted you to work on the greens, you really knew you were in.

'Might let you mow the first fairway, next week,' said the boss. And Ben realized in a flash that he hadn't been trusted on the first fairway for his first outing with the big tractor and the gang mowers. The first hole was visible from the clubhouse windows, and any clumsiness in the lines left from his cutting would have been all too evident to the members in the bar. But telling him that he might now be trusted there was telling him that he had done all right.

Ben Freeman said, 'Do you want me to move on to the fourth now?' Always show willing, however near it is to break time.

At that moment, the Head Greenkeeper's mobile phone screeched in his pocket. He pulled it out, pressed the button and put it to his ear, with the wariness of a man who does not trust such things. He listened, nodded, looked cautiously at the man who sat on the tractor above him as he spoke. 'You're to go to the clubhouse, lad. Secretary wants to see you. There's two coppers come in to talk to you, apparently.'

Ben Freeman's bright day seemed suddenly a little darker.

The grass was also beginning to grow on the neat lawns around Marton Towers. Neville Holloway knew that it would need attention in the next week or two, if the mansion was to have the elegant emerald surround which had set it off so admirably over the last few years.

With Cartwright dead and no regular outdoor staff now available, it was a situation which would demand his attention before long. At present, he had two men coming in on an hourly basis to keep things tidy outside. But the future was uncertain, with the owner of the Towers in custody and by all accounts likely to stay there. Richard Crouch's instructions from jail were to carry on as usual for the present: there was plenty of money in the bank for staff wages. But no one, and perhaps least of all Crouch, knew what was the long-term future of the estate and its employees.

Neville Holloway had more immediate concerns. He looked out at the reflection of the trees in the still waters of the lakes beside the deserted driveway, saw no sign of a human presence and locked the door of his office. Then he set the shredder to work on the documents he had selected over the last two hours.

With the police about and prying into everyone's business, it was time to cover your tracks.

The secretary of the golf club looked at his new employee curiously, then said, 'These two officers would like to have a word with you. You can use the Committee Room: you won't be disturbed in there.'

Ben Freeman looked round uneasily at this big room with the huge table in the middle of it, where he had never been before. When invited to sit down, he set his buttocks uneasily on the edge of a chair with arms, which seemed hugely above his status. Feeling a need to break the heavy silence, he blurted out nervously and meaninglessly, 'I haven't done anything, you know.'

'Then you won't have anything to fear from us,' said the woman with dark-red hair, who had made him self-conscious by watching his every movement. 'I'm Detective Sergeant Blake, of Brunton CID, and this is Detective Constable Northcott.'

A tall, unsmiling black man who looked as if he was made of ebony; a man you wouldn't want to tangle with. Ben looked at the contrasting pair and tried unsuccessfully to muster a little aggression as he said, 'Well, what is this about, then?'

'Murder, Mr Freeman.' DS Blake looked him calmly in the face, searching for a re-action, using the single word of the worst and most ancient of crimes as a weapon to frighten this young, open-faced man, who had looked so apprehensive from the outset. She was watchful but perfectly calm, delivering the sinister word as coolly as if it had been an item on a shopping list. 'Arson as well, perhaps, but let's all concentrate our attention on murder, for the moment.'

'You're talking about Marton Towers. I've left there.' Ben was stalling, buying himself time. But he found he couldn't use that precious time: his brain was racing out of control and refusing to perform, at this moment when he most needed it.

'Yes. Very interesting, that. We shall want to know the reason for your sudden departure, in due course. The important thing at the moment is that you were around at the time when Neil Cartwright died.'

He felt like throwing in the towel at the start. He had never been good with words, and they were going to out-smart him, whatever he said. The teachers at school had always been able to reduce him to a helpless silence, because they were so much better with words than he was. But this was much, much more serious than anything at school. He said helplessly, 'Neil Cartwright was my boss.'

'Yes. So you knew him well. How did you get on with him, Mr Freeman?'

Ben wished she wouldn't keep giving him the title. No one else spoke to him like that, and it unnerved him. 'Well enough.' He knew he needed to give them something more than that, if they weren't to come after him like dogs cornering a cat. 'I liked Neil. We worked together a lot, around the estate. And he taught me things, things that I didn't know before. Mainly things about gardening.' He forced out the phrases. Nothing came naturally or sounded right, even to him, who was producing these words.

'But you probably had disagreements with him. Most people who work closely together have those, from time to time.'

How pretty and persuasive she was, when she smiled, this woman who was only a few years older than him but who seemed to know so much more about the world. He had to resist again the temptation simply to agree with her, to give them what they wanted and have it over with. 'We didn't fall out with each other. Neil was my boss, but we got on well. I learned things from him, and he told me I was doing well.'

Again that smile, bathing him in warmth, assuring him that much the best policy was cooperation. 'Then why did you leave, Ben? Why throw up a good job at the Towers, when you felt you were doing well and your employers were quite pleased with your efforts?'

'Fancied the job here more.' He'd tried to prepare an argument on these lines, but he couldn't produce anything which sounded right to him now that the moment was at hand.

'And why would that be?'

'Better prospects.' He'd had more than that to say, when he'd rehearsed it last night, but now the words wouldn't come.

'Assistant Greenkeeper, the secretary here told us. On probation, at the lowest wages. Better prospects in that than in being Deputy Estate Manager at Marton Towers?'

He wanted to tell her that he had never had that title, that the job hadn't been anything like as grand as that. But he was beguiled by the thought of it, by the importance it seemed to give to what he had been doing up at the Towers. And she was right, of course she was: he'd loved the work up there, the variety of it, the sense that all the time he was learning and improving himself. If it hadn't been for bloody Neil Cartwright...

But he couldn't admit these things, however much this woman made it sound as if they already knew them. Ben Freeman said desperately, 'I've always wanted to work at a golf club. To work outdoors and make the grass as good as you can possibly make it.' Someone had told him to say that when he went for interview at the golf club, and he'd duly delivered the phrases at interview, though the people who had spoken with him then hadn't seemed very impressed by them. He tried hard to convince DS Blake by the earnestness he forced into his face now.

But just when he had focused all his attention and efforts upon her, it was the unsmiling, hard-as-granite black man who spoke. 'Why'd you leave the Towers, Ben?'

'I told you, I—'

'You did, and we didn't buy it. So cut the crap and tell us why, boy.'

'All right. I'd had a bust-up with Cartwright. He told me to go. Said to get my arse out of the place and find myself another job.' Suddenly and surprisingly, Ben found it easier to speak.

'Big bust-up, was it?'

'Quite big, yes. I was glad to get out, in the end. And I've found a job here that—'

'Did you kill Neil Cartwright, Ben?'

'No! No, of course I didn't.' Ben strove to convince them with the vehemence of his tone, to find words which would make it apparent that this was a ridiculous notion. He failed in both attempts.

'Because the facts suggest that, don't they? You've just told us you had a big row with Cartwright, as a result of which he kicked you out of a job you liked. It seems very likely that as a consequence of that, you lost your temper and attacked him.'

'No!'

'Perhaps you'd no intention of killing him, when it happened. Perhaps things just got out of hand. Perhaps you were even in fear for your own life, when you grabbed that piece of cable or whatever it was that killed Cartwright. You might even get away with manslaughter, if you get a good brief on it and tell him it was like that.'

'But it wasn't! I didn't do it!' Ben Freeman heard the panic rising in his own voice and could do nothing about it.

'So who did, Ben?'

'I don't know. I was scared, when I heard about it. That was the reason I got out.'

Clyde Northcott shook his closely shaven head, gave his first small, mirthless grin at the sorry creature in front of him. 'Not true, that, Ben. You'd been here asking after this job before the news of this murder was ever released to press and radio.'

'I don't remember. I'm sure—'

'We can remind you, then. The news of the fire and the murder became public on Thursday last. The secretary here tells us that you came here after a job three days earlier than that. On the Monday, in fact. You're telling us that isn't correct?'

'No. If he—'

'Because those days are significant, to simple people like us, who have to try to piece together what happened last week. They mean that you were out of Marton Towers before the police raid and the fire on Wednesday night, but you left *after* the murder of Neil Cartwright, who was probably killed on the Sunday. Doesn't look good, does it?'

'It may not look good, but—'

'It all supports a view of events which goes something like this. Ben Freeman has a row with his boss, Neil Cartwright. A serious row, which results in a fight, in which Ben kills Cartwright and hides the body in a place where he knows it won't be found, for a few days at least. He gets out of Marton Towers, as fast as his panic-stricken legs will carry him, and hot-foots it to begin a new life at Brunton Golf Club. Whether he starts Wednesday night's fire in the stable block himself, as seems overwhelmingly probable, or whether fate or some other person intervenes to help him, remains to be seen. As do a lot of other things in this case. But frankly, if we have an arrest for murder, all of that is secondary.'

'But I didn't do it,' said Ben dully, sounding almost resigned to his fate.

Lucy Blake considered his bowed head for a moment before she said softly, 'Then who did, Ben?'

'I don't know. One of the resident staff at the Towers, I should think. Or maybe that Mr Simmons, Neil's stepfather. They didn't get on at all, you know: Neil told me that.'

'Which one of these, Ben?'

'I don't know.'

'Come on, you must have some ideas. That's if DC Northcott is wrong and you didn't do it yourself.'

'I didn't! And I don't know who did. I don't know much about them, apart from Neil. I only went in each day to work there, you know. And I was outside all day, working on the gardens or in the grounds. I hardly saw anyone, apart from Neil.'

He looked exhausted, and Lucy Blake was almost willing to let it go at that. She glanced at the relentless black face beside her and received the slightest of nods. Clyde Northcott said, suddenly gentle, 'Would you turn out your pockets for us, please, Ben?'

At the beginning of the exchanges, Ben Freeman might have refused, but all resistance was gone now. He pulled out the pockets of his jeans without a word and put the contents on the table in front of him. The keys for the lock with which he chained his bike and the front door of the house where he lived with his mother. Three strips of chewing gum. Two pounds and fourteen pence in coins. A credit card. A torn Riverside Stand ticket for last Saturday's Rovers game. Nothing remarkable. He stared at the two officers, trying to muster a little defiance in the face of this innocent collection.

Northcott gestured towards the garment Ben had put carefully on the back of a chair when he came into this warm room. 'The anorak as well, please.'

Ben cast his eyes down to the dark green carpet beneath his feet. But not before they had caught the glint of fear in the dark-blue irises. He fumbled in the side pockets of the garment, produced two empty sweet papers, a used tissue, an even dirtier handkerchief, and added them to the pathetic collection on the table in front of him. They were grubby but innocent, his belongings: Ben wanted to muster some truculent defiance to throw into the faces of these CID torturers, but no words would come to him.

Instead, Clyde Northcott reached unhurriedly across to the inside pocket of the anorak, the one with the zip across the top of it, which most people forgot. He unzipped the pocket, produced the small white rock from within it, looked steadily at Freeman as he said, 'Coke, Ben. You're in possession of a Class C illegal drug. That leaves you with a little explaining to do, doesn't it?'

Sixteen

DCI Peach looked up and down the narrow terraced street before he got out of his car. There were places where it wasn't wise to leave a car unattended nowadays, in this part of Brunton. But this street looked respectable enough. The houses were well kept, with clean curtains and newly painted doors. No one bothered to rub the doorsteps every week with the yellow or white stone, as his mother had still done when he was a lad in the early seventies, but everywhere was clean and tidy.

The door opened almost before he had finished knocking. The man looked at him apprehensively, asked him in reluctantly, told him as such people always did that he didn't see how he could be of any help. But within two minutes they were sitting opposite each other in well-worn, comfortable armchairs.

Derek Simmons cleared his throat and said, 'We won't be disturbed. Brenda's gone round to her sister's. She needs a bit of company.' He wouldn't tell this sharply dressed observant man that he himself was no company at all for Neil Cartwright's grieving mother, because he hadn't got on with the dead man; or that this death had dropped like a wall between a husband and wife who had never had secrets from each other; or that he'd worked very hard indeed to get Brenda out of the house for this meeting.

Peach looked round for a moment, quite content to let a man who was patently nervous become even more so. Like a lot of these small terraced houses, this one was unexpectedly comfortable inside. The walls had been stripped of the paper they had carried for years and painted in an off-white emulsion, to make a small room look bigger. The three-piece suite was comfortable and of excellent quality, and the oval mirror in its heavy Victorian frame sat comfortably on the wall opposite the fireplace.

Peach eventually said, 'Routine, this is. Or at least I hope that's all it is.'

'I hope so too. Brenda and I said everything we could say to the constable who took our statements on Friday.'

Peach gave him a bland smile. 'That's why we're here, sir. When there are discrepancies in people's statements, we follow them up and clarify things. That's the routine I mentioned.'

'Discrepancies?'

'That's the thing, sir. Discrepancies. To be precise, we're interested in what happened on the Sunday night, which is almost certainly the time when your stepson was killed.'

Derek determined to keep calm. 'That's straightforward, as far as I can see. I was at the snooker club for the whole of the evening. Brenda was here. You're surely not suggesting that the lad's mother's been lying to you?'

Men of forty-three were always lads to the generation in front of them. 'No, sir. We've no reason to doubt that Mrs Simmons was here for the whole of the evening, as she stated. Or that you were out from around six forty-five until a quarter to eleven, as both of you stated.'

'Then where's the discrepancy?'

Peach made a show of consulting his notes, though he knew perfectly well what he was about to say. 'There seems to be a little confusion about where you were during those four hours, Mr Simmons.'

'No confusion. I was at the snooker club.' He paused a moment, looked into the black, unblinking eyes, and was drawn into saying, 'Ask Harry Barnard. He was with me through most of the evening.'

'We've asked Mr Barnard about it, Mr Simmons. That's why we're here. *He* said you were with him, but no one else in the club that night remembers you being there for so long. The steward was behind the bar all evening: his recall is that you came into the place somewhere around half-past eight. So we went back to your friend Harry Barnard and pressed him a little. He now agrees with the steward that you didn't come into the snooker club until around half-past eight.'

Derek wondered whether to deny it, to bluster it out, to challenge them to break his story. But if they'd demolished Harry Barnard, he couldn't hope to convince them. He tried to keep his voice steady as he said, 'So I must have got it wrong. I'm sorry about that.'

'So are we, Mr Simmons. You've wasted a lot of police time. And tried to deceive us, when we're looking for a man who has committed murder. We have to ask ourselves why you did something so foolish. That's why I'm here now.'

Derek wondered whether to change his story, to say that he'd gone out much later on that fateful night and get Brenda to back him up. She might do it, if he told her how vital it was to him. But he couldn't ask her to do it, not with her beloved son the victim at the heart of all this. He'd have to claw his way out of it as best he could. 'All right. I left here at the time I said. But those people you spoke to are right: I didn't get to the club until about half-past eight.'

Peach didn't bother with any of his range of smiles this time. Instead, he said grimly, 'I should warn you before you say any more that we know a little about your relationship with Neil Cartwright. You two didn't get on together, did you?'

'No.'

'Then it had better be the truth this time.'

'I went to see Neil at Marton Towers. Straight from home, I drove up there. Must have arrived there at about seven or just after seven.'

Peach looked at him keenly from beneath the black eyebrows. If this was correct, it would confirm that the dead man had been alive at this time. The latest sighting they had of him thus far was much earlier in the day. 'And what happened between you?'

'Nothing happened. He wasn't there. I hammered on his door in the stable block, but neither he nor Sally was in. I waited outside for nearly an hour in my car in the dark, getting colder and colder, thinking he must come home at any minute. But he didn't.'

'And have you any witnesses who can confirm that this is what happened?'

'No. It's a quiet place up there behind the main house at the best of times. I saw no one, and as far as I'm aware no one saw me.'

'Was this a pre-arranged meeting with your stepson?'

Derek paused, weighing the implications of the question, knowing that he was now a murder suspect. 'We'd sort of arranged it. We hadn't fixed a time, but Neil had said that he could arrange to see me on my own on most Sunday evenings.'

'And who had initiated this?'

'I had.'

'And what was the purpose of the meeting?'

Derek made himself take his time and arrange his thoughts into some sort of order. 'You're right about me and Neil. We didn't get on together. He never accepted me as the new man in his mother's bed. I know he was attached to his father, but he never gave me a chance. I'd have accepted that we'd never get on, if I'd been the only one involved, told him to bugger off and leave me be. But it upset Brenda when we were shouting and swearing at each other. I wanted to meet Neil to see if there was any way we could sort things out, for her sake.' Derek looked resolutely at the carpet between them, afraid that he would lose concentration if he looked up and saw disbelief in this copper's aggressive eyes. 'I'd tried the same kind of approach before, and he'd told me to get lost. But I was determined to have one last go, for Brenda's sake.'

'A last go indeed.'

'Yes. Except that we never met. I never got the chance to put my case.'

'Or you put it and failed, as you had before. And the falling-out was a violent one. Got out of hand, perhaps.'

'It wasn't like that. I told you, Neil wasn't there.'

'Then why deceive us about it? Why try to

set up an alibi for yourself with your friend Mr Barnard?'

'I didn't think you'd believe me – not when people told you about how Neil and I could never exchange a civil word with each other. And – well, I've had a bit of trouble before. A long time ago.'

'Serious trouble, though. Flew into a rage and nearly throttled a man, didn't you?'

'It was twenty years ago. Just a fight that got out of hand, really. And it was self-defence.'

'Never established, that, was it? I'd say you were lucky you didn't kill the man.'

'You can see why I didn't want you to know that I'd been up to Marton Towers, can't you? Because of what happened twenty years ago, you've now got me down as a murder suspect.'

Peach shook his head firmly. 'Not because of what happened twenty years ago, Mr Simmons. That merely demonstrates to us that you have a capacity for violence. What makes you a suspect is that you saw fit to lie to the police about what you had been doing at around the time when a man you seem to have hated was killed. When you are now forced to reveal to us that you were at the probable scene of the crime at around the time it was committed, that makes you an even better candidate.' He nodded his head in satisfaction, as if he saw pieces of a jigsaw falling neatly into place.

'I didn't kill Neil.'

'You won't object to giving us a DNA sample, then.'

A flash of what looked like fear crossed Derek Simmons' too-revealing face. 'Do I have to?'

'No. We haven't the right to demand one. Not at this stage, anyway.' He made the last phrase heavy with menace.

The ageing face set like that of a sullen child. 'Then I'm not giving you one. I don't see why I should. I told you, I didn't kill Neil.'

Peach looked at him keenly, his head a little on one side. 'Have you any suggestions about who might have killed him, then?'

'No. I don't know the people who worked with him up at the Towers. Because we didn't get on, I've not been involved with his life.'

Peach pursed his lips as he nodded slowly. 'Question we have to resolve, Mr Simmons, is whether you were involved in his death. Don't leave the area without telling us about your plans, will you?'

DCI Peach departed as abruptly as he had arrived. Derek had an hour of bleak contemplation of his situation before his wife came back from her sister's house. Brenda said, 'It was good that you made me go out, love. I feel better for seeing Edith and George, as you said I would. I just wish people wouldn't treat me with kid gloves, try to pretend that nothing has happened, when my son is dead. Anything happen whilst I was out?'

'No. Very quiet, it's been.'

Another lie. Another deception of the woman whom he had been determined never to deceive. Derek Simmons was beginning to wonder if the lying would ever end.

At Marton Towers, Tuesday night was very dark. The clouds were low, threatening rain or sleet before morning. Neither stars nor moon were visible, and there was no street lighting here. Even the lamps which usually illuminated the main drive had not been switched on since the events of the previous Wednesday.

Sally Cartwright was used to the night. When she had first come here five years ago, she had welcomed the darkness and the solitude, the confirmation that the city and all its tawdry glitter had been left far behind her. But in those days, which now seemed so innocent and so far away, she had never thought that it would come to this.

It was only just after nine o'clock, but it felt much later than that when you seemed to be the only one abroad in a sleeping world. She stood for a moment outside the door of her new cottage at the end of the stable block, letting her eyes become accustomed to the darkness and the eerie stillness of the night. The silhouette of the rear elevation of the big neo-Gothic mansion was the only thing she could see at first. The back of the big house was much less regular than the front, allowing for the multiple services which the affluent Victorians and their successors had demanded to supply the needs of the owner and his guests in the impressive main rooms of the house.

But in the darkness of this moonless March night, the shape became two-dimensional; only the basic, dominant outline, with its multiple turrets and towers, stood out against the dark sky and the scarcely moving clouds. The dead man's widow was reminded of Colditz, that earlier dark citadel, with its complex implications of imprisonment and escape. In that sombre moment, Sally Cartwright wondered if she would ever escape completely from what had happened at Marton Towers.

Sally told herself again that she wasn't frightened of the night. Hadn't she grown accustomed to its silence and its stillness over the years at the Towers? On a summer night, she had often ventured out alone, relishing the soft, warm, intimate obscurity, and the myriad sounds of the small animals who were active during the short hours of darkness. This March night was different. There was not even the sound of a distant screech-owl to remind her that she was not completely alone.

Her eyes were accustomed to the night now, utilizing the tiny amount of light there was to pick out the route she wanted to take. As she moved away from her door, she saw for the first time the only other visible sign of human existence around her. A hundred yards away, at the other end of the long, low stable block, there was a single soft orange glow behind thick curtains. The Naylors must have moved out of their temporary suite in the mansion and into their newly refurbished cottage. She wondered for a moment exactly what was going on in that other cottage, what kind of words the chef and his small, dark-haired attractive wife were exchanging with each other.

It was better not to think about that. She moved softly over the gravel she could scarcely see to the narrow path of tarmac which would take her to the main house. She had thought she knew every step of this route, but she moved very carefully now, happy to feel the soles of her trainers on the smooth surface, so that even the tiny scraping sounds she had made on the gravel were eliminated. As she drew level with the mansion, its black turrets towered impossibly high above her. She had a brief glimpse of the silent lakes on either side of the drive at the front of the mansion, still as black glass, with scarcely enough light even to catch their surfaces for her.

Then she turned away from the sight and towards the back of the house. There was no illumination to be seen anywhere, and you would have thought from here that the massive place was locked and deserted. But Sally knew better than that. As she moved nearer to the masonry, she felt she could smell the very stones of the familiar place, which had become strange and menacing to her.

All was darkness now under the mighty shadow of the Towers. She switched on the tiny torch she had brought with her for this last section of the route. With the outbuildings beginning to surround her and the first walls already higher than her head, surely no one would see the tiny, jerky circle of white light in front of her. She moved towards the north-facing portal of what had once been the dairy room of the house.

She needed her torch to find the lock when she reached the high, solid outer door. She stepped inside, thought about pressing a switch, decided instead to use her torch to find the security-system panel. Her fingers looked to her very white and frail as they tapped in the numbers of the code. She breathed a sigh of relief as the click told her that she had prevented the alarms screaming into action all over the ground floor of the big house.

She stood for a moment, waiting for her pulses to slow, gathering her resources for the different challenge which was coming. Then she turned the narrow beam of her torch upon the stone-flagged floor of the former dairy and moved through into the kitchen, and thence on to the carpeted floors of the front part of the mansion. She stood in the hall for a moment, her light fainter as she turned it on to the wide staircase twenty yards away from her, running up into the darkness of the first storey.

From somewhere away to her left, a man's voice called softly, 'Over here!'

She started a little, despite the fact that she had known there would have to be some form of contact. Then she turned and made her way towards the spot whence the words had come. At that moment, a light was switched on at last, high and brilliant, a long way above her in the elaborate patterned ceiling of the hall, but seeming to her harsh and dazzling after the darkness she had been negotiating for so long.

'We'll talk down here,' said the man who had called to her. 'You're right that we have things we need to discuss, but I didn't want my wife to hear any of this, and nor would you.'

Sally Cartwright nodded, not trusting herself to speak after being so long silent, and followed Neville Holloway into his office.

Seventeen

'It's six days now since the body of Neil Cartwright was discovered. We know a lot more now than we did then.'

DCI Peach made the simple statements sound like an ominous warning. James Naylor, the Marton Towers chef, who was intensely uncomfortable with words himself, shifted awkwardly on his hard upright chair. They were sitting in the Murder Room, which had been set up in an empty section of the stable block, the first one which had been unaffected by the fire. James, sitting isolated in the centre of the room, with no desk or table between him and the CID officers, felt already very exposed.

James should have kept quiet and waited for them to make the running. Instead, his nerves raced and drove him into speech. He looked hopefully at Lucy Blake and said nervously, 'I expect you've been putting together what people have said to you, and getting a good picture of what goes on around here.'

She did not answer his smile. 'Yes. As DCI Peach told you, we have a much fuller picture now. And as quite often happens, what people have left out is of much more interest than what they have told us.'

As James grinned weakly and decided not to trust his tongue any further, Peach followed up his partner's parry with a more definite thrust of his own. 'Almost amounts to lying, when people withhold information from the police, Mr Naylor. We take a very serious view of it.' He looked as if it was now going to give him a great deal of pleasure to take a serious view of the conduct of James Naylor.

'I can't think that *I* withheld anything from you.' The firmness James tried to give to his words was dissipated by the nervous laugh which followed hard upon them.

'Relationships, Mr Naylor. It looks like they might well be the key to the unlocking of this crime. And various people have been trying to deceive us. Including you.'

He made it a statement of fact. James wanted to argue, would in fact have argued, if it had come at him as merely a suggestion. He said feebly, 'If I deceived you, I didn't mean to.' He was even more conscious of his clumsiness with words. His evasions sounded like admissions.

Peach said calmly, 'You didn't like Neil Cartwright, did you? And he didn't like you.'

'That doesn't mean that I killed him.'

'I wasn't aware that you'd been accused of that. Yet.' Peach allowed himself a smile at this fascinating prospect.

'You can't say that because I know my way around the place I must have killed him.'

Peach merely nodded slowly to himself, as if weighing up that idea. Like many men who are unused to the shades which phrasing can give to ideas, Naylor gave more away than he intended to once he committed himself to words. He watched Peach's bald head moving as if it was hypnotizing him and said unwisely, 'Other people as well as me knew the room where the body was hidden before the fire.' Peach, with his eyes closed, continued to nod, as if accepting this, and his man was lured into more speculation. 'Surely Neil's wife had more reason to hate him than I had.'

Peach's eyes returned to his man's face, widening like those of a lion which had spotted today's meal. 'And why would that be, Mr Naylor?'

James, like many men unused to Peach's techniques, had concluded by now that the man knew far more than he actually did, that trying to deceive him further would only land him deeper into trouble. 'Well, she was the one whose husband was playing away, wasn't she?'

Both Peach and Blake were far too experienced in this game of cat and mouse to reveal by any flicker of their features that this was news to them. Peach relaxed a little and said, 'You'd better tell us all about this, hadn't you? In view of the fact that you concealed it when we spoke to you on Sunday, I should advise you to make every effort to be completely frank with us now. Then we shall be able to see how closely your account tallies with what other people have already told us, and with what they will tell us in the next day or two.'

He sounded to James Naylor like a man who knew everything that had gone on at Marton Towers in the days before the fire and the discovery of the body. James fought a rising sense of panic as he said, 'All I meant was that Sally Cartwright had every reason to hate Neil. She might well have killed her husband. I'm not saying she did, mind, but it happens, doesn't it? People lose their tempers when sex is involved. Sometimes they don't even mean to kill, but anger takes over.' His brow furrowed with the effort of so many words. 'There's a phrase for it, isn't there?'

Peach looked at the uncertain face in front of him. '*Crime passionnel*, the French call it. You're probably thinking of that. Crime of passion. It's an idea which British law doesn't recognize, as yet. No doubt some bloody idiot will introduce it, before long.' He shook his head sadly at the decadence of British jurisprudence, then looked eagerly at Naylor and said, 'So your suggestion is that Sally Cartwright did her old man in?'

'No! I'm not suggesting that. All I said was that she was bound to hate Neil, in the circumstances.'

DS Lucy Blake looked up from her notes. 'You said "She might well have killed her husband", Mr Naylor. Are you now withdrawing that suggestion?'

'Yes. Well, no, not really. I'm just saying she might have done it, I suppose.' James had a familiar sensation of things passing out of control, once he had to put thoughts into words and ventured beyond monosyllabic replies. It had all seemed very clear to him before they came: he had planned to divert suspicion away from himself by calmly pointing out that other people had better motives than him for this crime. Now he had no idea exactly how much these persistent, professional questioners knew, and they were saying things which he had never anticipated.

Peach pursed his lips and looked very serious indeed. He studied the fresh face beneath the tousled fair hair for a moment before he said, 'We'll need to re-examine Sally Cartwright's movements on the Sunday in question very carefully indeed, in the light of what you say, Mr Naylor. In view of the fact that you seem to think her guilty of murder, you'd better give us the details of the reasons she had to hate her husband, hadn't you?'

James Naylor shut his eyes, trying to summon the concentration which would allow him to speak the sentences which would divert attention away from him rather than towards him. You had to be fiendishly careful, when these things did not come naturally to you. 'All I'm saying is that Neil Cartwright and my wife weren't exactly discreet about their affair. Well, I suppose they were at first. I don't know how long it had been going on before I heard about it, do I?'

For an instant pain and passion flashed into the fresh face. Then he shut his eyes again and clasped his thick arms across his chest, as if they were the staves on a barrel, containing and disguising whatever forces lay within the powerful torso behind them. 'Sally must have found out at about the same time as I did – or perhaps a week or two earlier, for all I know. She's a clever woman, Sally. Not much passes her by.'

So the affair had been not between this man and Sally Cartwright, but between the dead man and the slim, pretty, very contained Michelle Naylor. The uneasy being who sat like a writhing schoolboy on the chair in front of them had been cuckolded, and was now pouring out information he thought they already possessed.

Peach controlled his elation as he said quietly and unemotionally, 'This is a powerful motive, Mr Naylor. One you should have revealed to us at the time of our first meeting on Sunday.'

'I didn't know how to tell you about it. I –

244

I didn't know how to find the right words. I thought you'd get it all from Sally Cartwright. I didn't think it was up to me to lead you to her.'

For a moment, his shiftiness, his assumption that you gave the police nothing that you could deny to them, reminded them of his past. This was a man who had been involved in an affray, who had offered serious, instinctive violence. Peach said slowly, 'What you're really telling us is that you think Sally Cartwright killed her husband. You've given us a motive. Do you have any real evidence to support it?'

'No. I'm not even saying she did it.'

'Just as well, that. Because the motive you've given to Mrs Cartwright applies just as strongly to you. In my experience, not too many men react calmly to the idea of their wives playing away.'

James felt the blood flooding into his fresh, too-revealing face, felt his fingers pressing hard into the muscles at the top of his arms as he strove to stay still. 'I didn't kill Cartwright.'

Peach gave the chef an affable smile. 'We'll need to be convinced of that. Especially since you chose to refrain from all mention of your wife's affair with the murder victim, when we spoke on Sunday.'

'I told you all about my movements on the day of the killing.'

'You told us something about them, yes.

You also told us that you got on quite well with Neil Cartwright. "Well enough", you said, I think. You then added that although you both lived on the site, you "didn't live in each other's pockets". Whereas what we now find is that the man had taken your wife into his bed and you hated his guts. Bit of a difference there, you'll agree. So we'll need to review what you said about your movements on the day of the murder with newly enlightened eyes and a degree of scepticism, won't we?'

James was bewildered and scared by this stocky, aggressive man with eyes like gimlets and a torrent of words at his disposal. It was disconcerting to find him quoting back at him the things he had said on Sunday. He kept his arms firmly folded and determined to say as little as possible. 'I told you what I was doing on that Sunday. I've nothing to add to it. I didn't even see Neil Cartwright on the day of his death.'

Peach nodded to Lucy Blake, who flicked back several pages in her neat notebook, though she knew well enough what she was going to say. It was dull stuff, but very necessary. 'Mr Naylor told us that he went to Tesco's with his wife in the morning. She has since confirmed that. The visit occupied them for no more than an hour. Mr Naylor went across to the mansion at around midday to discuss with Mr Holloway menus and times of meals for the guests who would be staying at Marton Towers in the middle of the week. According to the statement of Neville Holloway, this occupied them for no more than forty minutes. According to Mr Naylor's statement, he then spent the rest of the day on the site. There are so far no witnesses to that until seven o'clock in the evening. Mrs Naylor was away visiting her parents during the afternoon, but says that from seven o'clock onwards she was with her husband.'

'As she was,' said James, firmly but unnecessarily.

Peach smiled at him. 'Convenient, that. Spouses are always convenient, when they're providing alibis for each other. When we discover that one of them had been playing away and they're at daggers drawn with each other, we tend to be a little sceptical about quiet domestic evenings with no third party present and no other confirmation.'

'Make what you like of it. It's what happened.' James looked past his tormentor at the distant wall. They could go at this as hard as they liked, but they wouldn't shake it apart, if he and Michelle both held firmly to what they'd agreed.

Peach nodded slowly, evidently agreeing with this thought. Then he said, 'Leaves the hours between one and seven unaccounted for, that does. Unfortunate, from your point of view.'

It was on the tip of James's tongue to produce the cliché about being innocent until proved guilty. Then he remembered that he'd used it at the last meeting with this man, and had it kicked firmly into touch by this damned Detective Chief Inspector. He said as sternly as he could, 'You won't prove that I killed Cartwright. That's because I didn't do it.'

Peach stood up as suddenly as he seemed to do everything else and moved towards the door. It was left to DS Blake to say to James Naylor, 'If you think of anyone else who can confirm where you were and what you were doing in the time between one o'clock and seven o'clock on that Sunday, it will be in your own interest to let us know of it immediately. Meanwhile, you shouldn't leave the area without letting us have the details of your intended movements. Good day to you, Mr Naylor.'

At one thirty on the same day, a young police constable made his way reluctantly towards the office of Chief Inspector Peach.

Peach was much respected in the station, as thief-taker and scourge of Lancashire villains. He was also much feared, especially by newer and less experienced members of the Brunton constabulary. This hapless constable had been told with some relish that Peach gave more fearsome bollockings than anyone else in the county. And this was certainly the occasion for a right royal bollocking.

PC Jeffries knocked tentatively at the Chief Inspector's door and tried not to flinch at the peremptory command to enter. He drew himself up to his full height and stood painfully to attention in front of the great man's desk. He'd been hoping DS Lucy Blake might be around, but there was no sign of the female presence which might have mollified the great man's wrath. 'PC Jeffries,' he said tentatively.

'I know who you are, lad,' said Percy. 'PC Nigel Jeffries, if I remember right, which I do. Bit of a poncey name, to my mind, but I suppose we can't blame you for that. You'd better sit down: you make me uneasy, standing there like a dopey stick of Blackpool rock.'

'I'd prefer not to, sir, if you don't mind. This won't take long.'

'You hope it won't, you mean. Well, at least stop standing as if the chief constable's rammed a poker up your arse. What can I do for you? Or, more to the point, what can you do for me?'

Jeffries felt his knees trembling as he tried to relax; he feared for a moment that he might collapse into a heap before the great man, like a boneless circus acrobat. 'Well, sir, it's about the scene-of-crime supervision at Marton Towers. After that body was discovered up there, before the SOCO team got to work on the place.' He poured out the phrases in quick succession, as if he feared that he might be hit over the head if he ceased to speak.

'Ay. Simple enough task, keeping an eye on a crime scene. We tend to give it to lads who are still wet behind the ears, so that they can get a bit of confidence out of something it's difficult to get wrong.'

Nigel Jeffries shut his eyes. 'I think I got it wrong, sir. A bit.'

There was such a long pause that Nigel opened his eyes again to see what was happening. The man was staring at him as if he was something he had just scraped off his shoe. DCI Peach said slowly, ominously, 'You don't get this sort of thing a bit wrong, lad. It's like getting a woman a bit pregnant.'

'I missed something out of my report, sir.' The syllables fell out as if they were all part of one word, like that long Welsh place name he could never remember.

Percy Peach waited until the man in front of him looked again into his face. It took a long time, but eventually the hapless constable's eyes returned tremulously to base, like those of a monkey hypnotized by the cobra which is going to kill it. In contrast to the way the man in uniform had spoken, every syllable was distinct as Peach said, 'Let's hope it's not something important, shall we, Constable Jeffries? I'm not quite sure what will happen to you if you've omitted something vital, but I don't think there is much call for eunuchs in the modern police service.'

Jeffries tittered, an involuntary, nervous sound, which rang round the small room and took a long time to disappear.

Peach did not join in this graveyard hilarity. He said, 'I'm not laughing, lad. And I hope some murderer isn't laughing at Brunton CID because of you.'

'All it is, sir, is that I forgot to mention something in my report. It's probably not important at all. Probably has no bearing at all on the killing that you're investigating.'

'Perhaps you'd better let more experienced officers be the judge of that, Constable Jeffries,' said Peach with ominous control.

'Yes, sir. Of course I should, sir. Well, it's just that a man came and looked at the crime site, sir. Came over the back wall of Marton Towers, I think. That's certainly the way he left, anyway. I started to follow him, but decided I couldn't leave the crime scene un-attended. I was on my own up there at the time.'

Peach gave him a withering look. Nigel Jeffries duly withered.

He said desperately, 'I acted according to the book, sir, which says that a crime scene should not be left unattended.' He glanced fearfully at the DCI, then ended tremulously on a dying fall. 'But I did forget to include this man's appearance in my report.'

'So you noted the precious facts of the

times of your attendance at the scene, and the names of the officers from whom you took over and to whom in due course you handed over this onerous task. And forgot to record the appearance and departure of a man who may in due course prove to be an arsonist and a murderer.'

'Yes, sir. That's about it, sir. Sorry, sir.'

Peach regarded him steadily for several seconds, then said, 'You're a bog-roll, PC Jeffries. A wet, useless, disintegrating bog-roll. Let's have your description of this man.'

Nigel sensed that the worst was over. He had this information at least ready to deliver, though his tongue felt like dry leather against the roof of his mouth. 'Young. Aged about twenty, I'd say. Caucasian. Height about five feet eleven. Weight difficult to assess, because he was wearing a loose-fitting navy anorak and lighter blue tracksuit trousers, but I'd say around a hundred and sixty pounds. Maybe a little less, because he was slightly built. Dark hair. He didn't come close enough for me to see the colour of his eyes or the shape of his features. No visible distinguishing marks.'

Peach regarded him balefully until he was sure there was nothing else to come. Then he said, 'If you forget something as important as this again, lad, you'll be on your bike and looking for other employment. You can get your arse out of here now.'

PC Jeffries was only too ready to do that.

He blurted a hasty, 'Thank you, sir!' and turned so rapidly upon his heel that he almost fell over. He had his hand upon the door handle when the voice behind him said, 'You were right to come in here and confess your sins, lad. You got one thing right, at least.'

Nigel Jeffries bolted to the male officers' washroom and followed a rapid and copious evacuation of his bowels with a series of deep breaths in the privacy of the cubicle.

In his office, DCI Peach looked up Lucy Blake's account of the interview she and DC Northcott had conducted at Brunton Golf Club. He decided that it looked as if Ben Freeman, cocaine user and former assistant to their murder victim, had visited the scene of his former employment at Marton Towers on the day after the fire.

Eighteen

Sally Cartwright had always had the capacity to look calm when her inner emotions were in turmoil. It had been a valuable asset to her in a rather chequered working life. It had certainly helped to get her the housekeeper's post at Marton Towers. The capacity to remain calm, or at the very least appear calm, when domestic arrangements failed was a most valuable thing in one responsible for ensuring that the daily arrangements in the great house went smoothly. Neville Holloway had recognized and rewarded this capacity to remain composed and dispassionate while others panicked in a crisis.

It was a virtue which did not fail Mrs Cartwright even now, in this most extreme of crises. She had never been in a situation like this before, and she was feeling her way, but no one would have known that to look at her. She sat with her hands in her lap in an armchair covered in a crimson which matched the two sofas at the edges of the comfortable, low-ceilinged room. The window was open on the wall which faced the low March sunshine, but all traces of the scents of wet charcoal and fireman's foam which had been evident on their last visit had now disappeared.

She offered them tea, which Peach refused. Lucy Blake complimented her upon the decor of her sitting room, and she accepted the comment with a little shrug of her shoulders. 'I was lucky, being in this end cottage of the stable block, I didn't have to move into new accommodation like some of the others.' She knew they had things to raise with her; she found that she wanted these harmless preliminaries to be over and out of the way as soon as possible.

As if he read her thoughts, Peach said bluntly, 'You weren't completely frank with us when we saw you on Saturday.'

Sally had already decided that she would not deny it if he opened with something like this. She would let them make the running. See how much they knew and not give away anything that she didn't have to. She said obliquely, 'I was a newly bereaved widow. I expect I am allowed a little leeway for that, even by the CID.'

'Indeed you are. I have to say that you haven't behaved like the bereaved widows we usually see.' It was bold, almost insulting, but Peach was nettled by the self-possession of this blonde woman with the blue eyes and pleasantly plump physique. She was into her forties and her pale skin showed a few lines around her sharply intelligent eyes; she was anything but the dumb blonde still beloved of Hollywood.

Sally Cartwright assessed him and his words for a moment, wondering whether to offer him any reaction at all. She glanced at the wedding photograph on the top of the television in the corner of the room and said quietly, 'There will be a time for grief, in due course. At the moment, I still feel stunned by Neil's death. When you are able to tell me who killed him, when you release his body for a funeral, I might be able to allow myself the luxury of grief.'

It was too composed, too much a clever argument, for a woman in her position. Peach said abrasively, 'If you want us to discover who killed him, you shouldn't conceal the reality of your relationship with him.'

This time she said nothing, acknowledging the challenge of his statement only by the slightest widening of those observant blue eyes. Without the assistance of a denial, Peach was forced to develop his theme for himself. 'When we saw you on Saturday, you didn't tell us about the breakdown in your marriage. You withheld all mention of your husband's sexual relationship with Michelle Naylor.' He thought he caught the first hint of anger in her features with the mention of that name, but it passed in a flash and he went on, 'That is hardly conduct which is calculated to help us find out who killed him.'

She transferred her hands slowly from her

lap to the arms of her chair, then looked down at them for a second or two before she spoke, as if congratulating herself on the fact that her fingers were so still and relaxed. 'I object to your word "breakdown", Mr Peach. You should not assume that a marriage is at an end because of an affair. Such things do not help many marriages, but nor do they necessarily destroy them.'

She sounded as if she was debating an interesting proposition which had no personal application for her. Peach tried not to let his irritation show as he said sourly, 'Are you now trying to argue that it was helpful to conceal this affair from us when we came here on Saturday?'

'No. That would be absurd. I can see that in your position I should want to know all the facts. But a little imagination would tell you that it was natural I should conceal this rather sordid interlude from you. It does not enhance Neil's memory, and an affair with a younger woman is scarcely flattering to me. I submit that it is something which few wives would wish to enlarge upon.'

'Maybe. But you are intelligent enough to realize that in a murder enquiry, things change. Important facts cannot be concealed.'

She gave him a small smile, which was a mixture of acknowledgement and denial. 'Perhaps concealing the sordid detail of his tumblings with Michelle Naylor was the last service I could render to a dead man.'

Peach had had enough of her calm prevarications. 'That might be the case if this was an ordinary death. It is emphatically not that. So why did you elect to deny us this knowledge – in effect, to lie to us about important aspects of your husband's final days?'

Sally Cartwright felt her pulses quickening at what she knew she must now deliver, but she remained as outwardly poised as ever. 'I didn't see any reason to make myself more of a suspect. I know perfectly well that the spouse of a murder victim is always a leading suspect. Telling you about Neil's squalid love life would have informed you also that I had a strong motive for wanting to dispatch him.'

Lucy Blake had so far contented herself with studying this remarkable widow. She felt a reluctant admiration for the woman's self-assurance in the face of Peach's annoyance, but she knew also that such aplomb was admirable equipment for a murderer. Lucy said quietly, 'The fact that you lied about this, or to put it charitably held things back, now makes it seem more likely that you killed Neil. You must see that.'

'I do. I did what seemed to me right at the time. Since you seem to be making notes of this conversation, I should like you to record my formal declaration that I did not kill my husband.'

'When did you last see him?'

'I told you that on Saturday. He was supposed to be visiting his sister in Scotland for a few days. I watched him drive his car out of here at about one o'clock on the Sunday when he appears to have died.'

Peach said, 'We needed to ask you that, in case you had chosen to modify that information also. Neil's car was found this morning.' He threw the fact in suddenly, watching for a reaction from this obstinately calm woman.

There was none that could be read in the open, unworried face. 'And where was it found?'

'On an unpaved road leading to a disused quarry near Clitheroe. It was under overhanging trees. A farmer out lambing noticed it earlier in the week. He didn't report it until two hours ago.'

'Does it take you any nearer to solving the mystery of Neil's death?'

'It may do. The forensic people are giving the vehicle the most thorough examination known to man at this very moment.' He looked again for apprehension in her, and saw none. 'I'm very hopeful that clothing fibres or hairs will tell us who drove the vehicle to that isolated spot.'

'Then let us hope that your optimism is justified.'

He thought he detected the faintest note of ironic amusement in her comment. Controlling his own reaction to that, he said tersely,

'We've been examining various bank accounts since this death. It's quite usual for us to be given access which wouldn't normally be accorded to us, when we're investigating a crime as serious as murder.'

'And no doubt you've found more than you expected in Neil's account.'

She was ahead of them, even here, controlling the tone of these exchanges, anticipating the revelation with which he had hoped to shock her. 'We did indeed. Mrs Cartwright, how did you know that we would discover this?'

A little shrug of the broad shoulders above the nicely rounded breasts. 'I didn't know. But I suspected that you might find something like that. We had a joint account into which our salaries from our work here were paid. This would be a separate individual account of Neil's. Probably with a different bank.'

It was so accurate that Peach wondered if it was knowledge rather than speculation with which she was teasing them. He did his best to appear unruffled as he said, 'There is a sum of over forty thousand pounds. Most of it seems to have accrued over the last eighteen months.'

She shook her head sadly. 'That doesn't surprise me.'

'In that case, please be good enough to tell us where this money came from.'

She shook her head again, this time with

the ghost of a smile, and in that moment Peach and Blake knew that she was relishing this, enjoying the little game of ploy and counter-ploy which she had done so much to introduce and control. 'I can't do that. I'm surprised that you don't already know the source of this money.'

'We have our own ideas about it. I think you have too.'

Sally nodded. This didn't threaten her: she could indulge herself a little with these two now, secure in the knowledge that this particular line of investigation wouldn't compromise her. 'Drugs, I should think. That wouldn't surprise you, in view of the raid you conducted here last Wednesday night. You must have been in possession of a lot of information, to swoop on Richard Crouch and his cronies like that.'

'You knew that the owner of Marton Towers was heavily involved in trafficking illegal drugs?'

She smiled more openly now. 'Suspected, Detective Inspector Peach. Not knew. In my opinion, practically everyone who was a full-time employee at Marton Towers must have had a fair idea of where the money to run all of this was coming from. But we had jobs and prospects which we wouldn't have had without Richard Crouch, so most of us were sensible enough not to ask many questions.'

That reflected exactly what Peach thought himself, but it did not improve his mood to find it voiced by this unflappable adversary. He made it sound as ominous as he could as he said, 'You're telling me that you think your late husband was himself involved in the sale of illegal drugs, that this is where this forty thousand pounds came from.'

'I suppose I am, yes. But if you're asking me to supply you with concrete evidence to support that view, I can't provide it. It's merely my opinion – honestly delivered, as you requested.'

'So who else around here was involved in the trafficking of drugs?'

'I can't tell you that. No one, as far as I know, but I decided long ago that ignorance was the best policy.'

'How would you describe your relationship with Michelle Naylor, Mrs Cartwright?'

She took her time, well aware that this was the area where she might give herself away. 'With my husband's mistress? I think "strained" might be the best word for it. You would hardly expect it to be better than that, would you?'

It was typical of this imperturbable woman to respond to his most embarrassing question with one of her own. He said, 'It can't be easy, living on the site together and working together, in these circumstances.'

'But it's in our mutual interest to do so. We both have jobs that we don't wish to jeopardize by behaving like fighting cats. You'll find that Mrs Naylor is well aware of which side her bread is buttered on.' There was something waspish in this aside; it was the nearest she had come to revealing her hatred of the younger woman. As if she felt that she had shown a little too much of herself, she quickly asserted her habitual control. 'I expect that the tension between us will slacken a little, now that someone has removed Neil from the scene. How long we shall both continue to work at Marton Towers remains to be seen.'

'As do a lot of other things. It's almost a recurring theme, in this case. Who do you think killed your husband, Mrs Cartwright?'

'I don't know. James Naylor would have the same motive that you imputed to me, having been cuckolded by Neil.' She paused for a moment, as if to relish the old-fashioned word. 'I'd say he was a man who might resort to instinctive violence more readily than I would, but I can hardly be seen as unbiased in the matter, can I? And of course Michelle Naylor herself might well have fallen out with her lover. I know my husband well enough to think that he wouldn't consider his coupling with Michelle as a long-term thing; perhaps she did. I should think that under that kittenish exterior there is probably a little tiger when she's annoyed, wouldn't you?'

'What do you know about Neil's assistant, Ben Freeman?'

'The lad who left last week? Practically

nothing. I know that Neil was satisfied with his work on the estate and in the gardens. As my work was wholly in the mansion itself, I saw very little of the outside staff. And Ben wasn't resident on the site.'

Peach nodded, his eyes never leaving her face. He said abruptly, 'And what can you tell us about Mr Holloway?'

She smiled at him openly, relaxing as the attention turned away from her. 'He's my boss, Mr Peach. I'm hardly likely to be indiscreet about him, with my job at stake. But as a matter of fact, there's nothing I can tell you. He's an efficient manager of the mansion and the estate, and he's been good to me, in that he's given me more and more responsibility and several pay rises. But I have nothing beyond a professional relationship with him.'

'You say you're not surprised to find that your husband was making large sums from an involvement in the illegal drugs trade. Who else among the staff at Marton Towers do you think was involved in drug dealing?'

'I've no idea. I told you, we tend not to ask many questions, partly because most of us have things in our own backgrounds that we should like to conceal, partly because we know that the unwritten law here is that we don't pry into things beyond our work.'

She saw them off the premises, watched the pretty, red-haired girl whom she had found so irritating drive the police Mondeo until it passed out of sight. Then she went back into the cottage to digest the implications of this second meeting with the CID.

She wasn't a woman given to complacency, but she thought it had gone well. She had decided before they came that she wouldn't play the grieving widow, and she congratulated herself that it had been the right decision.

More importantly, she thought she'd managed to conceal quite how delighted she was that the bastard who had slept beside her for sixteen years had burned to a black cinder in last week's fire.

Nineteen

Percy Peach climbed the stairs towards Chief Superintendent Tucker's penthouse office without the usual deadening of his spirits. He felt unwontedly cheered by the knowledge that he had something tangible with which to taunt the Head of Brunton CID.

Tucker waved a wide arm at the chair in front of his huge empty desk. 'Sit down and let's get down to business. I was wondering quite how long it was going to be before you deigned to come up and brief me on the latest developments.'

'Yes, sir. The team has been very busy this week. As I expect you have been yourself.' He let his gaze travel slowly from end to end of the large empty working surface in front of his chief.

Tucker said tetchily, 'If I am to give you my overview, I need to be fully acquainted with your findings.'

You've been fully briefed each day, if only you would trouble to read the documentation and my memos, Percy thought, without any relaxation of his inscrutable features. 'No doubt you will be wishing to keep the

266

Chairman of the Police Authority fully in touch with developments in the Neil Cartwright murder case, sir. In the interests of good public relations, which are so important in the modern police service.' It pleased him to quote Tommy Bloody Tucker's phrases back at him; it was always a reliable method of maximizing the man's embarrassment.

'No, Peach, I shall not.' Tucker's glare was lost on a man who seemed suddenly lost in contemplation of the ceiling.

'Charged with eleven counts of indecent assault, sir.' Peach spoke like one in a pleasant dream, his voice rising in wonder.

'I'm well aware of what has happened to Henry Rawcliffe, thank you, Peach.' Tucker strove hard to terminate the subject by the sternness he injected into his tone.

'Blow for you, sir, it must have been. You being a close mate of his and all that.'

'I am no friend of Henry Rawcliffe's, Peach, and never have been. I don't know where you could ever have gained that impression, and I'll thank you not to—'

'Golfing companions and all that.'

Tommy Bloody Tucker spluttered in what Percy considered a rather appealing manner. 'I've always had my suspicions about Rawcliffe, even though I was inveigled into giving the man a game of golf at my club. It's not always easy to avoid these things, you know.'

'Yes, sir, I do. But don't I remember you

saying on Monday that you'd been delighted to have a game with golf with Rawcliffe last Sunday? That it reflected how well you'd got on the previous Saturday night? That it showed what close buddies you were?'

Tucker glowered at the man who continued to stare so innocently at his ceiling. Peach must have known about Rawcliffe's fall from grace when they had last spoken, when he had encouraged his chief to emphasize how close he was to the Chairman of the Police Authority. The Chief Superintendent said desperately, 'I always suspected there was something wrong about Henry Rawcliffe, as I've just told you. Of course, I couldn't voice it at the time, but—'

'Really, sir? I thought that when I issued the counsel that a man in your position had to be careful about your choice of friends, you said something like, "I could hardly make a better friend than the Chairman of the Police Authority, could I?" But of course, you may well believe that Mr Rawcliffe is innocent. I know from experience just how resolute you are in the defence of your friends and colleagues.'

Tucker scowled at him suspiciously. 'There is no question of the man being innocent, as far as I'm concerned, Peach. Do you realize that the charges relate to child abuse years ago, during his time as a social worker in the nineteen eighties?'

'So I understand, sir. A sorry business, but

no doubt he'll be glad to have a steadfast friend like you in this time of crisis.'

Chief Superintendent Tucker spoke with what he hoped was dangerous clarity. 'Let me make it plain that Henry Rawcliffe is no friend of mine, Peach. He has never been more than an acquaintance that I met in the course of my duties. Is that absolutely clear?'

'Perfectly, sir. I'm sorry that I was misinformed.' By you, you tosser. By the man who drops his friends and colleagues like shit off a hot shovel as soon as danger threatens. 'You won't wish to inform Mr Rawcliffe about our progress in the Neil Cartwright murder case, then, sir, as you were planning to do when we spoke on Saturday night and on Monday?'

'Henry Rawcliffe is no longer Chairman of the Police Authority. All connections are severed. I hope he goes down for a long time.'

Percy wondered about a little sally on the 'innocent until proved guilty' theme, and then reluctantly decided that he had squeezed the maximum amount of fun for himself and embarrassment for his chief out of the unfortunate Henry Rawcliffe.

He said briskly, 'It's still possible the butler did it, sir,' and watched Tucker's jaw drop slackly open in bewilderment; it was predictable, but still enjoyable. 'Neville Holloway, sir. Calls himself the General Manager up at Marton Towers, but he's the nearest thing to an old-fashioned butler, to my mind. Knows everything that goes on in that place, including his master's activities as a drug baron, and isn't telling us more than he has to. Therefore a candidate for our murderer, to my mind.'

'But you've unearthed nothing to connect him directly with this killing, so far. Disappointing that.' Tucker strove hard to reassert himself.

'Enquiries are proceeding, sir. Deceased's wife's odds have shortened.'

'This is not a betting exercise, Peach. The wife of a murder victim is always a leading suspect, you know.'

'Yes, I do, sir, as a matter of fact. But thank you for the reminder. Sally Cartwright wasn't conducting an affair with the chef at the mansion, as you suggested.'

Tucker couldn't remember quite what he had suggested to this bewildering man, who sidestepped his lunges like an elusive rugby back. 'Then that surely makes her a less likely candidate for this?'

'Would do, sir, except that our detailed enquiries have revealed that her husband was having it off with one of her domestic staff in the mansion. An affair between Neil Cartwright and Michelle Naylor had been going on for several months. Both Sally Cartwright and the woman enjoying the nooky concealed it from us when we first spoke to them. Intensive work by the team has now revealed it.'

'It's quite possible, you know, that this Mrs Cartwright was insanely jealous, that she did away with her husband after some blazing row about his adulterous relationship with another woman.'

Percy wondered whether his chief spent his afternoons of leisure watching black-and-white movies from the fifties. He decided not to enlarge upon any similarities between Sally Cartwright and Barbara Stanwyck. 'This Michelle Naylor is a cool one, sir. She made no mention of her passionate relationship with the dead man when we spoke to her. She's now got to account both for that omission and for her own movements around the time of the murder.'

'This Naylor woman might have killed him in fury if he said he was breaking up the affair, Peach. Lovers' tiffs can escalate very quickly, in these circumstances; fornication often leads to violence.'

'Yes, sir. I bow to your superior knowledge and experience in these things.' Peach wondered if he should enlarge upon a certain resemblance between the small, neat, dark-haired Michelle Naylor and Audrey Hepburn, but decided he now needed to keep this exchange as short as possible. 'Husband is James Naylor, sir. Chef at Marton Towers. Stocky and powerful man, sir. I wouldn't like to get on the wrong side of him.'

Tucker's face brightened with inspiration.

'Might well have seen his wife's lover off in a fit of blind fury, you know, Peach, if he felt he wanted to be rid of this rival for her affections.'

Peach reflected for a moment on his chief's unrivalled predilection for the blindin' bleedin' obvious. Then he said heavily, 'That had occurred to us, sir. Particularly as Naylor's got no alibi for the hours between one and seven on the day of Cartwright's death.'

'Ah! It sounds to me as if we're closing the net on our man!'

Tucker always switched effortlessly from 'you' to 'we' when he scented success. Peach's control deserted him for a moment and he gave the Head of Brunton CID the sourest of his range of smiles. Then he said, 'There's another candidate, sir. A young man who's been in trouble with the police before. Who left Marton Towers hastily immediately after the murder. Who was very possibly involved in drug dealing, though in a fairly minor way.'

Tucker nodded sagely and switched his ground as effortlessly as a politician hungry for office. 'This sounds to me like the profile of a serious criminal. What's his name?'

'Ben Freeman, sir.'

'Freeman, eh? But perhaps not a free man for very much longer, when our police machine ensures that justice takes its course!'

Tucker could not restrain a half-smothered guffaw at the excellence of his wit. Percy

Peach remained impassive. 'There's one other suspect, sir. This one has no connection with Marton Towers, as far as we know so far. It's the dead man's stepfather, sir.'

'Often don't get on with their stepchildren, you know, second husbands. Difficult relationships to sort out.'

'Yes, sir. I had heard that. This man's called Derek Simmons. Neil Cartwright refused to change his name to Simmons – that's not at all surprising, since he was almost an adult at the time of his mother's second marriage. But he remained very attached to his real father, apparently. Simmons went to some trouble to arrange an alibi for what he thought was the time of the murder, sir. He now admits that he was at Marton Towers at that time, trying to see Neil Cartwright. He claims he never found him.'

'That might be significant, you know.'

Peach's sigh was audible. 'We thought that, sir. Especially as we've now exposed this alibi Derek Simmons set up for himself.'

A frown furrowed the noble brow of Thomas Bulstrode Tucker. 'You've brought me too many suspects, Peach. It's your job to make arrests, not speculate like this.'

'Just thought you'd like to be brought up to date with the case as it stands at this moment, sir. Especially as you told me at our last meeting how important it was for you to keep the Chairman of the Police Authority thoroughly briefed on our activities.'

Peach went back down the stairs consoling himself that he had contrived to leave on a final mention of the egregious Henry Rawcliffe.

It would be difficult to imagine a greater contrast, Lucy Blake thought, as Michelle Naylor came into the murder room.

The dead man's lover was petite, attractive, very pale, with small, pretty features which were so perfect as to be almost doll-like. DC Clyde Northcott, who sat beside her and studied this woman he had not seen before, was six feet three and very black. The woman opposite her was pretending to be calm, whatever she was really feeling; the man beside her made no attempt to disguise his intensity.

DS Blake dispensed quickly with the formalities of introduction and then said, 'Mrs Naylor, why did you choose to conceal from us your relationship with a murder victim?'

'Because it seemed the best thing for his memory and for all of us who remained alive.'

'But you were warned that there could be no secrets when you were involved in a murder investigation.'

'Yes, I was made aware of that. But I didn't want to cause problems for either Sally Cartwright or myself, and I didn't want Neil to be remembered as an adulterer. So I concealed our affair from you. It seems to me

now that I may have been wrong to do so.'
Michelle glanced from the young female face, with its light skin, its hint of freckles and its frame of chestnut hair, to the implacable black features and piercing dark brown eyes to the right of it, and found comfort in neither of them.

Just when she thought the black officer was going to remain silent and watchful throughout, he said, 'How would you describe your present relationship with your husband?'

She had been prepared for more questioning about Neil rather than this sudden switch. She made herself take her time, wondering how James would expect her to answer, how her husband might have responded to the same question about her. 'Not as bad as you might think. It may not be an ideal marriage, but we're not about to tear each other's throats out.'

'How long has James known about your relationship with Neil Cartwright?'

She was perfectly cool now, remembering what she and James had agreed, what it was in both their interests to say. 'About a month. Maybe a little more.' Even if that bitch Sally Cartwright said something different, it wouldn't undermine them. Sally might have rumbled what was going on at a different time from James.

'And how did your husband react?'

'He wasn't pleased. No man would be. But this is the twenty-first century, Detective

Constable Northcott, and these things aren't uncommon. We are working things out in a civilized way: I use the present tense because we were still trying to resolve things at the time of Neil's death. We'll be all right, James and I, in the long run.' She gave him a confident, insolent smile, implying that whatever things were like where he had grown up as a piccaninny, they were different in her more sophisticated world.

Clyde Northcott, who had been born and raised in Lancashire and only rarely moved beyond its boundaries, understood much more of her contempt than she realized, but he did not react to it. He said coldly, 'In our experience, men react violently to discoveries like this. And in your case, the men knew each other well and were living close to each other on the site at Marton Towers, which must have made reactions much more intense. Don't you think it possible that your husband might have killed your lover?'

'No. I know James and he isn't like that.' She tried hard to be firm and dismissive.

'So how do you think Neil Cartwright died?'

'I've no idea.' She resisted the temptation to tell them that this was their job, not hers. 'I told you, I saw him drive away from here on Sunday. En route to a Scotland which he never reached. It seems likely that his death took place away from here, that he was killed by someone with no connection with

Marton Towers.'

A scenario which would of course be very convenient for this sharp-eyed woman and everyone else who lived here. Lucy Blake said quietly, 'That would require someone with no knowledge of the place to have killed him elsewhere and brought the body back here. To have known of a place where the body might be left undiscovered until a fire could destroy it, or at least burn so much of it away that forensic evidence was removed.'

She watched the woman closely as she spoke, expecting some reaction from her to this brutal description of her lover's end, but Michelle Naylor remained outwardly calm. 'I see the logic of that, when you point it out to me. But I can't think that anyone I know here could possibly have killed Neil. None of us was an angel in our previous lives, as you've been at pains to point out to us, but none of us has the profile of a murderer.'

Lucy wondered just how much the strange collection of personalities at Marton Towers had exchanged notes on their previous police interviews. Neville Holloway and the two women in particular seemed very composed, even when their deceptions were exposed. Perhaps it was the fact that all of them had been in trouble with the police years earlier in their lives which made them seem so calm under questioning. She said irritably, 'Where was your relationship with Neil Cartwright going at the time of his death?'

All the questions she had anticipated were coming at her, but not in the order she had expected them. Michelle allowed herself a small smile: it was a good thing that she and James had agreed what they would say beforehand on this. 'We weren't going to break up our marriages, or anything drastic like that. Neither of us wanted that. It's a pity Neil isn't here to speak for himself about it. I say that because it's my opinion that the affair had pretty well run its course by the time of Neil's death.'

'By the time your respective spouses had found out about it, you mean?'

She smiled again, trying to show them that she understood what they were doing and was proof against it. 'I didn't mean that, no. But I don't deny that the fact that we'd been rumbled had something to do with the way I felt. It's not easy to come home to the marital bed when your husband knows you're coming from someone else's. And people say that secrecy is one of the things which gives an affair its excitement. They may well be right.'

Clyde Northcott said suddenly, 'We haven't been able to pin down the time of death. When exactly do *you* think Neil Cartwright died, Mrs Naylor?'

This was something she hadn't expected. She went back quickly in her mind over her previous account of how she had spent that fateful Sunday, but she couldn't see anything there to excite their suspicions. 'No. If I knew that, I might be able to tell you who killed him, mightn't I?'

'You might even have killed him yourself, Mrs Naylor.' Clyde Northcott did not smile as he said the words. 'Had you fallen out with Neil Cartwright in the period immediately before his death?'

'No.' Michelle could feel her pulses racing, but she kept her body and her hands very still.

'You appear strangely unaffected by his death.'

She had thought there might be something like this from them, but she had not expected anything so blunt and unapologetic, so openly challenging. 'You have no idea what I feel. If I keep my emotions under control when I speak to you, that is surely to everyone's advantage.'

Lucy Blake had contented herself for several minutes with watching the reactions of this woman who, although not much older than her, was physically so different from herself. She now said slowly, 'Everyone we have spoken to at Marton Towers has been holding things back. Can you think of a reason for that?'

Michelle Naylor looked hard into the eyes beneath the broad forehead; they were a distinctive aquamarine colour, but they seemed to change from green to blue with the intensity of the light. She allowed herself a little smile of contempt at this woman whom she found she so disliked. 'Perhaps it's because we've all had experiences of police interrogation before. Perhaps those experiences have made us cautious. Perhaps we have learned not to trust the police.'

'And perhaps one of you is concealing murder.'

Michelle shrugged her small, neat shoulders. 'You wouldn't expect me to comment on that, Detective Sergeant Blake. I've already assured you that I didn't kill Neil.'

'And perhaps someone who didn't commit this murder is protecting the person who did. Becoming an accessory after the fact can lead to very serious charges.'

Michelle wondered what had happened to the 'hard cop and soft cop' routine. These two seemed only concerned to press her hard. She said carefully, with just a touch of insolence, 'It's as well that I'm not doing that, then, isn't it? I can't speak for anyone else, of course.'

She wondered when they had gone whether she should have played the distressed lover deprived of her man. They had picked her up on her lack of any obvious grief over Neil. But fortunately he wasn't here any more to clarify the temperature of the affair for them.

Twenty

Ben Freeman was pleasantly tired at the end of his work at Brunton Golf Club.

With the lengthening days, the grass was beginning to grow and it was time to get the last of the winter tasks out of the way before the hectic burgeoning of spring increased its demands on all of the green staff. He had spent the morning planting rhododendrons, which would make a brave show behind the greens on two of the par-three holes during the coming May and in many Mays to come. In the afternoon, Ben had watched in wonder as a lorry delivered two twenty-foot-tall oaks and planted them with the special digger which enabled trees of this maturity to be set with little disturbance to their roots.

'This is one of the things we couldn't do when I started this job,' the Head Green-keeper told him, as they completed the planting and tidied the site when the special-ist tree firm had departed. 'Until ten years or so ago, we just had to plant six-foot-high saplings and wait for them to grow. Now we can bring in sturdy young trees and watch them replace the old ones which have fallen with the minimum of delay. A young lad like you will see these fellows in full maturity before you reach retiring age.'

They stood for a moment in the March twilight, looking up at the slim, healthy young branches high above their heads against the darkening blue of the sky, marvelling at this combination of ancient nature and modern technology. Then the greenkeeper put his spade on his shoulder and said contentedly, 'That's enough work for one day, lad. We'll have a brew before you go, if you've got the time.'

They drove the tractor back to the big greenkeepers' shed, with its smells of oil and soil and grass, its machines which looked twice as big as they did outside when they were housed in this safe haven for the night. The other three members of the staff had already left; course workers began work early, at half-past seven each morning, to get on with as much work as possible before golfers appeared on the course, and finished correspondingly early.

They went into the familiar room at the end of the huge shed, with the battered armchairs which had been brought here when they became too shabby for the club lounge, the scratched wooden lockers, the Pirelli girlie calendar ten years out of date, the little electric stove and kettle. The Head Greenkeeper switched on the two-bar electric fire and filled the kettle. He nodded at the girl on the calendar as he waited for the water to boil. 'Do you a bit of good, she could!' he said, with a leer which was as much part of his unthinking male ritual as the tea.

Jim Burns had resisted all attempts to bring in more modern and daring porn to replace the Pirelli. Although he couldn't have explained it, he considered that the old and well-thumbed calendar gave a sort of antique distinction to male lust. He had his own cottage by the clubhouse and was happily married, with three grown-up daughters. But like most people who worked with the seasons, he was a traditionalist. This grizzled, growling, kindly fifty-year-old liked to be assured that the younger men who worked for him were heterosexual and lubricious; it was part of his insulation against what he saw as the increasingly varied and dangerous world outside his work.

They chatted happily over strong, hot tea, enclosed by the cosy intimacy that drops upon men who have worked hard together for most of the day when they sit down to rest. The Head Greenkeeper took a long, appreciative pull at his mug of tea, then exhaled noisily, in a way his wife would certainly have disapproved. 'You're doing all right, lad,' he said.

From Jim Burns, that was high praise, and Ben Freeman dimly understood it as such. Burns was not a man with any gift for small talk, but Ben asked him things about the history of the course and the plans for the future, and the older man was unexpectedly forthcoming. Like many taciturn men, he became quite voluble once his enthusiasm was kindled, and this was the area of both his expertise and his interest. When they eventually finished their conversation, Jim Burns found himself following the familiar route back to the cottage in near darkness, with a light, chill wind which was cool enough to remind him that it was still only late March. The clocks would go forward on Saturday; that was always the date which marked the real beginning of spring for a greenkeeper.

Ben Freeman was in a contented frame of mind as he went to the side of the long hut, unlocked the chain on his bike and switched on the lights. They were getting rather dim, but from next week on the light evenings would be here and he'd hardly need them. Maybe when he was established here he'd get himself the little motorbike which his mother was so much against.

It looked as if he was going to get away with what he had done at Marton Towers. He realized that he'd managed not to think about events up there for a full four hours this afternoon. That must be some sort of record.

As he turned on to the four hundred yards of private road which led away from the golf club and back to the public highway, Ben was glad of even the minimal light from the lamp at the front of his bike. There was no street lighting here, and no moon yet in a sky where there was now just a tiny residue of daylight in the west behind him. He pedalled steadily, searching for the rhythm which would come through his fatigue and carry him home. He was still young enough to have been considerably revived by the tea and the rest he had enjoyed during his chat with the boss.

The small van had no lights, but it did not need them on this road. Probably some chap having a quiet kip and a skive before he went back to work, Ben thought; it was a bit early for snogging. Ben realized as he moved out to pass the vehicle that its engine was switched on, but he was taken completely by surprise when the side of the van moved swiftly towards his bike.

He shouted, twisted his handlebars violently away from the wall of moving metal, stood and thrust his weight frantically on the pedals to accelerate, but it was hopeless. The van cruised alongside him, followed his movement across the lane, thrust him inexorably into darkness and thorny vegetation, as his wheels slid from the road and on to the verge.

He hadn't a chance. He was still face down, clawing at the brambles, tasting the blood in his mouth from the scratches, when the men set about him. There were two of them, he thought, but he couldn't even be sure of that. They had baseball bats or coshes, and they used them systematically, unemotionally, upon the body beneath them.

Ben had thought that with the arrest of the drug barons at Marton Towers he might be off the hook. But someone else must have taken over the empire, or the men lower down the hierarchy were continuing to operate the system. Now he felt that he was going to die. There was a blow to his cheek, and he flung his hands over the back of his head and buried his face in the brambles, yelling with the pain as the blows fell upon his back, his ribs, his thighs, blubbering with the thought that this was an absurd place to die, after what he had been through in the past month.

Then a voice said, 'Just a taste of what could come to you, Freeman, if you don't keep your mouth shut. We don't like people who leave us without permission. We'll be watching you and listening to you. One word about what went on at the Towers, and you're dead.'

Ben didn't recognize the voice, didn't dare to turn his face in the darkness. He sensed that it would be better for him if he saw nothing of his assailants; he had a dim hope now that he might survive, if he did not move at all.

They had ceased to hit him whilst the man

spoke over his victim, uttering the warning which was the real purpose of this visit. But now, just when Ben had thought it might be over, they gave him two final blows to the ribs, one on each side of the body, and pain flashed white and livid against his closed eyelids. Through the groans he scarcely recognized as sounds from him, he heard the doors slam and the van accelerate away.

It was a long time before Ben Freeman crawled, shivering with cold and shock, towards what was left of his bicycle.

Neville Holloway chose to see them in his office, even at seven o'clock in the evening. He wanted to keep them away from his wife, not just because of what her innocence might reveal to them, but because of some obscure instinct which made him reluctant to taint his domestic world with what had gone on in the mansion.

The Chief Inspector whom he feared brought with him not the consoling female presence of Detective Sergeant Blake, who had come with him last time, but a tall, muscular, unsmiling black man, who looked very tough and said nothing to revise that impression.

'Come with me and frighten the butler!' Percy Peach had said at Oldford nick. 'It needs a hard bastard who's handy with his fists to ruffle the Jeeves-like surface of the man.'

DC Clyde Northcott nodded and followed his man out of the station without argument. What Peach said went, as far as Clyde was concerned. He asked no questions, but he had no idea who this Jeeves was; Pelham Grenville Wodehouse wasn't Northcott's sort of reading.

Holloway began with the safe formalities. 'Is there any news on Mr Crouch? We are all naturally interested to know when he might be back.'

Peach gave him a grim smile. 'Probably not at all. Certainly not for several years. He's been charged with serious drug offences, along with the rest of the gang we arrested here last Wednesday night. That's merely an informed opinion, by the way. Drugs aren't my concern, thank God. I'm interested in arresting a murderer. Which is why I'm here at this time of night.' He looked with some distaste around the tidy, presently disused office. His gaze came to rest on the cabinet which the occupant had recently cleared of incriminating evidence, and Neville fought to rid himself of the idea that this disturbing man knew all about his efforts to cover his tracks.

He said, 'I'm as anxious as you to find out who killed Neil Cartwright. But I've already told you what little I know of the circumstances of his death.'

'No, Mr Holloway. Like everyone else we have seen at Marton Towers, you told us as little as you possibly could in our previous meetings, and concealed as much as you thought you could get away with.' Peach spoke as unemotionally as if he were reading a train timetable, but the content of what he said was uncompromising.

'I can't think that I can possibly—'

'You concealed the fact that a minor drug-dealing ring was centred here. That Neil Cartwright was involved in it.' This was Clyde Northcott, as physically threatening as if he was on the other side of the law, where rules did not apply, though he made no physical move towards the man who was almost thirty years older than him.

Neville Holloway wished that he had not allowed them to sit with their backs to the single light in the large room, which fell fully upon his own face as he sat behind his desk. He could see the flash of the black man's eyes, and the teeth beneath them as he spoke, but little else of his features. Those teeth looked very white and very large, and his office in the mansion felt very quiet and very isolated. He found himself too unnerved to challenge Northcott's assertions. He said weakly, 'You may be right about this. I had my suspicions, but I knew very little.'

Peach noted that weakness, even whilst he approved Northcott's ability to make bricks with the very little straw which they possessed. He said, 'I think you had better now tell us everything that you do know, Mr Holloway, whilst there is still time.'

Neville didn't like the implication in that last sinister phrase. He said slowly, 'Well, it's true that I suspected that my employer was involved in drugs in a big way. I also suspected that the people who came here on occasions like the one you interrupted last Wednesday night were people involved in the international trafficking of drugs. But it was suspicion, and no more than that. It was made clear to me when I came here that I should keep my nose out of my employer's business. I have tried to do that.'

It had some of the ring of a prepared statement, and that was probably what it was. Peach nodded. 'You also made that policy clear to the people you in turn employed to work in the house and on the estate. And you recruited people who like you had been in trouble with the law before, and thus had every reason to be as unseeing, as unhearing and as silent as the three wise monkeys.'

'I won't deny any of that.'

'Good. And on my side I'll say that I can understand, if not approve, that attitude. No doubt it's what Crouch expected of you. But this is murder I'm investigating. It's time to come clean, Mr Holloway.'

Neville glanced nervously from the round white face to the taut and equally unsmiling black one beside it. He licked his lips and ran a hand over his immaculately parted, silvering hair. 'You're right. I think there was a minor drugs ring which was centred on this site. Perhaps it happened because the supply was easy. I – I want you to know that I wasn't involved in it myself.'

'Then who was?'

'I think Neil Cartwright was. I think he began by dealing, then moved up a rung in the organization, so that he was running his own small ring of dealers himself.' He looked again from one to the other of the contrasting but equally unyielding faces. 'All this is no more than speculation, you understand. I have no definite knowledge.'

'I understand, Mr Holloway. I understand that you can end up as a corpse in the canal if you reveal anything about the boys in this particular racket. Do you think that's what happened to Cartwright? That he got too big for his boots and was taken out by someone in the organization?'

For a moment, Neville was tempted to nod and say he thought that is what had happened, to shrug off this killing on to the anonymous shoulders of the dangerous world of illegal drugs. But he did not know how much these men knew, and to be caught out in further deceptions might land him in very deep water. He said reluctantly, 'No. I don't know, but I doubt it. For one thing, I don't think Neil Cartwright was that important. And for another, people who die like that are usually dispatched away from home, and

their bodies dumped somewhere anonymous like a canal or a building site, as you
suggested they might be a few minutes ago.
I don't think they would have killed Cartwright here.'

It was almost a summary of Peach's own
thoughts on the matter, which he had
confirmed with the Drugs Squad earlier in
the day. That meant it was almost certainly
someone in Neil Cartwright's family or
someone who had worked with him on this
site who had killed him. The question in
Peach's mind at the moment was whether
this urbane, experienced man in front of
him, who was so smoothly shrugging away
his own connections with the dead man,
could possibly have been the one who
removed Cartwright from the scene.

It was DC Northcott who voiced that
thought. 'You know more than you've
admitted previously about this small ring of
dealers. How do we know that you weren't
involved yourself? How do we know that you
didn't kill Cartwright, either for your own
purposes or on orders from above?'

Neville Holloway was not outwardly ruffled, either by the questions or Northcott's
uncompromising attitude. He had dealt with
Fraud Squad detectives in the past, intelligent men who had pitted their wits against
his and won. But he was confident now that
these men knew very little about his own
role in anything dubious at Marton Towers;

they were fishing for information rather than confronting him with unpleasant facts. He said carefully, 'You will have to take my word on these things. One cannot easily prove a negative, as I'm sure you often find in your own work.'

Clyde Northcott, who had endured a varied and difficult working life before being encouraged by Peach to join the police service, had an instinctive dislike for men like Holloway, who in his experience spoke smoothly and acted ruthlessly once you were out of the room. He said, 'You have proved yourself untrustworthy by withholding full information from us in previous meetings. We have to keep you in the frame for this.'

'Then so be it. In the light of your attitude, it would obviously be in my interests to point you towards the real culprit, but I have to assure you that I don't know who killed Neil Cartwright.'

Peach received that statement with the slow smile of a predator. 'In the light of your undoubted innocence, you won't object to giving us a DNA sample.'

'And why should I do that?'

'Because you are anxious to give us hard-working coppers every assistance in this investigation. More specifically, because the dead man's car has been found and is being given detailed forensic attention.'

'This is blackmail. If I refuse, you'll say that I've something to hide.'

Peach's smile grew wider. 'I said a voluntary DNA sample, so you'd be within your rights to refuse. Of course, we'd be entitled to draw our own conclusions from any such action.'

Neville Holloway was definitely ruffled. He glared at his two visitors for a moment and then said. 'All right. You can have your sample.'

Peach's smile became a positive beam. 'Just a simple saliva test, Mr Holloway. And who knows, it may help to eliminate you from our enquiries. But I wouldn't bank on it.'

The CID men were in their car on the way back to the station when a disgruntled Northcott said, 'That bugger still knows more than he's telling us.'

For a long time, he didn't think his chief was going to offer any comment. They had gone fully half a mile further towards Brunton before Peach said, 'If a man got in his way, Holloway would certainly be cool enough and ruthless enough to dispose of him. Even your hard-man techniques didn't break him down.'

Then he grinned. 'The butler's still in the frame.'

A week after the fire at Marton Towers and the grisly discovery of that charred corpse, the mother of the victim was still struggling to come to terms with the death of her only son.

Her second marriage was an unusually happy one. Before this death, Brenda and Derek Simmons had chatted happily on most evenings on all kinds of topics, and almost invariably found that their views coincided. But Neil's murder had thrown a shadow between them, which seemed to become only darker with the passing days. Neither of them wanted to say that it was a week tonight since the fire at Marton Towers, though each of them became more aware of it as the hours dragged past.

Derek as usual was in charge of the television remote control, and their sporadic words of consultation about what they should watch were almost the only ones they exchanged during the evening. The set flickered in the corner, but most of the content of the programmes was lost on the couple, who stared at it steadily but found their thoughts equally steadily elsewhere.

At ten thirty, Brenda went into the kitchen and made two cups of tea. She felt guilty as she went automatically through the simple process: it was a welcome respite to be on her own, away from the observant eyes of her husband. She had never felt like this before, in all their years together. Her husband's animosity towards his stepson hung between them like a tangible thing, seeming more of an obstacle now than it had been when Neil was alive. In those days, Derek had done his best with his stepson, for her sake.

When she took the tea back into the sitting room, Brenda sat for a long time staring at the newspaper she was not reading. On the other side of the room, Derek was worrying about the DNA test he had given at the police station that morning. He had eventually changed his mind about refusing the test, because he thought it would only make him look guiltier to deny that smiling man Peach, but he was uneasy about what use the police would make of it. He wanted to talk about his fears with Brenda, as they would normally have discussed each other's anxieties, but he knew that was impossible.

It was Derek, who usually lingered for a while after she had gone up the stairs, who said an hour later, 'Time for bed, old girl!' and stood up determinedly. He realized only then that his tea still sat untouched and cold upon the little table beside him. He went and put his palm tentatively upon Brenda's shoulder, and after a few seconds her small hand crept up and sat on top of his. It felt very cold.

They were undressed and into bed very quickly. The central heating was off by this time, and they pretended that their haste was because of the cold, but each of them knew that darkness and the end of the day would be a relief to the other. They lay apart in the big bed, carefully avoiding contact with each other, as they had never done before this death.

Brenda was tortured as she had been several times during the last week by that incident in Derek's past which they never mentioned and which she had almost forgotten, until Neil's murder. Twenty years ago, Derek had almost killed a man. She didn't want the details, and had never wanted them, until now. Hadn't he tried to throttle the man?

At one o'clock, Derek was asleep and snoring very softly. Brenda lay on her back, staring at the invisible ceiling and contemplating the idea she had tried all day to thrust out of her mind. Was it possible that the man asleep beside her had killed her only son?

Twenty-One

On Thursday morning, the murder team had a full and very detailed report of the forensic tests done on Neil Cartwright's car. They were comprehensive, but in the end not very illuminating.

Eventually, and with varying degrees of reluctance, all the leading suspects had agreed to voluntary DNA tests. None of them had appeared very happy to give the simple saliva sample which could nowadays be so much more revealing than fingerprint tests, but only Derek Simmons had refused, and in the end even the stepfather whom the dead man had so detested had reluctantly come round to the idea that refusal would look suspicious for him.

Hairs had been found on the front passenger seat of the car from both Sally Cartwright and Michelle Naylor, but in view of what the murder team now knew, this was no more than would have been expected. Various minute samples of clothing fibres had been picked up from the seats of the car, but because of the incinerated state of the corpse, it was difficult to establish and eliminate what clothing Neil Cartwright himself had been wearing at the time of his death. A small bag containing sweaters, shirts, under-clothing, a pair of shoes and a digital camera was found untouched in the boot of the car. This appeared to confirm the dead man's declared intention to visit his sister in Scotland.

There was one strange fact, which might eventually prove either totally irrelevant or highly significant. The windows were shut and the car was locked, but there had been no car keys discovered on what was left of the incinerated corpse of Neil Cartwright.

The staff nurse was watchful at the door of the ward. You had to protect your patients. The police might only be trying to find out who had attacked them, but they were still fragile and unable to take too much stress.

She whispered to the young uniformed constable who had mounted guard in the corridor outside the ward for several hours, 'She doesn't even look like a police officer, that woman who's with him.'

The fresh-faced young man looked very young without his hat. He poked his nose cautiously round the door lintel, as if to re-assure himself before he spoke. The curtains had been drawn around the patient's bed to give the exchanges a little more privacy. 'That's Detective Sergeant Blake. She's a high-flier, they say. The DS will know what she's about.' He tried hard to keep the respect out of his voice; it came partly for the rarefied realms of CID and murder investigations, and partly from his wholly male reverence for the buxom charms and aquamarine eyes of Lucy Blake. He whispered even more breathlessly, 'I think your patient might even be a murder suspect.'

'All the same, Mr Freeman has the same rights as anyone else in my ward. He's got concussion and multiple minor injuries. He must be treated with care.' But the staff nurse peered through the doorway towards the curtained rectangle with a new respect: as far as she was aware, she'd never nursed a murder suspect before.

Inside the high room, with its eight beds and clutter of expensive medical machinery, Lucy Blake tried to ignore the livid bruising and stitches on one side of Ben Freeman's face and focus on the one eye which remained open. She said with all the confidence she could muster, 'We need to know who did this to you, Ben. We'll put them away, with your help.'

'I don't know. I didn't see them. They never gave me a chance.' Ben said what he knew he must say in a monotone, trying hard to concentrate through the pain which throbbed in his head.

'How many of them were there?'

'Two, I think.' There couldn't be anything wrong with telling her that, surely. But as an insurance policy, he added lamely, 'There might just have been three of them, I could not see in the dark. But I think there were two.'

DS Blake sighed, knowing now what was coming, sensing that the frightened man in the bed was too scared to give her the co-operation she needed. 'And no doubt you didn't see their faces. Were they wearing balaclavas?'

'They might have been. I'm not sure.' Ben Freeman realized that he could be perfectly honest about the details of the attack: he really hadn't seen anything of the brutal men whom he had feared were going to kill him. 'They had me face down in the brambles, and it was dark. I think they had baseball bats, or something like that.' He passed a hand cautiously over his face, wincing as he touched the stitches on his cheek, nodding as the lesser scratches on his forehead confirmed the damage of the bramble thorns.

Lucy Blake glanced through the gap where the curtains met towards the doorway of the ward, knowing her time to question this victim who was also a murder suspect was going to be limited. 'Who did this to you, Ben? Who sent these men to attack you?'

Even his one eye was half shut, giving a soft-focus effect to his view of this shimmering presence at his bedside. Ben Freeman saw a dazzling aureole of red-brown hair, eyes which were not only an impossible shade of green-blue but which seemed to be brimming with concern for his welfare, a delicious, untouchable curve of breast beneath the small, firm chin. This vision was a few years older than him. She was also that most dangerous of things for an impressionable young man, a highly desirable woman who was also mothering him in his wounded state. He fought back a huge urge to tell her everything, to make a clean breast of it, to lie back and leave his fate in her delicate and sympathetic hands.

Ben shut his one good eye and said to the blackness, 'I don't know why they did this to me. I don't know why they picked on me.'

'I think you know a little more than you're telling me, don't you, Ben?'

He thought she was going to touch him, to wipe his hot forehead with a cool cloth, as nurses did in films. But there was no contact. He said faintly, 'I think it was a random attack.'

'But they took nothing, Ben. They didn't want your bike, and they didn't go through your pockets. They could have killed you, but they didn't. They did just as much damage as they'd been ordered to do. I believe it was a warning to you, Ben. Perhaps next time it might be worse than that.'

It was so accurate a summary of what had happened in those awful moments when he had thought he was going to die that he thought for a moment that she must know everything about him, that this gentle, persuasive voice was just giving him the chance to make the best of it for himself. He didn't dare to open his eye and look at her again, sensing that if he added the spectacle of her to what he was hearing he would capitulate entirely. He said dully, 'I can't help you. I don't know any more.'

'This attack was connected with what you had done whilst you were at Marton Towers, wasn't it, Ben?'

'I don't know what you mean.' He knew it was feeble. He had the absurd illusion that his resistance was ebbing away through the bandaged wounds beneath the sheets.

'Oh, but you do, Ben.' The denial came in a voice of sadness, as if she were a therapist assisting him to rid himself of a burden. 'You were dealing when you were at the Towers, weren't you? Working for Neil Cartwright. You were one of his ring of drug dealers, weren't you?'

Now it was he who sighed, wincing a little with the pain the exhalation gave to his ribs. They knew, then. He was surprised at the relief he felt. 'How did you find that out?'

Lucy Blake smiled, paused, waited for him to open his eye, which he eventually did. She said quietly, 'We have our sources, Ben.' It wouldn't do to let him know just how much had been conjecture, before his admission.

'I was getting out, you know. I didn't want to deal any more. I wanted to go straight, have a proper career.' He turned his head painfully to look her full in the face. 'Will this affect my job at Brunton Golf Club? I'm doing well there: the boss told me that, just before this happened. We had a cup of tea and a chat. That's why I was riding home in the dark when – when they got me.'

She pursed those desirable, unattainable lips and her forehead wrinkled attractively. 'It's possible no action will be taken about your dealing. A lot depends how cooperative you are with us now. Those thugs were sent after you by the drugs bosses, weren't they?'

'Yes.'

'They knocked you about as a warning that you weren't to talk. Probably gave you notice that it would be much worse next time if you opened your mouth about them.'

'Yes.' This time it was the man in the bed who glanced anxiously towards the gap in the surrounding curtains, as if he feared that even now there might be some sinister presence listening to what he was saying. 'But I don't know anything. Neil Cartwright never told me anything about his suppliers, and I didn't want to know.'

It was probably true. People at the lowest level in the illicit trade, who ran the risks of dealing drugs in public places and were always likely to be caught, were kept completely in the dark about those above them. The muscle who had beaten up Freeman had probably just been sent in as an extra insurance that he would keep his mouth shut about any information he might have picked up.

Lucy was surprised she had been allowed as long as this with the patient. She said, 'You had a row with Neil.'

Ben was not sure whether it was a question or merely a statement. They seemed to know so much more than he had imagined they did. He said wearily, 'Yes. Neil didn't like me giving up dealing for him. He said I didn't have a choice about it. He – he told me things would happen, if I tried to stop dealing. He said that the men above him would expect him to put me straight.'

Lucy nodded seriously. 'Let's just get the sequence of events correct then, Ben. You decided you were going to give up dealing. Neil Cartwright, as your supplier, said it wasn't on and threatened you with violence. Immediately after this, he is murdered. And immediately after that, you abruptly cease your employment at Marton Towers.'

'Yes.' His single eye widened in horror and even the blackened lid of the closed one flickered with movement for a moment as the implications of this dawned on him. 'But you can't think that I – that it was me who...'

'Doesn't look good for you, does it, Ben? Especially as you approached the scene of the crime on the Thursday morning after the fire, and made off in a highly suspicious manner before the constable there could challenge you.'

'I – I just wanted to see what had been going on.' He couldn't manage anything better, and it sounded ridiculously feeble, even in his own ears.

'Or wanted to see whether the body you had hidden in the stables had been discovered as a result of the fire.' Lucy shook her head sadly over that thought, in a manner which the redoubtable Percy Peach would certainly have approved.

'I didn't! I didn't kill Neil Cartwright!'

His voice rose in panic, and the staff nurse thrust her head belatedly through the gap in the curtain. 'That's all the time I can allow you, DS Blake,' she said severely. 'You can see that my patient is exhausted. I'd have been here earlier if we hadn't had an emergency in the next ward.'

Lucy made a business of gathering up her belongings and leaving the bedside chair. As she did so, she said casually, 'Can you drive a car, Ben?'

'I can, yes. I don't have one of my own yet, but I sometimes drove Neil's, when he wanted me to collect something for the estate.' He was almost boasting over this modest skill, in his relief that she was leaving him at last.

'So you could easily have dumped his car, after you had deposited the body in that disused room at Marton Towers.'

DS Blake didn't need any reply; the horror on his damaged face was quite enough as she took her leave, thanking the staff nurse for the access to her patient.

The nurse took Ben Freeman's blood pressure and temperature, and remarked that both were higher than she would have hoped. She examined the bruises on his back and his ribs, then ran the back of her fingers lightly over his livid cheek. 'You're a good healer,' she said approvingly. 'Things could have been a lot worse, you know! You're really quite lucky.'

Ben lay on his back and watched the high ceiling swimming before the vision of his single eye. 'They've got me lined up for a murder rap,' he said faintly.

Percy Peach sat back on the sofa in Lucy Blake's neat modern flat and stretched his powerful but rather short legs as far as they would go. 'Nice place, this. Hardly big enough for two, though, when you make an honest man of me.'

Lucy loved the flat she had bought when this small block had been built three years ago. It was on the second and top floor, with extensive views over the old cotton town and out towards the Ribble Valley beyond it. And with the curtains closed on the winter evenings, it was a cosy place, where you could shut yourself away from the cares of the day and get on with the rest of your life. Percy's talk of marriage and of sharing made her feel very protective about this first residence she had owned. She said acidly, 'Everything here works, if that's what you mean. Including the central heating, unlike your place.'

'Tha won't need much heating when tha's wed to me, lass.'

She liked it when he thee'd and thou'd her, but this wasn't the moment to encourage it, when he was coupling it with the marriage which he was anxious to push on and she was anxious to postpone. She said firmly, 'You wanted me to bring you up to date on my visit to the hospital to question Ben Freeman.'

'Eeh, tha were always one for the Protestant work ethic. I never thought I'd find that attractive in a woman, but in thee, lass, it's fair champion!' Percy reached out to stroke his partner's rear as she set the two cups of coffee on the table beside them, but she moved out of his reach with a swift grace which came from much practice.

Lucy sat firmly at the other end of the sofa and thumped a cushion into place between them. 'Young Ben Freeman is a suspect,' she said firmly.

Peach resigned himself to the inevitable, assuring himself that the inevitable could still be quite short. 'In spite of being beaten up?'

'Because of it, if you like. He was roughed over because he'd given up dealing drugs. It was a warning to keep his mouth shut about anything he might know. Which appears to be zilch, incidentally.'

'He was dealing for Neil Cartwright?'

'Yes. He was one of the ring Cartwright was establishing to increase his earnings from drugs.'

Peach nodded, suddenly fully professional. 'The Drugs Squad tells me that Cartwright's supplier has now been arrested, as a result of information gathered after last week's seizure of the big boys at Marton Towers. So that chapter is closed, as far as they're concerned. But it leaves us with Freeman as a suspect for our killing.'

'Yes. Ben Freeman admitted that Cartwright cut up rough when he said he wanted out from his ring of dealers. Threatened him with violence, he says. Whether Ben responded with violence of his own remains to be seen.'

'Like too many other things in this case. Did Freeman seem like a killer to you?'

Lucy thought of that damaged, confused, rather pathetic figure she had seen a few hours earlier. She was far too experienced a CID officer now to make a murder judgement on appearances. 'I don't think he'd plan a killing in cold blood. But if he got into an argument with Cartwright, if he panicked, he might have done anything. If someone hid Cartwright's body away in that room without quite knowing how he was going to dispose of it, without any clear plan, that sounds like the kind of thing Ben Freeman would have done. He fled from Marton Towers immediately after the murder, and he approached the crime scene after the fire. He's certainly scared. But he was still in shock when I questioned him.'

'Aye. I think I'd be a bit scared, when the ministering angel at my bedside turned into a gauleiter.' Peach was a man of very different background and experience from young Freeman, but he had the male knowledge of the effect his partner could have on impressionable men. 'At twenty, he's our youngest candidate. I'd say he's just as likely as the oldest one, the stepfather, who's sixty-six.'

'Derek Simmons? He isn't the conventional wicked stepfather, though, is he? For one thing, he only appeared on the scene when Neil Cartwright was an adult, and for another, he seems to have done everything he could to be friendly to Neil. All the hostility seems to have come from the stepson, even according to his mother.'

'Nevertheless, Simmons went to some trouble to establish a bogus alibi, asking a snooker pal to lie on his behalf. And he was at Marton Towers on the Sunday evening when Cartwright died, on his own admission. Motive and opportunity, if the two of them fell out there. And he admits that he nearly throttled a man, twenty years ago. "A fight that got out of hand", Derek Simmons called it. This might have been another one.'

'I'd rather it was one of the women in the

case.' Lucy hastened to justify her prejudices. 'The wronged wife and the lover. Always good candidates. Sally Cartwright seems singularly unaffected by her husband's death. And she too had motive and ample opportunity.'

'As did Michelle Naylor, if we posit that the lovers had fallen out. If, for instance, Cartwright had pretended the affair was going to be long-term when he had no intention that it should be more than an exciting interlude. That little spitfire wouldn't have taken kindly to that.'

Lucy sought for some method of defending her sex against this clichéd approach, and found none. 'In their different ways, both those women are very cool characters. I don't think I've ever met anyone quite so cool under questioning as Michelle Naylor. She's certainly got the temperament to plan and carry out a murder.'

'So has her husband, I would think. James Naylor wasn't quite as calm under fire as his wife. But then he might have more reason to fear our investigation.'

'He's a chef. They're not supposed to be good with words: it's not part of their job description.' Lucy remembered how she had at one point been sorry for James Naylor, as he faltered under the stress of Percy Peach's interrogation.

'Doesn't mean they're not good with their fists, does it? Or with a length of rope round a man's neck.' Percy stretched his legs out again, examined the shine on the leather toecaps of his shoes, and said reflectively, 'Of course, it could still be the butler.'

'Neville Holloway? He's a smoothie, who obviously knew everything that was going on at the Towers. But he's a fraudster, rather than a killer, to my mind. I think you only fancy him for this because he's the butler. Or because you insist on calling him that to annoy Tommy Bloody Tucker.'

'Holloway's capable of killing, if he decided it was necessary to him.' Percy brightened visibly. 'But if he proves to have no connection with this, we could hire him to take charge of our wedding. I fancy taking over the Towers for the day and having a butler in charge of arrangements.'

Lucy hastened to be firm. 'Well, I don't! And I think Marton Towers will be sold and Holloway will be gone, long before we get wed!'

'Your mum would like it to be at the Towers. Perhaps I should discuss it with her.' Percy stared dreamily into space, a sure sign that he was at his most mischievous.

Lucy decided it was time for drastic diversion. She shuffled a little nearer to him on the sofa, took his hand, examined his immaculately groomed fingernails, and said, 'I'm finding it difficult to sleep, with all these people to think about as suspects. I was rather hoping for an early night.' She focused on the spot on the wall Percy seemed to be studying, and looked just as ruminative.

Percy turned and looked into those disturbing, humorous, aquamarine eyes. 'You're transparent, Lucy Blake. But I like it. Putty in your hands, I am.'

'Oh dear! I was rather hoping that the bit I planned to handle wouldn't be putty at all.'

'Eeh, I luv it when tha talks dirty, lass. I might need careful treatment, though, an innocent lad like me. Tha'd better make sure to warm thy 'ands.'

Lucy led him swiftly into the pleasantly warm bedroom. The wedding talk had gone. And she liked being thee'd and thou'd, under the duvet.

It was a considerable time later, after an interval of high pleasure and a splendid spending of energy, that Percy Peach lay on his back and contentedly stared at the invisible ceiling of Lucy Blake's comfortable bedroom. He wasn't conscious that he was thinking of anything, just of being suffused in a warm glow of post-coital fulfilment. Yet the human brain is still more complex and certainly more unpredictable than any computer. For it was in that moment of delicious relaxation that the one significant fact which he had overlooked in the case struck him with stunning force.

Twenty-Two

Neville Holloway was glad to be conducting business in his familiar office. He felt in control again, as he hadn't done since his employer and the important visitors had been arrested in that police raid nine days earlier. Things would certainly never be the same again, and the future was uncertain for him and for all of the employees at Marton Towers, but a measure of normality was being restored. Holloway had his remaining full-time members of staff with him in his office and they seemed as anxious as he was to be working again.

Richard Crouch, the owner of Marton Towers, had been charged with serious drug offences and was still in custody, but he had given permission for certain commercial developments at the Towers, which would help to keep the place going. Holloway and his skeleton staff were going to make the place available for wedding receptions and other functions, bringing in part-time help as they needed it. It was an obvious use of the place, to Holloway's mind. Neville had drafted an advert for the local papers and for *Lancashire Life*; he was discussing it and some of the menus they might offer with James and Michelle Naylor and Sally Cartwright.

The chef and the two women were also glad to be back at work. Even if this catering represented merely a stay of execution on their employment, it would increase their reputations and experience. Even if the worst came to the worst and the Towers passed into new hands, this new work would look good on their CVs, and it was even possible that new owners might re-employ them, if they made a success of this.

The quartet passed a happy and productive hour discussing the facilities they could provide for weddings and similar celebratory functions, and the different demands which such work would make on them and the other staff at Marton Towers, such as cleaners and outside workers, who came in on a daily basis.

'There will be more use of the public areas, such as the main lounge and the reception hall,' said Neville. 'Can you cope with that, Sally?'

Sally Cartwright smiled. 'I'm sure that Michelle and I will be able to cope.' It was a coded acknowledgement that she would need to work with her dead husband's lover in the months to come, that the old era was behind them and she was determined to look forward.

Michelle Naylor said coolly, 'Sally and I

have worked efficiently together in the past. There is no reason why we shouldn't do so in a new situation. We shall need part-time workers at different times, but we have a good list of people to call on. Sally and I both know reliable people who will be glad of the work.'

Holloway nodded. 'The catering demands will also be very different. From serving very high-class food to a few people, we shall have to move to providing acceptable menus for perhaps a hundred people. Can that be done, James?'

James Naylor was ready for the question. 'I think so. I've given it some thought, over the last few days, since you first came up with the idea. High-quality meals will be needed, especially in the early weeks, when we are creating our reputation. Word-of-mouth recommendations are more effective than all the advertising in the world, where food is concerned, and when you're developing something new like this. I think the kitchen facilities here can cope with it, as long as we offer set menus and we know in advance the number of covers we have to provide.'

It was a long speech for this man of few words, one he had prepared in advance of this meeting. He blushed a little as he concluded it and saw the others nodding their approval.

Neville Holloway, normally so unemotional, found himself caught up in the prevailing enthusiasm. 'The great advantage we have, the trump card in our hand, is the location. No one competing with us will be able to match the setting of Marton Towers. The photographers will love it, for a start. I can see them posing their wedding groups against our impressive entrance. And they'll certainly want background shots of things like the lakes by the main drive and those two huge copper beeches.'

'We'll need people to maintain the estate, though, if it's going to be such a feature. Everything's going to start growing like mad in another month or so.' Sally Cartwright spoke almost apologetically about these gaps in the team which had been headed by her dead husband, the absence in this gathering no one in the room wanted to declare.

Neville Holloway said hastily, 'You're right. Young Ben Freeman left us in the lurch, departing as suddenly as he did last week.'

Michelle Naylor said, 'I hear he's in hospital. Came off his bike on his way home from his new job at the golf club, apparently.'

If anyone in the room knew anything more accurate about what had happened to the young man who had so recently been their colleague, they didn't reveal it. James Naylor made a comment about Ben Freeman and Derek Simmons, the dead man's stepfather, being interviewed by the police about last week's fire. The others all nodded gravely, as if they were totally unaware that a greater crime than arson was what was interesting the CID.

Neville Holloway said, 'At the moment, I've got two gardeners coming in part-time, to ensure that things don't get out of hand. If our new venture takes off and we become a little clearer about what the future holds for Marton Towers and for all of us, I might be able to consider a full-time employee for the estate work, but at present the funds won't run to it.'

There followed a discussion of the kind of money they needed to raise from their new enterprise, which naturally interested all of them because their futures depended on it. It was Sally Cartwright who eventually raised the factor which none of them had chosen to mention. 'We'll be able to plan developments properly once we get the police off the site and we can think about restoring the stable block.'

They looked automatically towards that black-edged and ugly gap in the long, low regularity of the auxiliary building which had housed the recent dramas, and at the adjacent spot where the police had established what they called a Murder Room to accommodate their enquiry. Then, almost as if they were operated by one brain, the four pairs of eyes swung back towards the more cheering spectacle of the grandeur of the long drive up from the gatehouse, as it ran between the twin rectangular lakes, with their water-fowl and the water-lilies showing their first green of the season.

At that moment, as if answering a cue in a film, a police car turned in between the high, distant gates and moved steadily up the tarmac towards the mansion. They heard the sound of tyres on gravel in the sudden prevailing silence, watched DCI Peach and his driver, DS Blake, leave the vehicle, and exchange words with each other which the watchers could not hear.

Then, almost as if he knew they were assembled in Holloway's office, Peach turned and raised his dark eyes in a long, unblinking look at the window beside the pillared entrance at the top of the steps.

He was with them in thirty seconds, during which no one spoke. As the detective stood in the high doorway of the panelled room, Holloway explained a little nervously, 'We've been planning what we can do to raise revenue and secure our futures. To allow the public access to this wonderful site and do a little to return it to the community.' He threw in a couple of phrases from the publicity brochure he was planning.

'Admirable,' was all that Peach said, in such a neutral and preoccupied tone that it was impossible to determine whether he was being ironic. 'In the meantime, I need to have words with Mr Naylor.'

'I do hope you're not planning to deprive us of our chef,' said Holloway with a smile

319

and a return to something like his normal panache. 'Mr Naylor is integral to our plans; we confidently expect him to be the star turn of many future wedding celebrations. But we've finished this morning's meeting. You may have my office for your little talk with James, if you would like it.'

'We'll do it in the Murder Room, I think,' said an unsmiling Peach. His tone permitted no discussion, and the others watched James Naylor leave the room with as good a grace as he could manage. They saw him crossing the gravel a few seconds later, moving unevenly as his trainers slid over the yielding surface, casting a last glance back towards the room he had left and his wife's white face at the window.

The officers left Naylor on his own for a good five minutes with just a uniformed constable sitting silently in the corner of the room, knowing that an already nervous man would only become more edgy with the waiting.

Even when they came into the room, they positioned themselves unhurriedly opposite James Naylor, as he sat awkwardly on his hard-edged upright chair, and stared at him impassively for several seconds. Eventually, his nerve broke and he said, 'Can we get this over with quickly, please? There are things in the mansion that I need to be getting on with.'

Peach gave him his predator's smile. 'How long this takes is very much in your hands, Mr Naylor.'

'I – I don't see how that can be.'

Peach waited for the eyes which were flashing their gaze wildly around the room to come back to his, as he knew they must do. 'I mean simply that a confession would simplify matters, for you as well as for us.'

James Naylor tried desperately to stem the pulses he felt racing in his head. They couldn't know anything they hadn't known before, surely. No one would have shopped him, would they? Surely no one *could* have shopped him? The police hadn't charged him with anything. They must surely be bluffing. He fancied he could feel the blood rushing into his face, then draining away, but that must surely be no more than an illusion. Chefs were used to the heat of the kitchen, lived with it all the time. But this was a greater heat than he had ever felt in his life.

He said, 'I'm not going to confess. You've got the wrong person here.' He wanted stronger words, but they would not come to him.

'I don't think so, Mr Naylor. You gave yourself away, you know.'

He knew it. He'd never in his life been confident with words, and now they'd let him down, in this, his greatest crisis. James Naylor felt in his heart that the game was up even as he said woodenly, 'I don't know what you're talking about.'

'You knew that the body of Neil Cart-wright had been stowed away in the room above the office where the fire was started. That was information which could only have been possessed by the man who killed him.'

'No. You're mistaken. I never knew that.' He heard his voice rising in panic, and was powerless to control it.

'You told us about it when we saw you on Wednesday, Mr Naylor. We reminded you that you knew all about the geography of this place, and you then maintained that other people as well as you knew the place where the body had been hidden. But apart from us, only Neil Cartwright's murderer knew that the body had been hidden away like that.' Whereas the chef's voice had risen towards hysteria, Peach's tone seemed to become ever calmer and more confident with his announcement.

'No! No. I told you about my Michelle's affair with Cartwright on Wednesday, that's all. Nothing more.' He wanted it to be true, wanted to state it again in different words, to shout it at them, as if by repetition he could make it true. But words as usual were not his friends.

Peach was inexorable. 'We knew that the body had been stowed away in that locked room for three days before Wednesday night's fire. The information was not reveal-ed to anyone else. It was not contained in any of the bulletins released to radio, television or the press.'

This man whose dark eyes never seemed to blink found words easy, was able to torment his victim with them, whereas James found it so hard to summon the phrases he needed. It was unfair. James fought the unfairness of it, struggled against the urge to throw in his hand and have done with it. 'I didn't know about it. I didn't say that I did. You must be mistaken.'

Peach said calmly, 'Recall Mr Naylor's words to him, will you, please, DS Blake.'

Lucy flicked over the pages of her small notebook to the words she already knew by heart. 'Mr Naylor, you said to us on Wednesday morning, "Other people as well as me knew the room where the body was hidden before the fire". No mention had been made by any CID officer of the body of Neil Cartwright being hidden in such a manner.'

Now her eyes as well as Peach's were on him. They were soft, green, almost sorrowing, it seemed to James. They made him feel as he looked into them that all further resistance was futile, that confession would from now on be the best option for him, as well as for them and everyone else concerned. Including Michelle. He thought of his wife's face, regular and pretty beneath her black hair, so different from the softer beauty of this face in front of him, with its colour and its suggestion of freckles within the frame of chestnut hair.

James Naylor looked deliberately away from DS Blake's persuasive face, down at the carpetless floor. His words surprised him as well as his listeners as he said, 'Michelle had nothing to do with this.'

Lucy Blake said softly, 'Tell us what happened on that Sunday, James.'

It was the first time that either of them had used his forename: it seemed to him an acknowledgement that it was all over. And with that thought, his tongue was miraculously loosened.

'I met him. Out in the country, away from everyone else. That was Neil's idea. I'd said to him that we needed to talk, if we were going to continue to work together and live alongside each other on the site, and he said that it needed to be where no one else could see us.'

'He didn't think you were going to kill him, then.'

He glanced up at her, then dropped his eyes again, as if he could afford no distraction to his concentration. 'I didn't mean to kill him. Not when we set up the meeting.'

Months later, Lucy thought, this would be material for a defending counsel, arguing for mitigation on the grounds that this was an impulsive, not a premeditated killing. Not her concern, that. 'So you set up this meeting. For what time on that Sunday?'

'Neil set it up, not me. He was going off to

see his sister in Scotland, leaving the Towers at about one. He said the easiest thing was for me to follow him out a little later. He'd wait for me at the place we arranged: it was out on the slopes of Pendle Hill. He said he knew a lane off the road which was only used by farm traffic; we wouldn't be disturbed there, even on a Sunday, Neil said.'

She wondered if Cartwright had been out there with his lover, if he knew it was private because he had taken this man's wife there in the past. James Naylor was broken now, and all of them knew it. Her role was merely to keep him talking. She said gently, 'So you followed Cartwright in your own car.'

He nodded. 'About twenty minutes later. So that no one would think I was following Neil. But I don't think anyone even saw me go.'

He was probably right. Certainly no one had reported it. Lucy already had a feeling that the cool and thoughtful Michelle Naylor might turn out to be an accessory after the fact, but that might be difficult to prove, if this man chose to protect her. 'And what happened at the meeting, James?'

'I said I wanted to be sure that it was all over between him and Michelle. I said I'd forgiven Michelle, and I hoped that Sally had forgiven Neil. I pointed out that all of us needed our jobs at Marton Towers, so I wanted to discuss how we were going to recover from this and go on living and working together.'

There was a naivety about this man that was quite touching. Lucy thought as she had done before that it is not always the most evil or naturally vicious people who commit murder. She said, 'But your meeting didn't go as you planned it, did it, James?'

'No. Neil said that Michelle had been mistaken if she'd ever thought it was anything very serious. He said she'd never been anything more than an easy screw for him.' His face twisted in pain as he brought out the coarse phrase.

'So you quarrelled.'

'He said he wasn't the first she'd had and he wouldn't be the last. Said I'd need to watch her in the future, if she wasn't to go over the wall again. I hit him then.'

His fair-skinned face was just for an instant as proud as a boasting schoolboy's. Then it clouded again with the thought of his present situation. Lucy Blake offered the latest of her prompts. 'And it got out of hand, I suppose.'

She seemed to understand. James felt absurdly, disproportionately grateful to her for that. 'I thought he'd be sorry for what he'd done; that he'd be anxious to wipe the slate clean and get on with the rest of our lives. I thought I was being generous, when I told him I was willing to forget what had happened between him and Michelle.' He stopped, looked from one to the other of the two very different faces in front of him, and said with an air of wonder, 'I love my wife, you know. We were going to be all right, until I did this.'

Lucy Blake spoke into the silence. 'You were saying that Neil Cartwright just would not let it go.'

'He taunted me. Said I was a loser, that I'd asked for it. It was when he said that it would happen again that I lost it. He'd broken a young shoot off a tree before I got there. A willow, he said it was: Neil knew about these things, even when the trees weren't in leaf.' He paused for a moment; in that instant, precision about which tree was involved seemed of supreme importance to him. 'Neil had been swishing the tops off weeds with this whippy shoot whilst he waited for me. He threw it away when he turned to go to his car. I grabbed it and threw it round his neck from behind, pulled it against his throat until he stopped struggling. I just wanted to stop him using those words. He didn't have a chance. I'm pretty strong, you know, when I lose my temper.'

It was half a boast, half an apology. For a moment, he was a callow, overgrown school-boy who is proud of his new-found strength, even as he apologizes for a minor breakage. They had to remind themselves that this fresh-faced, awkward, seemingly gauche creature was a killer who had just confessed to garrotting the man who had taken his wife to bed.

It was Peach who now growled, 'I think you had better tell us what happened next, Mr Naylor.'

'I put the shoot of wood into my car – I flung it over the hedge on my way home, when I was miles away from where Neil had died. Well, it was a murder weapon, wasn't it?' He smiled a little at his cleverness, seemingly prepared to ignore the irony that he was now giving them every detail they needed of his crime.

'You had a corpse on your hands.'

'Yes. I thought about leaving Neil's body in his car, hoping you'd think it had been a random killing.' Now that he had given up and the tension was broken, he felt almost unnaturally calm. 'But I knew you'd come back to the people who'd worked with him at Marton Towers, and I didn't want that. I – I didn't want people to find out about what had been going on between him and Michelle.' He was suddenly blushing over his desire to protect his wife's reputation, despite the desperate nature of his own situation.

Peach thought that other people at the Towers had probably known all about the relationship between Neil Cartwright and Michelle Naylor: lovers were usually absurdly optimistic about their liaisons remaining secret. 'So you took him back to Marton Towers.'

'Yes. I had Neil's keys. I thought I could put his body in his office and lock the door on it. It's not much more than a box room, but he kept his bits of paperwork and a few bags of fertilizer in there. No one else but Neil and Ben Freeman ever went into that room, and Freeman didn't have a key. I had the idea that if I waited for a day or two, I'd be able to take him out and dump him somewhere where he would never be found; in the sea perhaps, or in a lake somewhere, with weights on the corpse. So I put his body into the boot of my car. I moved Neil's car on to an unpaved road leading to an old quarry, so that it wouldn't be easily found. Then I locked it up and took the keys away with me. It was still quiet when I got back to the Towers. I left him in the boot for an hour or so, until it was dark. Then I transferred him to his office, locked the door and took the key away. That gave me time to think.'

'But the body was still there three days later.'

'Yes. We were too busy at the beginning of the week for me to get away for any lengthy period, because of the guests who were coming in on the Wednesday. I was busy ordering food and preparing menus, and I had to be around for Mr Holloway to consult me.' For a second, he was proud of his importance in that vanished system, of the Head Chef status which was now gone for ever.

'The police raid on Wednesday night must

have come as a shock to you.'

'Yes. It was a shock to all of us, but to me more than anyone else. The place was suddenly swarming with police. I thought it was only a matter of time before they went through the stable block and found the body. I don't know much about fingerprints – about what surfaces you can take them from and so forth – but mine must have been all over him. I was panicking when I saw Mr Crouch and the others being taken away in handcuffs.'

'So you set the place on fire.'

'Yes. I knew that there were cans of petrol for the estate machines in Neil Cartwright's shed. I still had his keys. Once Ben Freeman had left, no one needed to get into that shed. So I got a couple of cans from there and set up the fire under Neil's office, where the body was.' He paused for a minute, as if the pleasing irony of raiding the dead man's province to destroy his remains had just struck him for the first time.

Then he ran his fingers vigorously through his tousled fair hair, as if the gesture was necessary to his concentration. 'I made sure that no one was in the area at the time before I threw a match into the room and set things going. All the residents were in the main house, discussing the arrest of Mr Crouch and his visitors and being questioned by the police. The flames had got a good hold before some passing motorist set up the alarm.'

Peach nodded to his colleague, and Lucy Blake stepped forward and pronounced the formal words of arrest. James Naylor smiled at her, trying to catch her eye as she spoke the words carefully and clearly, as if he was glad that it was DS Blake and not that grimmer dark-eyed presence beneath the bald pate which was ending his freedom.

He said only, 'Michelle had nothing to do with this, you know. I want you to record that. Whatever she might say to you, I want you to remember that I did this on my own.'

As DS Blake drove slowly over the gravel and on to the now familiar drive between the twin lakes of Marton Towers, Peach sat beside the passive handcuffed figure of James Naylor in the back of the vehicle. The DCI looked up the steps and at the window of Neville Holloway's office beside the impressive stone entrance to the mansion, where faces at the window were following every yard of their exit.

A single white-faced figure stood between the pillars at the top of the stone steps to the entrance. Michelle Naylor was as motionless as a marble statue as she watched her husband's departure.

NEATH PORT TALBOT LIBRARY AND INFORMATION SERVICES

1		25		49		73	
2		26		50		74	
3		27		51		75	
4		28		52	3/20	76	
5		29		53		77	
6		30		54		78	
7		31		55		79	
8		32		56		80	
9		33		57		81	
10		34		58		82	
11		35		59		83	
12	٦/١٦	36		60		84	
13		37		61		85	
14		38		62		86	
15		39		63		87	
16		40		64		88	
17		41		65		89	
18		42		66		90	
19		43		67		91	
20		44		68		92	
21		45		69		COMMUNITY SERVICES	
22		46		70			
23		47		71		NPT/111	
		48		72			